I0763481

outlaw otp

t.k. riggins

Outlaw OTP

Published in 2020 in accordance with Franchise Publishing.

Cover design and Interior Formatting by:
Edge of Water Designs, edgeofwater.com

Issued in print and electronic formats.
ISBN 978-0-9959002-8-8 (Book)
ISBN 978-0-9959002-9-5 (Hardcover Book)
ISBN 978-0-9959002-6-4 (E-book)

Franchise Publishing
Vancouver, British Columbia

For the lost ones,
Forever in my heart.

Table of Contents

CHAPTER 1

Doing What We Like To Do, Our Way

"Tell me all the reasons why you love me," Amelia said. She twirled in her new silk gown in front of the mirror.

"That's going to be a short list," Mardious replied with a grin. He was sitting on the bed and admiring a golden dagger he'd found on the desk. It looked like something a king would own.

"That's so cruel!" Amelia turned to Mardious with a wicked smile. "I love it."

Mardious looked up and forgot where he was. Amelia's green dress was far from a perfect fit. It was loose around the waist where it should have been tight. The neckline was so gaping that it almost fell off her shoulders and revealed her own, threadbare shirt beneath. The sleeves were so long, they dangled beyond her fingertips. And yet she still looked radiant.

Amelia slowly strolled across the bedroom, modelling her dress and trying not to trip as she kept her eyes locked on Mardious' eyes. Putting her hands on Mardious' shoulders, she straddled him on the bed. She tried to grab the dagger, but he hid it behind his back.

"I want to see." She crossed her arms and pouted.

"It's pretty sharp," Mardious replied slyly. "I wouldn't want you to get hurt."

"How sharp?" Amelia whispered. Her head moved so close their noses touched, but her mouth stopped just short of his.

The couple stared at each other in silence. Mardious put his arms around Amelia, but instead of pulling her closer, he turned and flipped her. She shrieked and then started giggling. He pinned her to the bed and held the knife at her neck. He pressed the cold blade against her skin. His heart beat a little faster.

Amelia's fingers crawled up his back. Her nails playfully scraped his fancy new jacket. "Do it." She closed her eyes. She was helpless, but looked comfortable with that loss of control. She was fierce. She was crazy. She was free. Those were just three reasons why he loved her.

Mardious loosened his grip on the dagger. He removed the blade from Amelia's neck and used the tip to brush the loose hair away from her face.

"Chicken," she muttered. She peeked with one eye, grabbed his head and pulled him in for a passionate kiss. Her plump lips were firm but tender. As she disengaged, she lightly dragged her teeth across his lower lip. It always drove him wild, and she knew it.

Mardious leant back, but resisted going in for another kiss. The late afternoon sunshine crept through the glass window, making Amelia's sapphire eyes dazzle. "Your dress is hideous," he said with a straight face.

Amelia's jaw dropped open in sarcastic astonishment. "This dress is fit for a monarch," she replied in a distinguished tone. "Warriors would have swordfights over this dress. Scholars would devise schemes to get their hands on it. Wizards would … " Amelia burst into laughter, which made Mardious laugh too. "I do feel pretty ridiculous," she admitted in her normal voice.

"Try another one on." Mardious grabbed her neckline, poked a hole in it with his knife and ripped it. He was careful not to damage her normal, rustic attire beneath the dress.

Amelia pushed him off and stood up. She looked at the pieces dangling from her shoulders. She smiled seductively, gripped the edges of the torn dress, and yanked it off.

"That was fun." Amelia giggled and held her hand out. "My turn."

Mardious raised his eyebrow as he handed her the blade. Amelia grabbed the collar of his black jacket, and examined the crest on the left breast. "What do you think this means? It looks prestigious."

"Who cares?" Mardious replied with a shrug.

Amelia giggled again as she placed the edge of the knife behind one of the buttons. She pushed down and it sliced through his clothing. Unlike Mardious, Amelia was not careful to only cut his fancy clothes. Instead, she pressed the tip of the blade too deep and slashed through his jacket, his own garments, and his skin.

Mardious cringed as the pain sliced through him and he pushed Amelia away on instinct. Anger bubbled up to match the burning sensation. He stood, clutched his bleeding chest, and stumbled towards the mirror. Pain and anger warmed him in equal measures. Amelia laughed softly as she watched him struggle.

He looked at his hand in the mirror. Blood seeped from between his fingers, as if in response to the rage pounding in his heart. He immersed himself in fury, allowing the pain to overtake his body. A scream escaped him, releasing the pent-up feelings. His voice bounced off the stone walls, seeming to amplify as it reverberated.

He clenched his hand, leant back, and punched the mirror with all his might. It left the mirror looking like a spiderweb, but it left him shaking in discomfort.

"Babe," said Amelia in a soft, sultry tone. "It's just a scratch."

Mardious couldn't help but laugh. His emotions were on fire. He stumbled around the room, unable to control himself. He wasn't sure he wanted to.

He crashed into a set of drawers and ripped out the top one. Its contents scattered everywhere when he threw it across the room. He stumbled into a stand that held a beautiful ceramic vase. He choked its neck as he picked it up, and then smashed it on the stone floor. The sound of it breaking excited him.

Amelia sat on the edge of the bed. "Babe," she said again, "let me heal you."

Mardious whipped his head towards her, but as soon as their eyes met, his muscles relaxed with a shudder. Slowly, he crept over and sat down beside her, not raising his eyes.

Amelia reached across Mardious' body and helped him lie down. She tried to move his blood-soaked hand away from his chest, but he didn't want to let her. He didn't put up much of a fight, though. After a few easy tugs, he dropped his hand down to his side.

Amelia pulled back and sat up straight, reaching for the small golden medal that she always wore. Mardious knew it well. It had three symbols etched onto its surface: a sword, a flame, and a quill. There was an inscription on the back, which read 'Strength in Unity.'

Amelia clutched the medal and pressed her free hand down on his chest. She closed her eyes, and a soft white glow shone from her palm. At first, her touch felt cold, but then it was instantly hot. She kept both hands steady, but Mardious could tell from the expression on her face that she was struggling. His skin crawled as her healing power took over.

She screamed out in pain, and then laughed violently as she embraced it. Mardious looked down. Even though Amelia's hand was still pushing hard, it felt like she was pulling him inside out. She screamed again. The pain was transferring from his body to hers. She laughed again.

Without warning, Amelia leant back, threw both her hands up into the air, and collapsed beside him. Her chest heaved as she tried to catch her breath. She slowly traced a small line across her chest, over her heart.

Mardious checked his wound. He moved his fingers through the tear in his robe, mimicking Amelia's motion, and felt the small scar that had replaced the bloody cut. He rubbed his index finger along the scar and slowed his breathing. He wasn't in pain anymore.

"You're getting better at this," he said.

"Now we'll remember this day forever." Amelia rolled over onto her side and lifted her shirt. "It's a lot like this day, remember?" she said, pointing to a triangular scar on her side.

"Of course," Mardious said. He felt guilty about her scars, because he was never able to heal her wounds. He didn't know how to use his magic that way. He rolled up the sleeve of his jacket and shirt, and showed off the time Amelia had put a knife right through his arm. "What about this one?"

She giggled. "That was a fun morning." She leant in close. "We're so bad," she whispered, and kissed Mardious gently. Her wickedness was another reason why he loved her.

Amelia pulled back and slid off the bed. She danced her way back towards the rack of dresses that dangled in the closet. Mardious looked on in amazement at his beautiful partner in crime.

"I'm hungry." Mardious stood up. "Pick out another dress. I'm heading downstairs to find some food."

"Try to find some dates." Amelia grabbed an orange dress and threw it across the room in disgust. She turned and gave Mardious a genuine, happy smile. "I'll be down in just a minute."

Mardious raced down the hallway towards the stairs. He destroyed everything he could along the way: a painting of a gallant knight that he knocked off the wall; a banner with a three-headed dragon that he ripped down; a commemorative plate displayed on a side table that he picked up and tossed. It shattered gloriously.

The home that Mardious and Amelia were in was three storeys tall, with five bedrooms, four bathrooms, a dining room, kitchen, and library. It was the largest house that either of them had ever been in, and was in an area of the capital city where only the rich and famous could afford to live. It belonged to a retired scholar couple that might have been wise enough to acquire the castle-like home and all the riches strewn about, but they weren't smart enough to keep any criminals out. It was easy to break into, once Mardious had spent some time scouting the venue. The couple usually left for the evening, so he figured that he and Amelia would be alone all night.

Mardious made his way into the kitchen, and his eyes lit up when he saw a side table stacked with food. There were peaches, strawberries, and bananas in a fruit bowl. Walnuts, dates, and peanuts were each separated into jars. A breadbox sported a variety of rolls, muffins, and buns. There was even an entire jar of sugar cookies, just beckoning for him to taste.

He quickly washed his blood off his hands, and then grabbed a plate from the cupboard. He delicately loaded it with food, trying to make it look pretty for Amelia. He put some fruit on one side, rolls on another, and dates in the shape of a heart in the middle. He took the plate to the dining room table—while snacking on a few cookies, of course—and carefully placed it between two of the seats. He found a bottle of wine, poured two glasses, lit a single candle, and patiently waited for her to arrive.

He heard her coming down the steps, and watched the dining room entrance eagerly.

Instead of coming through right away, she stepped her left leg into the doorway. She pulled her dress up, along with her rags underneath. Mardious recognized her favourite scar, shaped like an arrowhead, decorating her leg. He heard her giggle as she peeked around the corner. When she saw the food on the table, she stopped her seductive act and jumped into view.

"Wine!" she exclaimed. "What a nice treat!"

"There's also these dates, shaped like a spade." He stood up and his face relaxed as he spoke from his heart. "You look lovely: like a princess. Princess Amelia Jane."

He pulled out a chair for her to sit in. Amelia made her way over, gracefully swinging her dress in grand fashion. This red, short-sleeved dress, also made of silk, fit a little better than the last one, but was still too big. She wore white gloves that were supposed to reach her elbows, but they were so loose that they were already falling down. The only thing that fit perfectly was the silver, red-jewelled tiara that she wore atop her apple-like head.

"Thank you," she replied with a smile. "You're such a gentleman." She covered her mouth and tried not to laugh, but Mardious giggled as they both sat down.

The two of them ate, drank, and pretended like they were royalty. They made a toast with their wine, delicately handled their food, and laughed boisterously at each other's jokes.

As they were snacking on some after-dinner sweets, they heard a door open from down the hallway. Both delinquents froze and waited cautiously. Loud chatter announced the owners' return.

"And then Reginald ..." An old man laughed as he breathed in hard. "Reginald said," the old man stopped his story and wheezed again. "Reginald said, 'for a second, I thought you were a minotaur!'"

The couple's laughter echoed down the hall and into the dining room. Mardious quietly got up and grabbed Amelia's arm. He pulled her out of her chair, but she knocked it over in distress.

The laughter stopped. “Is someone there?” asked the old man.

The dining room had two entrances. One was out into the hallway, and the other led to the kitchen behind them. Mardious tried to pull Amelia towards the kitchen and the back exit of the house, but she resisted, reaching to grab her glass of wine from the table. She tried to drink the last little bit before they had to leave.

“Let’s go!” Mardious whispered angrily.

Amelia looked back at him playfully, and then threw the glass out into the hallway.

They both watched it fly through the air with wide eyes. It moved like it was in a slow dance with destiny: elegant and timeless. The dance concluded with a loud crash as the glass finally hit the ground. It shattered magnificently.

The owners stumbled down the hallway, but the loud and heavy steps of the old were no match for the light and quick steps of the young. Mardious and Amelia made it through the kitchen and out the back exit with ease, giggling as they fled the scene.

The sun was setting, and the orange sky brightened the narrow alleyway behind the house. The large stone building was one of many in a row, stacked next to each other in the core of the city of Kimroad. There were no spaces between the houses on the block, just a wide street in the front and a narrow one behind.

Mardious and Amelia turned to their right and started running, hand in hand. They moved as quickly as their feet could carry them away from their crime scene.

The old man screamed, “Stop, thieves!”

Mardious turned his head. The old man was hobbling after them, shaking his fist in frustration and anger.

“He looks so funny!” Amelia said. She looked back as she ran too. “Look how red his face is.”

“I think I see steam coming out of his ears,” Mardious agreed. He noticed there was a busy street ahead. “Let’s lose him in the crowd.”

Mardious pulled Amelia’s hand harder and raced towards freedom.

He could tell that she loved the fact that they'd gotten caught, but knew she didn't actually want the old man to catch them now. Luckily for them, the old man chasing them was a retired scholar. If he had been a warrior, the two young wizards would have been stopped easily.

As soon as they exited the alley, Mardious led Amelia around peddlers, underneath carts, and around some horses. They slowed down to a brisk walk, blending in well because of the fancy clothes they wore.

They stayed low so that the old man wouldn't be able to see the tops of their heads as they weaved their way through the crowd. Even though the main street was noisy and busy with business, they could faintly make out the old man's screams. "Stop, thieves!"

They curled around a couple of tall, burly men, but came face-to-face with a horse wearing the common headdress of the High Guardians of the realm. Mardious and Amelia froze.

Mardious kept his eyes down, but he could tell that Amelia was looking up at the warrior riding this majestic steed. He hoped they hadn't drawn attention, but he got a bad feeling in his stomach. He decided to look up. He had never seen a Guardian wearing a helmet with horns on it before. They were slightly curved, like those of a bull.

As they made their way past the High Guardian, Mardious and Amelia found themselves on an open part of the street. The businesses that lined this part of the block weren't as popular as the previous ones. Mardious saw an alleyway past the flower shop at the end of the row. They had to get there. He remembered the layout of the city well, and the alley was a shortcut to the nearest portal gateway.

"Run," he whispered to Amelia. He let go of her hand, and they both sprinted down the street.

When they were halfway towards the alley, they heard a lower, louder bellow. "Stop, thieves!" Mardious looked back. It was the High Guardian with the horned helmet that they had passed moments before. The old man was beside him, scowling and pointing at them.

The Guardian's horse broke into a gallop. Mardious glanced ahead. They were still a long way from the alley. He turned to Amelia. She was focused and determined. He looked back again. The High Guardian was gaining on them.

They couldn't outrun the horse. It was time for some magic of his own. He reached back while he ran, moving his fingers as if playing a piano to focus his power. He locked in on the horse's deep black eyes. His fingers moved a little more gracefully. He could feel the anger inside him stir.

The horse skittered on the cobble street and jerked its head up. The High Guardian knew that something was wrong, and he tried to steady his trusty steed. He was too late. Mardious was connected to the animal, and was now in total control.

The horse came to an abrupt halt and stood on its hind legs. It was going wild, jumping and bucking while the High Guardian tried to calm it down. Everyone on the street was now looking at the warrior, their eyes full of wonder and astonishment. With one last buck, the horse sent the High Guardian crashing to the ground. Mardious turned his head back towards the alley. They were nearly there.

They ran around the corner and hugged the stone building. They stood with their backs against the wall and tried to catch their breath. Mardious peeked around the corner, and saw the High Guardian stand up and rub his leg. He hoped the warrior was injured. The crowd seemed bewildered by all the commotion.

"That was too close," Amelia said.

Mardious turned back to her and smiled. He knew that although they had escaped trouble for the moment, they weren't free just yet. "If we can make it through here, then over a few more blocks, we can get to the portal gates," he said, pointing down the alley. He was focused. He was strong. He was powerful.

He thought he heard Amelia sigh. Her beautiful eyes looked at him dreamily. Her admiration for him was another reason why he loved her.

Amelia put her arms around him and peered around the corner. "Let's hurry." She stepped back to peel the too-large dress away from her shoulders, letting it fall to the ground. She removed the gloves that dangled from her fingers, and plucked the tiara from her head. She dropped it, to leave everything on the alley floor.

Mardious removed his ripped jacket, and they quickly made their escape. By the time the High Guardian could get to the alley entrance, they would be nowhere to be seen.

They were more cautious for the rest of their journey so that they wouldn't draw attention to themselves. They stayed close to buildings, slipped in and out of alleys, and remained in the shadows.

Mardious could see the castle of the Triple Crown in the distance. He used it as a guide to lead them to their destination. As much as he liked looking at it, and dreaming of being a ruler of the realm, it wasn't the right time to fantasize about the future. He needed to stay focused now, for Amelia. They needed to escape. They needed to be free.

It didn't take them much longer to reach the portal gateway. There were nine doorways at this particular station. Each doorway consisted of a triangular stone arch with two sliding doors, about twenty feet high at its point and twenty feet wide at its base. Each door had ancient markings engraved on it, although Mardious didn't know what the symbols meant. He assumed it was the language of the giant masons that had built the gateway.

In front of each doorway was a keystone, where travellers would insert their Aileron coins and choose their destination. A pulsating white light would find its way through the cracks in the doors as the magic portal calibrated itself to the correct destination. The two stone doors would then slide out of the way to disappear into the edges of the frame. Once a glimmer of the destination could be seen in the doorway, the travellers were able to move through to another part of the realm.

Since Mardious and Amelia never had any Aileron, they normally snuck through one of the open portals illegally with another group before the doors closed. They didn't need to wait for an exact destination to reveal itself; they just needed to pick one that was close to home.

To his left, Mardious saw two woodsmen on a rickety old cart rolling through a portal that led to Hazelwood Forest. It was a familiar destination for him and Amelia, and was the second-best escape route they could have hoped for.

"This one," he said to Amelia. He grabbed her hand and yanked her hard.

Before the two men could disappear through the portal, Mardious and Amelia hid behind the cart. They walked through the doorway at the same time, keeping one eye on the woodsmen and one on any onlookers. They didn't need anyone alarming Guardians of their illegal transportation manoeuvre and cause another chase.

As soon as they were on the other side, the two cunning crooks turned in the opposite direction from the woodsmen and sprinted into the forest. They ran as fast as they could, deeper and deeper into the woods, until the air in their lungs felt heavy. Neither of them was physically gifted, so it didn't take long. Mardious let go of Amelia's hand and leant against a tree. She collapsed on the ground after a few more steps.

Mardious could feel his heart trying to escape his chest, but didn't know if it was from the physical exhaustion or the excitement of the chase. He put his hand over his newest scar and traced it with his finger. He closed his eyes and smiled as his breathing slowed.

"Why does it feel so good to be so bad?" Amelia said. She was gasping for air, but started to giggle through the panting.

"We were lucky." Mardious sank down and sat at the base of the tree. "That High Guardian should have caught us." He let his legs relax while he kept his eyes on Amelia. Her smile brightened as their eyes locked. He didn't know what he would do if he lost her to the Guardians' law.

Amelia's smile disappeared. "You broke the rule."

"What?" Mardious replied innocently.

Amelia tightened her lips and squinted. She was angry, but she remained quiet. She didn't even move from her uncomfortable spot on the forest floor.

Mardious tried to remain strong, but he felt the guilt building up inside. He crawled towards her, placing his hands and knees carefully to avoid any sharp rocks. He rested his elbow a few feet from her head, and leant on his open palm. His other arm dangled behind his back.

Without saying anything, Amelia reached out and grabbed the handle of the dagger that was sticking out from his belt. She looked up and their eyes met. She sighed as she removed the weapon from its hiding place.

Mardious looked away. "I thought we could sell it for a few Aileron," he mumbled in defence.

"We don't need Aileron," Amelia said sternly. "All we need is each other. We are from the shadows. We will stay in the shadows. If we start taking things and selling them, we'll draw too much attention to ourselves. People will start asking too many questions, and it will expose us. Didn't we agree on that?" she pleaded.

"I just thought I could get you something nice," Mardious said. He looked back at her with sad eyes. "I want you to feel like a princess. You deserve to be treated like royalty. Princess Amelia Jane."

"Babe." Amelia sighed. "I don't need a tiara, or nice dresses, or a fancy house in the city. Other people can have all that. All I need is you. You are my king, and I am your queen. These adventures together give me more pleasure than any item we could find, or any amount of Aileron we could ever collect."

Mardious smiled. Amelia was right. He was the only thing that mattered to her, and she was the only thing that mattered to him. That was why she was his true love. "I'm sorry." He extended his face towards hers. "Forgive me?"

His queen's lips met his, and she kissed him deeply.

After a hot moment, she broke the kiss and looked him in the eyes. "You're forgiven." She placed the tip of the dirty knife on his chest and traced his new scar with it. When she got to the end, she let go of the dagger. It fell to the ground.

"Let's go home." Mardious stood and extended his hand. After he helped Amelia get back on her feet, she moved his hand around her waist and pressed her body against his.

"I am home." Amelia wrapped her arms around him and buried her head into his chest. Mardious felt his heart flutter as they walked deeper into the forest.

They left the dagger behind, because they both knew they didn't need it. They didn't need anything. They had each other.

CHAPTER 2

The World Is Mine

"Hey, bruh. Can I get another drink?" Darcy waved his empty glass in the air.

Mardious suppressed a sigh. He hated being called 'bruh.' "Yes, sir." He smiled and grabbed a glass from behind the bar. Although he felt like the pub was sometimes sucking the soul from his body, he could always pretend like he loved his job.

"Hey, bruh," said Brantley, the grizzled man sitting beside Darcy. "I'll get another one too." He hiccupped, and his head bobbed from side to side.

Mardious felt his skin crawl with disgust. "Yes, sir." He grabbed another glass. He took a couple of bottles from the shelf behind him and started pouring.

Mardious was a talented mixologist, and even though he was young, his skills were known throughout the Badlands. He had a gift for sensing just how much of each ingredient he needed. This time, he made a couple of Mali-mali-boo-yahs, which were made up of pineapple elixir and dwarf-colada mix. When he was almost finished pouring the round, the waitress tried to get his attention.

"Hey, bruh," Amelia said with a grin. "Can you hurry up? I need you to make some drinks for me, too."

Mardious looked up at her slyly. She knew what bothered him at work, and loved to tease him. He was about to make a witty remark of his own, but noticed he wasn't pouring into the glasses anymore. He jumped back a little, but still ended up spilling some on himself.

"Bruh," Amelia said solemnly. She slowly shook her head.

"Shut it," Mardious retorted. He chuckled and grabbed the drinks. He could hear Amelia's laughter as he walked away.

Darcy and Brantley didn't even thank him. They wrapped their drunken fingers around their new beverages and quickly quenched their thirst. He marked their tabs and returned to Amelia at the other end of the bar.

"Isn't your shift over yet?" he asked sarcastically.

"Is that what you want?" Amelia fluttered her eyes flirtatiously with a pout.

"I just want you to keep it ten by ten," Mardious said emphatically. "One hundred."

Amelia smirked and shook her head again. "You think that's going to catch on, but it isn't."

"I can see why you might think that," he replied. He puffed out his chest proudly. "But that's because you're not as cool as me."

Amelia rolled her eyes dramatically, and leant on the bar with one hand. "Okay, cool guy. Can you just make my drinks please?" She sighed. "And to think, I was going to give you a really good tip tonight."

Mardious looked at his lover and smiled. The 'tip' that Amelia was referring to was a kiss. "Can I get a tip now?" He leant in closer to her.

The bar still separated them, so Amelia had to lean in a little too. Before their lips could touch, Amelia stopped. "After you make my drinks, bruh," she whispered.

Mardious couldn't help but laugh. He quickly grabbed some bottles and made a few cocktails as Amelia rattled them off. He selected some different glasses and poured ale from the wooden kegs at the other end of the bar. He was fast, efficient, and clean. When he finished, he closed his eyes and puckered up again.

Instead of fulfilling her promise, Amelia giggled, grabbed the tray of drinks, and walked away.

Although the pub could seat over one hundred people, it was pretty empty. Two couples sat at tables on the far end, where Amelia was currently serving. There was a small group of Guardians drinking ale on the other side of the room, and a few harmless travellers sitting at an open table in the middle.

There were ten stools at the bar, but only two were filled. It made for an easy work shift, but time crept by sluggishly.

Mardious and Amelia had been working together at the pub for almost two years. Since they didn't steal from anyone in their hometown, they were obligated to make honest Aileron to pay the bills. Their wages weren't great, but it kept a roof over their heads and food on their plates.

The pub was named Sugarplum, after the owner's mother. It had a mostly wood interior, with a heavy wooden bar, slatted walls, thick timber pillars, hardwood floors and handcrafted tables. It smelled like a forest, mixed with the scent of victory and defeat.

There used to be a piano in the corner, but the owner had removed it to add more tables. On quiet nights, Mardious would play music for the limited patrons, rather than standing obediently behind the bar. The songs he played were a great escape from the daily struggle, and brought him peace and inspiration. It was even more enjoyable when Amelia danced to the melody. She loved the slow songs, because they felt more soulful to her, but watching her move to the rhythm sometimes made it harder for him to concentrate.

Sugarplum was located on the edge of Camptown, which was the main trading city in the segregated district of the Badlands. Since it was a poor community, the pub was frequented more by travellers than locals. It brought in a great mix of strangers, which made things exciting at times, but that excitement led to unpredictability some nights.

The owner was an ex-convict named Gerard, who took over from his parents after being released from prison. He never told Mardious why he was locked up, but there were rumours that he used to be a member of a gang known as the Tyco. He was certainly always nice to other gang members, showing them respect whenever they came to his pub.

Although Gerard wasn't an official member anymore, Mardious knew that he still had connections to the gang. The Tyco were a bunch of thugs who lived by their own rules and disrespected those that opposed them. They were reckless and violent, even if they claimed that there was a method to their madness.

But Gerard knew how to deal with the gang, and had a successful business because of it. Mardious wasn't sure exactly what was done in order to keep the peace, but he knew it wasn't necessarily legal. In fact, Gerard was away from Sugarplum this very night because he had a meeting with the gang leaders.

"Hey, bruh. Can I get another drink?" Darcy waved his empty glass in the air.

Mardious shuddered. He looked at Darcy and smiled, and the night went on. More ale was poured. More cocktails were made. More time was spent flirting. More time was spent being flirted with.

Just as it seemed like the night was wrapping up, five members of the Tyco walked through the door. They were all branded with the gang symbol, a circle with a line down the centre. Some showed it off proudly on their arms, but others had it covered by long sleeves. They stood still, surveying the scene quietly.

Of all the things Mardious hated about his job, he hated serving gang members most of all.

"Porkchop!" exclaimed Amelia. She ran over and gave him a big hug.

Porkchop was a stout young man with thick biceps and a belly that almost busted out of his shirt. Mardious didn't know if Porkchop's nickname originated because he really liked pork, or because he looked like a pig. Amelia could barely get her arms halfway around him.

"Hey, beautiful," Porkchop said in a low, boisterous tone. "You look radiant today. How's my favourite girl?"

"I'm well, thanks for asking," replied Amelia.

As she tried to pull away, Porkchop kept one arm around her. He leant down and whispered something in her ear.

Mardious watched him like a hawk.

Amelia giggled. "Stop," she said playfully.

Porkchop's hand moved down Amelia's back. His fingertips were gentle, like a spider crawling across its web. It seemed like he had only one thing on his mind.

Mardious felt his blood heating in his chest.

Before Porkchop's hand could get any lower, Amelia reached behind her and moved it away. "I'll show you to your seat."

Porkchop smiled and followed obediently. He looked back at the bar, sniffled as if he had something stuck in his nose, and nodded.

Mardious didn't nod in return. He didn't fake a smile.

Amelia took the order for the Tyco members and returned to the bar. Before she could tell Mardious what they wanted, he was already mixing their drinks. He had a good memory, and remembered what all five of them had ordered the last few times they were in. He used the same recipe, but this time he felt like adding something special.

"Why do you put up with that?" he asked.

"C'mon, babe." Amelia rolled her eyes. "It's part of the job."

"No, it's not." Mardious grabbed a bottle labelled 'The Tempest.' "How many times do we have to talk about this? They can't treat you like a piece of meat. You don't have to act like—"

"Don't tell me how to act!" Amelia snapped. "You do your job the way you want to. I'll do mine the way I want to."

Mardious sighed and nodded instead of arguing. He hated disagreeing with her. He took the bottle and added a drop to each drink.

Amelia angrily grabbed the order and took it back to the table, but Mardious felt a little happier. He watched as she placed the cocktails in front of the Tyco members, and then walked away to check on her other tables.

Porkchop's right hand man, D'Angello, grabbed his drink and took a sip. He licked his lips as he set it down. After a few moments, he squealed like a tiny mouse. The rest of the Tyco laughed at him, but his face was full of panic.

"What is this?" D'Angello yelled in a very high pitch. His voice had changed completely, and he was now talking with a beautiful, uncontrollable falsetto. His friends laughed harder.

Mardious smiled as he looked on in pleasure.

D'Angello grabbed the drink and threw it across the room. The glass shattered splendidly when it hit the floor: shards of it bounced as far as the table of Guardians.

Everyone in the pub turned. Even the warriors stopped drinking and talking, their attention on the Tyco.

"Porkchop, what happened?" Amelia's voice cut through the silence.

Porkchop lifted his own glass to his nose and took a whiff. He looked at Amelia, stretched out his arm, and dumped the contents on the floor. He snorted a couple times. "There's something wrong with our drinks." He calmly shook the glass so the last few drops would fall out.

Amelia turned to Mardious and glared at him. He didn't feel guilty.

Because of their silent quarrel, Mardious didn't see who threw the next cup, but it nearly hit Amelia in the head. It flew straight past her and broke against the wall, sending glass and liquid everywhere.

Mardious eyed the Tyco. "Get out!" he yelled.

"We want new drinks," squealed D'Angello. This time, no one was laughing.

A Guardian got up from his table and made his way across to the bar. His footsteps landed heavily on the wooden floor. His comrades followed him closely. "Gentlemen, is there a problem here?" he asked.

All eight of them halted between the bar and the Tyco's seats, forming a perfect united front. Unlike their noble brethren in the rest of the realm, Guardians in the Badlands had a reputation for looking for an excuse to fight. The drinks they had been pounding back amplified their blood lust.

The ensuing quiet was so tense, it was almost as if the air in the room had stopped moving.

Porkchop and his gang stood from their table. They strutted across the pub to meet the Guardians halfway. Porkchop turned and looked at Mardious. He snorted again. "Let's go," he said. He tilted his head towards the door.

The Tyco all glared at Mardious as they exited, but they left without any more trouble. The Guardians stood strong until the gang had left the building, and then they returned to their seats.

"You're welcome," the lead Guardian said, nodding towards the bar.

Mardious didn't know who he hated more in that moment, the Tyco or the Guardians.

He headed to the back room in order to grab a broom, but Amelia stopped him on the way. Her eyes were full of rage. She pushed him as hard as she could, knocking him back a few steps. They stared at each other for a moment, but then her face relaxed and she reached out. He hugged her gently.

Mardious and Amelia cleaned up the mess made by the Tyco while the pub slowly filtered out. The 'bruhs' at the bar paid their tabs and went on their merry way. The Guardians were done with their ales and left together.

When the last patrons exited the pub, Mardious locked the doors behind them. Sugarplum was closed for the night.

"I'm going to the back to settle my Aileron," said Amelia. She gathered her sac of tips from the evening.

"I just have to take out the trash." Mardious shook the sac he was holding, and the broken glass rattled. "I'll meet you in a few minutes."

He walked towards the side door, trying to hold the sac carefully so it wouldn't rip open from the inside. The cool night breeze wafted over him when he exited the pub. He looked up at the glimmering stars and crescent moon, and was glad his night was over.

He walked the ten yards to the trash bin that rested against the wall and tossed the garbage inside. As he turned back to the pub, five shadows approached him from the opposite end of the building. The shadows crept forwards until the light from inside the pub shone on their faces. D'Angello was at the front of the pack, glaring at Mardious.

"That was some trick you pulled," he said. His voice was no longer high-pitched, and was now filled with hate.

Mardious looked behind him. Since Sugarplum was on the outskirts of Camptown, there were miles of open land beyond it. He thought about running. He was smaller and skinnier than each of the gang members, and likely not as fast, but he was a survivor.

He took a deep breath and then looked again at D'Angello. He started walking towards the power of the Tyco. "I don't know what you're talking about," he said.

"How dare you," snarled D'Angello. He had pulled out a knife, and now pointed the tip of the blade towards Mardious. "You know exactly what you did. You disrespected me, and you disrespected the Tyco. Now you're going to pay for it, and there's no muscle around to help you this time."

"I don't need those Guardians," said Mardious. He stood tall, clenched his fists and glared back at D'Angello. "I've never backed down from the Tyco, and I'm not about to pick today to start running."

D'Angello tilted his head from side to side and shook his arms out. He gripped his dagger, smiled, and reached out to grab Mardious.

"Stop." Porkchop calmly raised his arm and waved his hand.

D'Angello froze. "What?" He whipped around to face Porkchop, disappointment plain on his face.

Porkchop snorted again. "This is over." He stepped towards Mardious.

Although D'Angello was still fuming, he acknowledged his leader's request. He glared again at Mardious, spat at the ground in front of him, and then reluctantly moved back to join the rest of the pack.

Mardious stood proud as Porchop approached, but kept his fists clenched. He noticed he was breathing heavily, so he focused on slowing it down. He pretended to be confident and unafraid.

"Mardious Hood," Porkchop said, shaking his head. "You're either the stupidest person I've ever met, or one of the bravest." He leant in close to Mardious.

Mardious felt like Porkchop was studying his face, his eyes, and ultimately his soul. He remained quiet and continued to stand strong. He didn't want to show any emotion. His heavy breathing was noticeably louder, but his legs stood still.

Porkchop leant back. "You might not know this, but I've been watching you for months now. You're a good worker, you're smart, you have connections, and you have a strong will to survive. You would make a great asset to the Tyco. Have you ever thought about joining us?"

Mardious clenched his fists tighter and looked Porkchop in the eyes. "Never."

Porkchop held his belly and laughed. "Easy, easy," he said, and snorted a couple times. "The Tyco own this town, and everyone in it. One day, they might even rule the entire realm. It's better to be on the right side of history, so why don't you take some time to think about it first?"

Porkchop turned and motioned to the rest of his crew. They all started to leave. Before they were out of sight, he stopped and glanced back. "Oh, but in the meantime, if you ever disrespect us again ..." He dragged his index finger across his neck in a slicing motion.

The Tyco returned to the shadows, leaving Mardious alone.

Mardious kept staring straight ahead. He wanted to chase after them and put them in their place. His legs didn't move, but his mind raced. He felt like screaming, and clenched his fists even tighter. He hated being threatened.

"No one owns me," he muttered.

CHAPTER 3

The More Money We Come Across, The More Problems We See

Mardious pulled a glass out of the rinse bin. He wiped it with a clean towel, and stacked it with the others. He glanced across the pub again, but no one had come in.

Amelia sighed. She was standing on a stool, pretending to dust around the ale barrels behind the bar. She hated doing side duties, but with Gerard hanging around in the back room and nobody to serve, she had to look busy.

Mardious grabbed another glass and walked over to Amelia while he dried it. "Want to have some fun tomorrow?" he asked.

Amelia stopped wiping and looked at him slyly. "What did you have in mind?"

"There's another house I scouted in Kimroad," he replied. "It belongs to a widowed scholar. He spends his days fishing, and sometimes camps overnight in the woods. I'm betting he's kept his wife's possessions, and all they're doing now is collecting dust."

Amelia's smile disappeared. "It's kind of mean to pick on someone who's lost a loved one," she said. "That's how curses start."

Mardious wasn't superstitious enough to believe in things like curses, but he had to agree with Amelia's assessment. He was disappointed in himself for overlooking that detail, since it was the only house he'd scouted recently. There was one other venue that they could hit, but he was hesitant.

"I was saving this for your birthday." He stopped wiping his glass. "There's an antique store in Lakerville that looks like it's pretty easy to break into."

Amelia's jaw dropped. "How long have you known about this?"

Mardious felt a little guilty; Amelia loved old artefacts. "It was supposed to be special."

Amelia put her hand on his arm and smiled. "It will be anyway."

"Mardious," Gerard's raspy voice echoed through the empty pub. Before Mardious could turn, a fly landed on the bar top. It rubbed its legs together, as if it was thinking of a brilliant scheme, but a swift hand crushed it before it could get away. Amelia lifted her hand, and wiped the guts off on her dusting rag.

Mardious looked back. "Yes, sir?"

"Let's go for a walk," Gerard said seriously. He was standing at the side exit, holding a ring of keys. His skinny arm shook, as if it was struggling with the weight. "I need to show you something."

Mardious put his glass on the stack. He draped the towel on the hook beside the wash bin, and followed Gerard outside. The sky was turning orange, the sun setting on another boring evening.

They walked behind the pub, past the trash bins, and around the far corner. On the end of the building was a set of doors that led down to the pub's underground storage. The heavy steel panels, angled into the ground, had dual locks and no visible hinges, which was perfect for security in this area.

"I heard about your situation with Porkchop and his friends the other night," Gerard said. He fiddled with his key ring, studying it carefully.

"They threw a glass at Amelia's head," Mardious said in defence. "I had to kick them out."

Gerard found the two keys he was looking for, and took them off the ring. "I meant your talk with him afterwards. He asked you to join the Tyco?"

Mardious clenched his fists. "They think they own this town. They use violence to intimidate people and gang up on anyone that opposes them. I wish there was a way to put them in their place."

Gerard smiled. His moustache twitched under his long nose, like the whiskers of a hungry rat. "There are many different ways to take on an enemy," he said. "Sometimes the best way isn't to attack them from the outside, but to strike from within."

Mardious nodded, but he had no idea what Gerard was talking about.

Instead of elaborating, Gerard held up both keys and then knelt down on the doors. "The left one goes in first. Turn it and wait until you hear a click." He inserted the key, and then waited five seconds. It sounded more like a thud to Mardious. "Then use the other key on the right. If you insert it too soon, it'll break."

There was another thud, and then a handle popped out of the middle of the right door. Gerard took the keys out of their sockets, and then pulled the first panel open.

Mardious moved closer to the entrance. He'd never been down in the storage space before. He'd assumed it was used for old signs, tools, or cleaning supplies. However, the aroma that slipped through the doors made it seem like there was a beautiful garden hidden underneath the pub.

Stone steps led down into darkness. It looked creepy, but Mardious wasn't afraid. It felt like a great escape from the dry, mundane environment surrounding him. At Gerard's invitation he stepped underground and waited.

Gerard followed. He pulled his fire starter out of his pocket, flicked it on, and handed it to Mardious. He reached back outside. "There's a bar on the back," Gerard said as he pulled the door closed. "Just push it across, and the locks will recalibrate so no one can follow you in." He slid the metal protrusion, and another thud rang from the door.

Gerard hustled down the steps and took the fire starter from Mardious. As soon as they reached the bottom, he went around the room and lit a few candles.

Mardious stood still and admired everything. Shelves lined the outer walls, holding hundreds of different potion bottles. Some were filled with liquid, others with powders, and a few had ingredients—usually parts of different animals—inside. He almost laughed when he saw an entire jar of tiny eyeballs.

"I call this room The Cage," Gerard said proudly. He lit a green candle on a table in the middle of the room. "It's where I come to experiment with different potion combinations, trying to create new beasts." He picked up a small jar filled with purple powder. "I call this one Medusa."

Mardious took the jar and cradled it in his hands. "What does it do?"

"It turns people to stone," Gerard said casually.

Mardious held his breath. He straightened his arms to get the jar away from him.

Gerard laughed. "Not really." He laughed again. "It's made with lemongrass, fermented grapes, and hairs from Kaber bears, among other things. It immobilizes someone for a short period, but it doesn't actually turn them into rock. That would be psychotic."

He took the jar from Mardious and placed it back on the table. There were notebooks and papers scattered all over, but he didn't seem too concerned about adding to the mess.

Mardious felt out of his element. "What am I doing here?" he asked.

"I need your help," Gerard said with a warm smile. "After your outburst with Porkchop, I realized that you might hate the Tyco just as much as I do, if not more." Gerard rubbed his upper arm. "I thought I had a plan, but I've come up a little short lately. I think you might be the missing link."

Mardious looked at the papers again. He wondered how long and detailed the plan was.

"The Tyco rules by fear, but its power comes from Aileron," Gerard continued. "The highest members have the most of it, while the lower members hoard any scraps given to them. But the reason why they have so much is not because they steal and threaten others, it's because they control the most valuable resource in the Badlands: Rosebud. They own all the grow-ops and distribute it exclusively."

Mardious nodded. He already knew that the gang sold the addictive herb around Camptown, but he hadn't realized it contributed so much to their power. "So how do we stop them?"

"We create a potion that's better than Rosebud," Gerard said. "We create a resource that they need to make more money. Then we give it to a single high-ranking member of the Tyco, and let it poison their group. We create chaos from within by giving them too much, and having them fight over it."

Mardious tried not to laugh. Create a new potion? Let the Tyco tear itself apart from within? It seemed like Gerard wasn't thinking through all the possibilities. "I'm not sure," Mardious said instead.

"Look." Gerard put his hands on Mardious' shoulders. His bony fingers didn't apply much pressure. "I'm just looking for a little help. You have a magical aptitude for mixing things together. I have some recipes here, but they require a bit more experimentation and creativity. All I want you to do is try. If you don't make a potion better than Rosebud, that's fine. But you might be surprised how just a little insignificant thing can inspire something grand."

Gerard moved to the corner of the room and lifted a black curtain. Underneath was the small piano that used to be in the pub. "I even have this to help inspire your magic," he said. He knew that Mardious' focus came from his experience with the instrument.

Mardious moved to the piano. He reached out and played a short, one-handed tune. He imagined Amelia dancing to it. When he was finished, the keys to The Cage dangled in front of him. Gerard's dark eyes looked desperate. Perhaps that was why the ideas behind them were borderline insane.

Mardious didn't have to think about it. He smiled and accepted the keys. He wanted the opportunity to play around with new potions, and if there was no risk involved on his part, it seemed like a good idea.

"Thank you," Gerard said. "I really owe you. I know that you'll succeed where I have failed."

Mardious had an idea of how to capitalize on Gerard's desperation even more. He rubbed his temple and tried to act confused. "This is a lot to handle," he said, shaking his head. "Is it okay if I take the rest of the day off?"

"Of course!" Gerard exclaimed. "Anything you want."

"And Amelia?" Mardious said. "I need her to—"

"Absolutely," Gerard said, waving away an explanation.

Mardious helped Gerard blow out the candles around the room, then let him lead the way back up the stairs. He slid the locking mechanism out of the way and opened the door. When they were back outside, Mardious almost ran for the side entrance to the pub.

He found Amelia still pretending to wipe the ale barrels. She hadn't moved, because the pub was still empty.

"Our shift is over for the day," Mardious said, barely containing his smile. "Want to go antique shopping?"

Amelia stopped dusting and stared at him. "Don't tease me."

"It's true," Gerard said from behind him. He closed the door and walked behind the bar. "You two have a great evening together. It doesn't seem like it will be busy here anyway."

Amelia tossed her dusting rag on the bar top and skipped towards Mardious. He grabbed her hand, and they exited the bar together. They were so excited that it felt like they ran home. Mardious barely had enough time to tell Amelia about The Cage, Gerard's plan, and how that led to them getting the day off.

Amelia and Mardious lived in a one-level complex that was split into ten separate living quarters, or blocks. Each had its own entrance, which opened up into a room large enough for a bed, but not much else.

In their block, the bed was centered in the room with the headboard against the left wall. A short nightstand rested beside it. There was a small closet filled with second-hand clothes on the opposite wall, and a wash bin and toilet tucked away in the corner. It might have been tiny and substandard, but it was home.

After the couple entered, Amelia went to the closet to find a change of clothes while Mardious collapsed onto the bed. He wasn't tired. Instead, he eagerly waited for his partner in crime.

Amelia removed her tight-fitting work shirt and tossed it on the floor. She rummaged through the closet, trying to find something more comfortable. The gold medal she always wore swayed and tapped her breasts lightly.

Mardious couldn't help but stare at her beautifully scarred skin. The nostalgia of all the danger that encompassed their lives flooded his mind. He could feel his heart beat faster as he thought about some of their greatest moments together. His excitement for their next adventure built.

Amelia had found a black shirt. She held it in front of herself instead of putting it on, covering her exposed body. She slid towards the bed, knelt on the edge, and then draped herself on top of him. He wrapped his arms around her, tracing his fingers along the scars on her naked back.

"Do you think we'll get any new ones today?" she whispered.

"Hopefully." He closed his eyes and smiled.

He felt Amelia push herself off his chest and straddle him. He assumed she was finally getting dressed, until he felt her hand slap his cheek. He embraced the sting as blood rushed to his head, but her laugh tickled his heart.

He peeked through one cracked eye, and noticed her extending her arms to put on her shirt. When her top was covering her face, he grabbed her by the waist and flipped her, causing her to laugh hysterically. He pinched his knees against her hips and pulled the neck of her shirt below her chin to expose her beautiful lips. "You're going to pay for that," he said slyly.

"You don't have the—," Amelia started.

He kissed her hard, and she kissed him hard back. The madness, the pleasure, and the pain all wrapped together. He pinned her arms on the bed, intertwining his fingers with hers. Their bodies moved together like waves in an angry ocean.

Mardious leant back and broke the kiss, dragging his teeth across her lower lip. Her hands clutched his harder, as she arched her back and tried to reach for more. He let go of her hands and pushed himself up. He smiled at her, and saw her answering grin.

"My turn," she whispered. She grabbed him by the waist, shifted his body, and flipped him to the other side of the bed. She flung herself on top of him, but he didn't try to fight it.

She looked to the table beside the bed, reached over, and grabbed a half-used candle and fire starter. She lit the wick and held the candle over Mardious' neck. With her other hand, she clutched her golden medal. She looked up to the ceiling while she concentrated.

Mardious closed his eyes. He could feel the warmth from the fire on his skin, but he didn't know what she was doing. The anticipation and uncertainty excited him even more. He could feel the flame flicker, tickling him like a snake slithering across his neck.

All of a sudden, the relaxing sparks turned into a burst of heat, as if the snake had bitten him. It was as if its hot venom was oozing into his body, burning its way through his skin. His excitement turned to fear.

He tried to scream, but couldn't. It felt like his throat was being ripped open from the inside. He reached out his hand and swung wildly at Amelia. He hit her in the shoulder, knocking her away. The candle went flying as she fell off the bed. He heard her hit the wood floor with a thud.

Mardious clutched his throat and tried to slow his breathing. The skin felt a little rough, but he wasn't badly injured. He closed his eyes and relaxed.

He heard Amelia rolling on the ground, fumbling around on the floor. He would check on her soon—he just needed a few more seconds. He inhaled and felt his chest expand. He exhaled and let it all out. His peace was returning.

"Why do you have this?" Amelia asked softly. It sounded like she could barely get the words out.

Mardious opened his eyes, and stared at the golden dagger she held. Her hand was shaking, and her eyes started to water. The pain from his neck disappeared, but now travelled to his stomach instead.

"I wanted a souvenir from our last adventure," he replied. He looked down to avoid her sad eyes. "I went back to Hazelwood Forest a few days ago and grabbed it."

"Liar," Amelia said, her voice cracking but not breaking. "Why do you have this?" she repeated slowly. Her voice was regaining its strength.

Mardious lifted his head and met Amelia's gaze. He saw her pain, and felt angry at himself for causing it by getting caught. "I was going to sell it," he said honestly. "I was saving up so that we could get out of this dump, out of this town, and run away to a fancier life."

"This 'dump' is our home," Amelia said, fighting back full tears.

"It doesn't have to be," Mardious said, trying to reassure her. "Gerard might have a plan to take down the Tyco, but he's going to fail. Nothing will change. We have an opportunity to escape this wasteland and build a more successful life together."

He moved to the edge of the bed and stood up. Amelia raised the dagger to hold the tip of it against his chest. He didn't move any closer.

"Don't you want to live out your dreams? Don't you want to create a life for yourself where you can live out all of your wildest fantasies? We're not doing that here. We're working at a pub, barely making enough to live in a home that has more rats than rooms. Don't you want to be better?"

"Be better?" Amelia clutched her medal. "I can't do that. I can't be anyone other than who I am. Camptown may not be as fancy as some of the places that we visit, but it's in my blood. I *am* the Badlands."

Mardious felt his heart sink. He knew he was losing this battle, but he wasn't about to give up. "I'm not asking you to change who you are," he pleaded. "All I'm saying is that we should relocate. I have enough Aileron under the bed to—"

"There's more?" Amelia said in disbelief.

Mardious could see the light go out in her eyes, and knew he'd made a mistake.

"There's more? You liar!" She lifted the knife above her head and swung it down at him.

This time Mardious was quick enough to move away. She fell onto the bed as her momentum carried her forwards. Instead of engaging her, he backed up slowly towards the door.

Amelia didn't even lift her head. She let go of the knife and started to sob.

"Babe, I ..." Mardious started, but he couldn't find the words he wanted.

"Get out," Amelia yelled into the mattress. "Get out!"

Mardious knew that he'd messed up, but didn't know how to make it right. The only thing he could do right now was obey her request.

He turned and reached for the handle. He wanted to look back but he couldn't. The weathered hinges creaked. He stepped outside, closed his eyes, and took a deep breath.

He slammed the door behind him.

CHAPTER 4

To The Left, To The Left

The antique store smelled like a wet dog huddled beside a campfire. It wasn't putrid, but it definitely wasn't fresh. Mardious took his flowered handkerchief out of his pocket and tied it around his neck. He pulled it up and over his nose to ease the stench.

He had bypassed two locks to get through the back door. The first was on the steel gate, which was supposed to be an extra guard, but its craftsmanship was a joke. The solid wooden door was a little tougher, but he'd had lots of practice with similar ones. Now he stood just inside the entrance, letting his eyes adjust to the darkness.

He'd never gone on an adventure without Amelia before. At first, it made him feel free. He didn't have to listen to her, or make decisions based on her preferences. He didn't have to wait for her to hurry up, or escape because she pushed the limits. It felt good to be alone.

On the other hand, he missed her presence. Her laugh made the good times more enjoyable. Her wickedness made the danger more enticing. Her love of being bad made him feel accepted. Her love for him made him feel more alive.

He took one step, and then another. The floor creaked under his feet, but it was a safe sound; it reminded him he was alone. He didn't need anyone to find him here.

He walked towards the front of the shop. He passed rows upon rows of artefacts to get there, but the moonlight shining through the windows made the front end a little easier to see. He felt around, trying to judge his surroundings as the shadows danced about.

He tried to pick the easiest path, but items from the shelves had spilled into the aisles. He didn't want to knock anything over—yet. He was waiting for just the right time to release his pent-up anger and annihilate the precious antiques.

A statue caught his eye near the window. It was of a lion sitting proud, its mouth open and its teeth bared angrily. It was taller than he was, but slender enough that it almost looked human. Wings came off its back, making it look like a feline angel.

He reached up and flicked one of its fangs. His finger bounced off the ceramic softly, which made him smile wider than the lion. He knew it would shatter magnificently.

He rubbed his hands together to get himself ready. He took a deep breath, and was about to push the statue over, but something behind it glimmered. That glimmer tugged at something inside him. He surrendered to the shine and moved closer.

There were a few medals dangling on the wall. They each had three circles etched on the front. The first had a sword, the middle one had a flame, and the last had a quill. He turned one of them around, and read the inscription on the back: Strength in Unity. It was like the medal that Amelia had, but shinier. He held it in his palm, and sadness crept into his heart.

He glanced around the room, blinking to get the water out of his eyes. His vision had adjusted to the darkness, so he could make out more shapes than before. There was so much to explore, and so many things to destroy, that he started to feel guilty.

He wanted Amelia there to live the experience with him. He wanted to hear her laughter as she embraced her bad side. He wanted to see the passion in her eyes when she scoured the artefacts. He wanted to witness her anger escape during the destruction.

He looked down and sighed. He decided it wasn't worth destroying the antique shop without her. He let go of the medal. It clunked dully against the wall.

He was about to leave, but he noticed a pile of books on the floor to his left. The top cover had a lightning bolt captured in a potion bottle. Clouds surrounded the rim, making it look like a wicked storm. He picked up the book and tilted it towards the moon to get a better look.

There were a few words indented into the cover, but he couldn't make them out. The book felt old and dirty. He blew across the top of it, but there wasn't any dust.

When he opened it, the pages crinkled together. The yellow parchment was thick and old, but the words and images were inscribed perfectly. The painting on the first page matched the cover, but was instead beautifully coloured. The title above it read: *Potion Genie.*

He flipped through the text and briefly scanned list after list of vibrant potions. There were truth serums, sleeping solutions, and smoke screens. There was a whole section on poisons and remedies. He couldn't help but smile as he thought about his new assignment from Gerard.

He tucked the book under his arm and grabbed the next one. It had a tornado on it, and this time the title was clearly legible: *Element Control 101*. He was about to flip through this one's pages, but he heard a creak from across the room.

He froze.

He held his breath and counted to ten. The silence settled heavily on his shoulders. He didn't know if someone else was there, or if his mind was playing tricks on him. He looked around without moving a muscle. He didn't see anything except for the artefacts closest to him.

He was a little shocked to notice that most of them looked like animals. There was an angry wolf staring directly at him. Two dragons blew stone fire at each other. There was even a human body with a bull's head attached to it. He thought about when they had almost been caught by the Guardian with the horned helmet. He didn't feel like getting chased again.

He heard another creak, and almost jumped out of his skin. He didn't think anyone was creeping around in the dark, but he didn't want to stick around to find out exactly what was making the noise. He had to move.

He tucked both books under his left arm and tiptoed down the closest aisle. His head swivelled, and his perception heightened. There were statues on the floor that he didn't want to step on. There were angry faces above him that he knew were going to add to his nightmares. He had to keep moving.

He made it to the end wall, and then sidled along it until he was at the rear entrance. He turned the handle gradually until he heard the click from the mechanism. He slid the door open just enough to fit through the gap and slipped outside.

He held the handle in a death grip. He looked about to make sure that no one else was in the alley, and then used his tools to relock the door. He pushed the gate closed, but didn't bother with the second lock. All he wanted to do was run.

He dropped his head down and hurried away. Keeping close to the wall of the building, he headed for the end of the alley. There were multiple businesses on this strip, most with doors out the back. Some of them were even open, the night hours being profitable for their chosen market. He didn't want to look inside any of them and risk getting seen.

Something dropped behind him, and the sound of broken glass echoed down the alley. It was probably someone taking out the trash, but he didn't look back. He heard a crash, and obeyed his legs' sudden urge to run.

He entered the main street the alley emptied into and kept running. The rich town of Lakerville had streetlamps lit along the cobblestone roads, so it was easy to see where he was going. A few people were walking about, but no one seemed to notice him. It was probably because no one was yelling for him to stop, or calling him a thief. It felt good to be free.

His lungs were starting to burn, so he pulled his handkerchief down from his mouth. His jog turned back into a brisk walk as he gasped for air. After a few more blocks, he was at the portal doors. He was almost done.

This time he didn't want to follow someone to a random destination. He wanted to go home, but it was unlikely anyone from Lakerville would travel directly to the Badlands. No one from this rich part of the realm would risk going to a place as dangerous, unwelcoming, and poverty-stricken as Camptown. He knew if *he* ever moved to a city as luxurious as this, he'd never return to the Badlands unless absolutely necessary.

He was alone in front of the row of portal doors. He glanced down the street, but no one was approaching. It might be better for him to wait for someone to return instead of going back out into the street. There were five doors at this gateway, so he stood in front of the third; he'd have to move quickly to whichever portal opened first.

Two doors slid open at the same time. The one to his right had a horse poke its head through, dragging its cart and driver past the glimmer. But to his left emerged an older couple, both wearing fur coats and laughing boisterously. They were the perfect mark.

Mardious tucked his books under his right arm, kept his head down, and walked towards them. Most men carried their Aileron in a pouch within their left inside coat pocket. He'd lifted money before, and was confident that he could do it again. He peeked up at his target; they didn't seem to notice him. He took a few quick steps and crashed into the man head-on.

He tossed his books up in the air, making the pages flutter as they dropped to the ground. The man grunted. Mardious' hand dipped in and out like a snake attacking its prey. The woman shrieked.

Mardious dropped to his knees. The execution was perfect.

"Oh, I'm so sorry," the old man said. He bent down to help Mardious pick up his books.

"I'm sorry, sir," Mardious replied, pretending to be contrite. He tucked the Aileron pouch into his own pocket and grabbed his potion book.

The man stood and studied the other book cover. "I've seen this before." He flipped open to the first page, and started scanning its contents.

Mardious froze. Did the old man know that it was an antique? Did he know the owner of the store? Was he the owner?

Before Mardious could run away, the old man laughed. "This class was the worst." He turned to his companion and showed her the book. "Do you remember this, Elaine? Professor Newman used to take naps in class while we did homework."

Elaine didn't look pleased. "I liked Professor Newman," she replied. "He was the wisest, most decorated professor at The Academy."

"Teacher's pet," the old man muttered. "Looks like you have your work cut out for you, son. Good luck with your studies." He handed the book back to Mardious.

"Thank you, sir." Mardious took his prize, his gaze on the stones below his feet, and turned the other way. He had no idea what the old man was talking about, but it didn't matter. He'd gotten what he needed.

He headed to the last portal door at the gateway and stopped at the keystone. He placed the correct number of Aileron into the slot and waited. A bright light shone through the cracks as the portal calibrated for travel to the Badlands. It pulsated thirteen times, and then the two panels slid open towards the edges of the frame.

Mardious saw nothing but darkness on the other side of the glimmer. He smiled as he walked through to his homeland.

Unlike the streets of Lakerville, no lights shone around the single portal door in the Badlands. Instead, there were four dark, stone guard towers, with wood fencing between them. They were unmanned, and the wooden gate between the two main corners was always left open. No one cared enough about the Badlands to regulate what went in or out, because there was never steady traffic. The locals couldn't afford to use the portals, and the rich didn't value anything here.

Past the towers, there was nothing but barren land. No beautiful trees to stand under or mountains to gaze at. No animals scurrying about. There were only patches of yellow grass spread about the brownish-grey soil, and the slight breeze that blew across it all.

Mardious walked the few miles to Camptown alone in the dark, guided only by the starlight. It was peaceful, and it gave him time to relax, even though all he wanted to do was look through his new books. He wondered what magical treasures lay ahead of him.

He came over a ridge and noticed a few flickers of light down in the valley. Compared to the steppe he had just travelled across, the valley was lively and refreshing. Camptown was situated at the intersection of three rivers, with budding greenery and shrubs to the east, but continued barrenness to the west. There were other towns in the Badlands, like Deadwood, Riderton, and North Krydor, but Camptown was the main trading post. The rest of the realm knew it as a city full of scum.

Mardious made his way through the brush, past the unimpressive town outbuildings, and on to the main strip. Only a few people slept against the walls of the old abandoned buildings surrounding the main drag, but he could hear the buzz of chatter from the city centre as he rounded another corner.

"Get away from me or I'll stab you, troll," an old woman yelled.

"That's my bread, you rat," a man yelled back.

It felt good to be home.

Most Camptown locals kept to the main street. It was the city that didn't sleep; everyone talked around small campfires night and day. The road was nothing more than a mixture of mud and loose soil, constantly being trampled by the crowd. Since people from Camptown were notorious hustlers, it was the place to be for anyone trying to sell their goods; the people were always on their game to trade for anything new and shiny.

Mardious ignored everyone he passed. He recognized a few faces from Sugarplum, but he didn't make eye contact or engage in conversation. He was good at not drawing attention to himself. He even had the books hidden under his garments, so no one would see and wonder at what he held.

He was almost at the end of the strip, but suddenly stopped and ducked around a corner. He peeked out and stared across the way. Amelia huddled against a wall. She was holding a bottle and laughing hysterically. Porkchop had his arm around her, and was snorting and chuckling, too.

Mardious couldn't breathe. He was so angry he wanted to rip Porkchop's arm off. He wanted to cut off his head and spit down his neck. He would bury the portly man, and take on the entire Tyco to do it.

Why would Amelia turn to the gang for comfort? They were nasty, pig-headed brutes. Was it because he'd almost gotten in a fight with them? Had Porkchop made the same offer to her to join the Tyco? They were scum that didn't deserve her company. And yet she seemed to have made the transition from him to someone else so effortlessly. What did she see in Porkchop?

Guilt filled the pit of his stomach. He knew it was his fault. He knew he didn't deserve her, either.

The same group that had caused trouble at the bar were there, along with a few other girls and Amelia. Mardious wanted to confront them, but he was outnumbered. He also knew that it didn't matter how many there were if Amelia was still mad at him. He needed a better plan. More than that: he needed a better position of power.

If Amelia was bent on staying in the Badlands, then he had to figure out a way to get her away from the Tyco and others like them. He had to find a way to make Camptown better, to make it into the city that she deserved.

He pulled his new books out from concealment. He had work to do.

He kept to the back roads until he reached the west edge of town. He didn't go into Sugarplum, or check in with Gerard, but went straight to The Cage.

He took out his keys, remembering the sequence with ease. He locked himself in, lit the candles around the room, and cleared a spot at the table. He opened the *Potion Genie* and started reading.

He was focused. He was inspired. He was evolving.

CHAPTER 5

Now I Know Only I Can Stop the Rain

"What?" Damian slammed his empty glass on the bar top. His eyebrows were raised, and his eyes looked like they were going to pop out of his skull.

"C'mon." Xavier stood from his bar stool and headed for the door. He'd only been there a few minutes, and had managed to chug his entire ale.

For a moment, Mardious thought he had dozed off while the two men were drinking. He hadn't slept much lately. He was pulling double shifts, and then spending all night studying and mixing potions. He'd been making so much progress he was too excited to rest, and opted for naps in The Cage to regain some energy.

He grabbed both empty mugs. He wasn't imagining things after all. He wondered why Damian and Xavier were in such a rush. They usually stayed for a few rounds, at least.

"Order," Tiff said from the server station. Amelia had been giving away all her shifts over the last few weeks, probably to avoid seeing Mardious. Gerard didn't mind, but since Tiff had picked up most of them, it made Mardious' job that much harder. Tiff was the worst.

He sauntered over and put the dirty mugs in the wash bin. He stood in front of the bar well and waited for Tiff to respond.

"Two ales, one Bloody Mage" she said.

Mardious picked up a glass with one hand, and reached back for a bottle with the other. His arms moved rapidly, even if his mind worked at a snail's pace. He picked up a couple more glasses, and filled them from the kegs. He put all the drinks on the bar for Tiff to take away.

"Wait," she said. Her short nose scrunched up in confusion. "I actually need one ale and two—"

"Got it," Mardious said impatiently. He pulled one of the ales off the bar top, and replaced it with an empty glass.

Tiff grabbed the first two drinks, and turned to take them to her tables. As she stepped forwards, she lost her balance and dropped the Bloody Mage. The glass shattered beautifully, but the red liquid sprayed everywhere.

Mardious calmly took another empty glass and placed it on the bar. He made two more drinks as Tiff scrambled to clean the liquid from her shoes. She was able to wipe it off, but she still seemed flustered.

Before she could start making excuses, Mardious volunteered to clean up her mess. "It's okay," he said. "I'll go grab a broom."

But instead of heading for the back room, he took an empty mug and knelt beside the puddle on the wooden floor. He relaxed and steadied his breathing. He was excited to try a new element technique he'd been studying.

He reached out with his right hand and started to play a slow tune on his imaginary piano. He had practiced with some liquids in the potion room, moving them from one bottle to another. The trick was to imagine rocking in a rowboat. Instead of fighting against the movement of the ocean, he needed to move with it. The feelings that stirred inside him shouldn't be opposed, but rather embraced, like rowing with the current.

His heart beat faster as his power took control. It was like something was reaching inside his chest and massaging him from the inside as he connected with the liquid.

As he focused, the Bloody Mage droplets coalesced into a single puddle. He tilted his mug so that the lip was against the floor, and twiddled his fingers a little faster. Like an eel hunting for prey, the puddle slithered towards the opening, filling the mug perfectly. He lifted the glass in triumph.

He placed the dirty drink into the washbasin and went to the back room to get the broom. Although he had practiced moving powders with his element control skills, the shards of glass were too big to move around. He would have to sweep up the mess.

When he finished, he noticed a new customer sitting at the bar. The woman's grey hair stood on edge, and looked as dusty as her tattered rags. Her arms were so pale and skinny that he thought she might be a banshee. He approached her cautiously.

She looked up at him and smiled. She had two, maybe three teeth. He tried to make eye contact with her, but her left one was a little lazy. Her wrinkles were so deep that the dirt on her face didn't conceal them at all.

"Hello, young man," she said politely. "What can I get with this?" She slid him a flat, circular token. It wasn't an Aileron coin, but a novelty piece. It had a silver edge, with brass in the middle. An 'M' was etched on its surface.

Mardious recognized it instantly. He had taken a small sac of the tokens from one of the houses he and Amelia had visited in Kimroad. He thought they looked special. But when he tried trading some of them in Camptown, he discovered they were worthless.

"Where did you get this?" he asked.

The old woman smiled brightly. "An angel gave it to me," she said. "She told me to come here and present my gift to the man at the bar."

Mardious nodded. Amelia had set it up. "It's good for one free drink," he said. He added a fake smile, even though he could feel the budding anger inside him. "What's your poison?"

"Anything hard," the old woman replied.

Mardious slid down to his well. There was an old fashioned bottle on the top shelf behind him that was more potent than the rest. No one ordered it, except for the odd elderly person. Mardious used it to make something to satisfy the woman's request.

For the rest of his shift, all Mardious thought about was his nest egg. If Amelia had given the worthless tokens away, what had she done with the valuables? Had she spread his hard-earned wealth throughout the Badlands? Had she given it to Porkchop and the Tyco? Or was it possible that she was just baiting him?

He needed to talk to her.

The old lady stayed for a couple more, but the night was nearly done. When the last few patrons left, Mardious hustled to finish his closing duties. He even did most of Tiff's so that she wouldn't slow him down.

When Tiff left, he locked the doors and raced to The Cage. He grabbed his black hooded sweater, a bottle of his improved Medusa concoction, and a truth serum just in case. He wasn't exactly sure where Amelia was, but he was confident she wouldn't be alone.

After he left The Cage, his first stop was home. He half-hoped to find Amelia there, waiting for him in their bed. He imagined her resting peacefully, snuggled with their heavy blanket. He tried not to think about her sharing it with someone else.

When he got to the door, he hesitated. He leant his ear against it, but didn't hear anything. He turned the handle, took a deep breath, and finally entered. The moonlight shone on their bed. He was disappointed, and yet a little relieved, not to find her there.

He stumbled around the room, searching for the candle. He found it propped on the nightstand, and lit it right away. The first thing he checked was his hiding spot beneath the bed. All he found was an empty sac.

He brought the cloth up to his face and screamed into it. How could he have been so careless? It had taken him months to gather up that loot, only to have it discovered by accident. He should have thought of a better hiding place—or maybe a few smaller, less obvious ones.

He sat on the bed with a sigh. He thought about the night Amelia had discovered it. He could have taken it then, but he knew it didn't really matter. He remembered the look in her eyes, and the tears that he'd caused. He'd lost more than just a few coins and fancy artefacts that night. He'd lost the only thing that meant anything to him.

He needed to get her back.

He blew out the candle and rushed out the door. The only time he'd seen her since their fight was on the main strip, so he decided to try there. He took the back roads to emerge at the same spot he'd seen her before.

His hunch had been correct.

Amelia leant against the wall. Porkchop and the other Tyco members were talking. This time she didn't have a bottle in hand, and she wasn't laughing. She looked bored and lonely, even though she was in the midst of the lively group.

There were twelve of them in total. Even though the street was as busy as usual, they had their own distinct space on the side of the road. No one bothered them, but some of the Tyco members watched the crowd intently. They were like a pack of wolves: keeping to themselves, but always aware of their surroundings.

Mardious pulled his hood over his head, and took his handkerchief out of his pocket. He tied it around his neck and pulled it up. He didn't need to accidentally breathe in any of his powder. He'd made that mistake a few times in The Cage.

He opened his Medusa bottle, and sprinkled some of the purple powder onto his palm. Anyone that inhaled the potion would be rendered immobile, but they'd still be able to hear and see everything around them. His book had come in handy, and his newfound knowledge was about to be tested.

He'd added a memory loss mixture to the Medusa potion in anticipation of needing to be sneakier—he figured anyone he used it on didn't need to remember that he'd done so. This time, the Tyco didn't need to be involved in his conversation with the woman he loved.

He set the bottle on the ground and started playing a slow tune on his imaginary piano with his free hand. He needed to control the particles as they floated through the air. It was similar to controlling liquids, but he found it a little easier. He could feel each component, rather than trying to move a fluid all together as a puddle.

He cautiously filled his lungs, and then exhaled sharply so the rush of air crossed his mask. The powder dissipated, but he was in control of it. The particles floated like a soft cloud.

He fluttered his other hand, and the powder sped across the street. He lifted it over the crowd, and steered it towards Porkchop and the Tyco. He split the cloud into eleven equal parts, and filled the lungs of the wicked.

When he could tell that every speck of powder had been inhaled, he relaxed.

The potion worked almost instantly. By the time Mardious picked up his bottle and crossed the street, it was already in effect. The Tyco members were all statuesque. Their eyes swirled like blue whirlpools. Amelia still stared hopelessly into the darkness, seemingly unaware of what had just happened.

She didn't even notice Mardious until he stood directly in front of her. She didn't seem to recognize him under his hood with his flowered mask. He pulled his handkerchief down. She stared at him, and then rolled her eyes.

Her lack of enthusiasm hurt, even if he half expected it. He opened his mouth, but no words came out.

Amelia reached for a bottle that one of the Tyco members was holding. She clutched the bottom of it, but couldn't get it out of his grasp. She yanked on it a couple times, and then stood straight. She noticed his swirling eyes, and moved in for a closer look. "Did you do this?" she asked.

Mardious took a deep breath. He pulled the potion from his pocket. "I call it the Forgetful Medusa," he said. "It's a combination of a few different things, but the effects are powerful. It basically turns someone to stone, but when it wears off, they don't remember what happened."

Amelia walked to the other Tyco members, taking in all of their swirling eyes. "Why aren't we affected?" she asked.

"I used element control to target the rest of your group," Mardious replied. "It's something I learned from a text I stole from the antique store."

Amelia tilted her head, and couldn't hide her wicked grin. "You've been busy," she said.

"So have you," he retorted.

Amelia turned to him with her arms crossed. Her eyes squinted as she studied him, but she remained quiet. He thought she might apologize for taking all his treasure away, but he knew she was too stubborn to admit any guilt. They stood in silence.

She walked over to him and put her hand on his bottle of Forgetful Medusa. He didn't stop her from taking it away.

She pulled the cork off the top, and sprinkled a little into her hand. She straightened her arm, extending her palm away from her nose as far as possible. "Show me," she said.

For a moment, Mardious thought about using the potion on her. He looked over his shoulder, and found a different target instead. He didn't know the man standing by the fire pit, but he was an easy victim.

He stretched his arms out and played Amelia's favourite song on his imaginary piano. He leant to the side and blew the dust away from her hand. The potion floated through the air towards the innocent man. When it moved into his lungs, Mardious stopped controlling it. The man stopped rubbing his palms together beside the fire.

"Well done," Amelia said from behind him. "That will come in handy when you're on your own, stealing Aileron and jewels from the rich. Living in a fancier city and having a better life."

Mardious closed his eyes. He felt sad. He didn't want Amelia to think he was weak, but he didn't see any other way to get her back.

He turned and locked eyes with her. She held his bottle out to him, but he ignored it. He felt a lump in his throat, but he pushed through it. "I'm sorry," he said simply.

Amelia squinted and crossed her arms again. "What are you sorry for?"

"I'm sorry I broke our rule," he said. "I know it was risky, and might have caused unnecessary attention, but I thought the treasure could help us build a future together."

Amelia shook her head and looked away. She wiggled the bottle, still trying to get him to take it, but he didn't.

"I'm sorry I walked away," he continued. "I should have stayed and fought with you, instead of leaving you alone. I wish you hadn't turned to the Tyco for support, but I understand why you did."

Amelia pulled the bottle back. She still didn't look at him. She pursed her lips, like she was holding back words.

Mardious took another deep breath. "I'm sorry I lied to you."

Amelia raised an eyebrow, and faced him again. Her expression softened.

"You know me better than anyone else," he admitted. "I shouldn't have hid things from you, or pretended to be something I'm not. I hope that one day you'll be able to trust me again."

Amelia took a step towards Mardious. She tucked her chin down and wrapped her arms around his waist. She pulled him close and nestled her head on his chest. "I do trust you," she said.

He embraced her tightly. He didn't want to let her go ever again. "I love you, babe." He kissed the top of her head.

Amelia looked up at him. "I love you too, babe," she said with a smile. "There's something I need to tell you, though."

Mardious kept his arms around her, but looked away.

"I gave all of your treasure away," she said.

He turned back to her and stared into her sapphire eyes. He was glad she hadn't said anything worse.

"The strange thing was, it actually made me feel *good*," she admitted.

"What do you mean?" he asked.

"I started handing it out to random people on the street," she explained. "Their faces, their thanks, their smiles: it was uplifting. It made me feel like I had a real purpose."

She rubbed his back and squeezed him tighter. "I wanted to do more, so I gave the rest to the shelter. They help way more people in need than I could ever track down on my own, and will make good use of the donation. But that's when Porkchop and his goons caught me."

Mardious glared at the statuesque Tyco members. He was a little disappointed that they'd forget her confession to him.

"He told me that if the rest of the Tyco found out I had that much gold, they'd either take it or make me work for them." Amelia rested her cheek against his chest. "So I paid everyone here for their protection."

Mardious rubbed her back gently. "We can always take it back," he suggested. "Or I know how to make a few poisons if we want to get rid of them for good."

Amelia let go of Mardious and stepped back. Her eyes looked sad. "I know I made it difficult for you, and pushed you away when all you wanted to do was make our lives better. But if I can be honest, I like that you took that treasure. It made me feel good to make the poor people here a little richer, even if Porkchop took some of it for himself. It made me feel like I was making a real difference in our community."

Mardious smiled. He was glad that Amelia was happy. He was also relieved that his bad deeds had done some good for their world. In that moment, he realized that instead of saving money to build a life away from the Badlands, they might be better off making their current home a more comfortable place to live.

"What if we were able to get more?" he asked. "What if we went to houses in Kimroad and brought riches back for everyone: the people, the shelter, the Tyco. We could help the Badlands become a more prosperous part of the realm. Would that break our rule?"

Amelia smiled. "Some rules are meant to be broken." Her eyes sparkled with wickedness.

"Well, then, it looks like we have work to do." He reached his hand out for the bottle. "Together," he added.

She didn't give the potion back to him, but grabbed his hand instead. "Always together," she said.

They left Porkchop and his gang and headed to The Cage. Mardious had more things to show her, and they needed a plan if they were going to be successful. He was excited to demonstrate his potion-making skills, and help her to practice her own element control techniques.

Even though they had a new reason to go on their adventures, they were both excited just to be together again. They talked about which areas of the realm they wanted to explore, and what items might be most valuable. They thought about their outfits, and how they'd want to blend more deeply into the shadows.

More importantly, they came up with ideas to make the Badlands a better place to live. They were ready to take care of their people and provide riches for everyone. They were ready to make the Badlands *their* home.

CHAPTER 6

Check, Right

Amelia slid her handkerchief up and made sure it was snug around her nose and mouth. Her hood was pulled up, but it didn't conceal her beautiful blue eyes. "Ready, babe," she whispered.

Mardious took out his lock picking tools. He inserted the tension wrench into the keyhole, careful not to make a sound. When it was set, he applied a little pressure, but not too much.

He slid the pick on top of the tension piece, and methodically pulled it towards him. It had a jagged edge, which was useful for lifting the locking pins enough for them to catch. The pressure applied on the wrench kept the pins from slipping once they reached their position.

It took a few tries, but the tension wrench finally twisted: the door was unlocked. Mardious turned the handle and pushed the front door open a crack. He was met by welcoming darkness.

It felt different breaking in somewhere when they knew the owners were home. He was used to spending time studying his prey, learning their routines and picking the correct time to strike. The houses they used to target were always empty, so that they could be as noisy as they wanted without alarming anyone.

Since their goal was to collect as many valuables as they could find, they didn't need to spend a lot of time in each location. They wanted to be in and out as seamlessly as possible. The potions that they were armed with would help ensure their success.

It was the perfect crime.

Mardious and Amelia slipped inside and gently closed the door behind them. Their eyes didn't need long to adjust to the dark room, because they had already been travelling through the night without any light. They leant against the entrance to study their unfamiliar surroundings.

Mardious identified the edges of the hallway in front of them. He unhooked a pouch from his beltline. Inside was a sleeping potion that he had concocted from valerian root, rainbow sloth hair, organic elderflower, and neon toadstool. Ideally, he wanted to find the owners of the house asleep upon arrival, and then make sure they remained that way.

He tiptoed down the hallway, leaving Amelia behind. He was a little concerned that the wooden floor would creak and give their position away, so he felt it best for him to venture alone. He made it to the first doorway on the left of the hall without making a sound, and peered inside.

Moonlight shone through the window; the light bounced off a pristine dining room table. Silver candleholders stood erect, but the rest of the table was clear. Mardious knew that there would be other valuables stored in the dining area, but he didn't hunt for them yet.

He glanced across to the opposite room, and made out a crib nestled in the corner. A mobile of a family of multi-coloured flying unicorns hung above. He cautiously moved towards it, emptying some powder from his pouch in the process.

There was a rocking chair beside the crib, but it was empty. He walked to the edge of the baby's bed, and studied the sleeping child. It couldn't have been more than a few months old. It had very little hair, but massively pudgy cheeks. He thought it looked like a miniature Porkchop.

It looked peaceful and innocent, and wasn't directly a threat to their mission. But it was an alarm waiting to sound, and Mardious had to take precautions.

He hadn't tested his potion on a baby, but lessening the dosage seemed logical. He put a small dab of powder on his index finger and held it under the baby's nose until it was all gone. The child stirred only briefly before returning to its peaceful slumber. He rubbed the baby's shoulder gently, and hoped it had pleasant dreams.

He left the room and crept to the end of the hall. On his left was the kitchen, but to his right was the master bedroom. He took a deep breath as he emptied more contents from his pouch, and then entered cautiously.

He stood at the base of a wood-framed bed. The posts reached to the roof, and delicate linens draped from the canopy. Two heads rested on their pillows, but the couple had their backs to each other. They didn't look like they were having as peaceful a slumber as their young child.

Mardious didn't want to get any closer, so instead of dabbing the powder under each of their noses, he blew the particles off his palm. He leisurely twiddled his fingers while he controlled the floating substance into the lungs of the rested. Both of them snorted a little, but neither of them woke.

He whistled like a songbird to signal his success.

He heard Amelia shuffle down the hallway towards him. She stood at his side as he secured his pouch to his beltline.

"Where do we start?" she asked.

Mardious glanced around the room. "You check the dressers, I'll take the bed," he instructed.

She handed him a sac, and they both went to work. She rummaged through the drawers while he studied the sleeping beauties. He took the rings from their fingers, and the necklace from around the woman's neck. He also grabbed a few Aileron that were sprinkled on the bedside table.

After the bedroom, they scoured the kitchen and dining room for anything of value. Mardious swiped the candlesticks he'd noticed earlier, while Amelia stole some silverware. Overall, they were satisfied with their haul, but their sacs had plenty of room for more.

Mardious turned the handle of their exit, but Amelia stopped him. She traced her finger from the back of his hand, up his arm, and then slowly turned him. She tugged on his handkerchief and uncovered his lips. He hoped there wasn't any powder lingering in the air.

"This is a lot better than our adventures before," she whispered.

She pulled at his collar and brought his lips to hers. He wrapped his arms around her, swung her around, and pressed her against the door. She bit his lower lip and giggled. He could feel his heart pumping wildly.

After a few more minutes, the crime duo returned to reality and left their first heist. They were in a suburb of the small town of West Tally; it was less likely for Guardians to be patrolling here compared to the larger cities. The houses were on larger plots of land, but they didn't mind the walk between properties. It didn't matter if they were out in the open if no one was awake to see them.

The second house was much like the first. They entered flawlessly, used the powdered sleeping potion on the family, and escaped with a little more loot in their sacs. The third and fourth houses were the same, too. Their confidence built with each successful robbery, along with their excitement.

When they reached the fifth house, Mardious found something different in the kitchen. It looked like a birdcage, but there was a blanket draped overtop. He would have left it alone, but something red glowed from behind the white cloth. Drawn to its power, he forgot about his mission entirely.

The closer Mardious moved towards the small table where the birdcage rested, the brighter it seemed to get. He peeled up the edge of the sheet. The bottom of the cage was lined with shredded pieces of parchment.

He removed the sheet entirely and stared at a bright, glowing bird. Its feathers were ruby red. It looked like a raven, but the ones he was familiar with were black. The colouring wasn't the only noticeable feature: the red raven had three legs.

He stared at the tripod bird and thought he must be missing something. It stood still, but its head slowly turned towards him. Its beady black eyes studied him as he moved his hand towards it. He wanted to take one of its beautiful red feathers.

A split second later, the three-legged red raven started squawking wildly.

Mardious took a step back and remembered where he was. He was too flustered to try his animal control technique, so he reached for his pouch containing the medusa potion—it was too late for the sleeping powder. He fumbled with it as he tried to unhook it from his belt. Rustling footsteps sped towards him from the hallway.

"Babe!" Amelia whispered. She leant on the doorway and stared at the luminescent bird.

Mardious pulled out the pouch and emptied some of its contents into his hand. He wasn't sure how much to give the creature, so he just tossed the entire handful at the bird in panic. After a few more squawks and a flapping of wings, the bird went so stiff that it fell off its perch and onto the papered base.

Mardious tickled his fingers, and tried to connect with any remaining floating particles of his potion. It had worked on the bird, but he didn't need it to affect him and Amelia accidentally. Luckily, he didn't feel anything in the air.

"Ruby?" said a male voice from down the hall.

Mardious stared at Amelia. Her eyes weren't swirling, but she was as still as a statue.

"Ruby, is everything okay?" the voice said again.

A soft light shone against Amelia. She slowly turned towards it, but Mardious couldn't see what was happening.

"Who are you?" the voice asked.

Mardious poured the rest of the potion out onto his palm. He started to play a faster tune on his imaginary piano. He lifted his concoction in front of his mask.

Amelia giggled. She stuck her arm out. "You're still dreaming," she said calmly. She waved her hand slowly. "There's no one here but you."

Mardious blew the potion towards the hall. He twiddled his fingers, trying to quickly send the substance towards his target. The light got brighter, and he heard footsteps race towards Amelia. Then they stopped abruptly.

Mardious peeked his head around the frame, and saw an elderly man holding a candle. He had a mean scowl and a dirty beard, but his sleepwear was clean and white. His eyes swirled due to the effects of the potion.

"That was close," Amelia said. She shoved Mardious' shoulder.

"I'm out," he admitted. He held up the empty pouch. "If there's anyone else here, it's over."

Amelia went silent. Mardious stood still. They both listened intently for any other movement, but the house remained quiet.

Mardious moved out into the hallway. Now that they had the old man's shining candlelight, it would be difficult to see into the shadows as crisply as before. He grabbed the candle. The man was clutching the holder, so Mardious had to remove the wax from its base.

He didn't have to be sneaky anymore. He had already checked the first room upon entry, so there were only two more to go. He raced into the man's bedroom, but found no one else there. The other room was a study, with papers and books scattered on a cluttered desk.

They were safe.

He returned to Amelia, who was already rummaging through the kitchen. He stood in the doorway, and held the light so she could see.

"Are we clear, babe?" she asked. She opened a cabinet, but didn't seem satisfied.

"Just an old man living alone with his bird." Mardious glanced down at the pet, and thought about stealing one of its feathers. It might prove valuable if he could match it to any ingredients in his potion book.

"I'm tired," Amelia said. She pulled a jar of prunes from the cabinet, twisted the lid, and then popped one in her mouth.

Mardious lifted his sac. It was more than half full; their night had already been successful. "Me too," he said with a smile.

They ate a few snacks, grabbed some more valuables from the house, and left their crime scene. They disappeared back into the shadows of the small town.

The portal gateway was silent. They used a few of their stolen Aileron to return directly to the rough terrain of the Badlands. When they finally arrived home, they both flopped onto the bed. They were so exhausted that they didn't even bother to close the door.

"Should we see what we got?" Mardious asked. He kissed Amelia on the cheek.

"I'm already asleep, babe," she responded.

He forced himself up. He tossed their sacs into the corner, and then wrapped the blanket around Amelia. He was about to change out of his dusty clothes, but a knock on the open door stopped him.

Mardious turned, and glared at the portly shadow standing in the entrance. It sniffed the air a few times.

"Is that my share?" Porkchop asked. He pointed to where Mardious had tossed the sacs.

Amelia shot out of bed, dropping the blanket. She grabbed her fire starter from the nightstand and lit the candle. She turned towards their guest. "That's part of it," she said. "We were going to split it up evenly tomorrow. A third for you, a third for me, and a third for Mardious; just like we agreed."

Porkchop raised his palms. "I trust you," he answered. He lowered his arms and glared at Mardious. "But I don't trust him."

Mardious clenched his fists. He could see a few members of the Tyco huddled outside the door. He wished he had more Medusa potion, but the rest of his supply was at The Cage.

"You're going to have to if this is going to work," Amelia replied. "We're all in this together. Isn't that right, babe?"

Mardious nodded. He knew that dealing with Porkchop was better than having to deal with the leaders of the Tyco, even if Porkchop was paranoid. "Should we divide it all right now?" he suggested.

Porkchop snorted and then nodded. Mardious grabbed both sacs and emptied them onto the bed. There were coins, rings, silverware, candleholders, necklaces, and a few red feathers. He was pretty proud of their haul, and knew that the people in Camptown would appreciate the score.

"That's it?" Porkchop asked.

Mardious scoffed. Porkchop took a step forwards, and reached for the loot. Mardious brushed his hand away. "Don't—"

Porkchop swung in a sudden backhand, hitting Mardious square in the nose.

"No!" Amelia shouted.

Mardious stumbled back and reached for his face. Tears blurred his vision as his body reacted to the blow. He tried blinking a few times to clear his eyes, but closed them when he felt his hair being pulled.

"Don't you ever lay a hand on me," Porkchop said. He yanked Mardious' head forwards, slamming it into the doorframe.

Mardious swayed. The black spots in his vision were worse than the tears. He wanted to fall down, but Porkchop still held his hair. The petty tyrant slammed his head into the doorframe again before letting go.

Mardious slumped to the floor. Blood ran from his nose and into his mouth. He licked his lips, tasting his wounds and trying to get up the energy to retaliate. He gasped for breath, choking a little on the blood.

"I'm going to honour our deal in the future," Porkchop said. "But for that I'm going to take a little more today."

"That's not right," Amelia said angrily.

"Think of it as an investment." Porkchop snorted again. "I take a little more up front, and use it to buy information so that we can come up with a better plan. That way, you two don't have to put so much effort into robbing the lower class. We can build something better by going after bigger scores."

Mardious unhooked his pouch from his beltline. Maybe there would be a few particles stuck inside. A boot stepped on his hand.

"No tricks," D'Angello warned.

Mardious winced as he looked up. D'Angello glared at him and handed a bag to Porkchop.

Porkchop stood over the bed and started scooping up treasure by the handful. After he was satisfied, he gave the sac back to D'Angello, who finally lifted his foot off Mardious' hand. Mardious tucked his fist to his body and rubbed it, tying to ease the pain.

"We'll see you again soon," Porkchop said. He nodded towards Amelia and smiled. He looked down at Mardious and glared. But he stepped over the fallen wizard without any more trouble.

Amelia rushed over to Mardious. She closed the door, locked it, and then knelt beside him. She helped him sit up against the wall.

"I'm sorry, babe," she said. She brushed the wet hair from his forehead.

Mardious hadn't realized he'd been sweating. "It's not your fault," he said. He wasn't angry, just disappointed that he hadn't foreseen Porkchop's aggressive behaviour. "Besides, I was kind of wondering when I'd get a souvenir from tonight." He chuckled, but then coughed on some of his own blood.

"Show me where it hurts," Amelia instructed. She pulled her medal out from under her shirt and clutched it tight.

Mardious guided Amelia's healing touch from his forehead, to his nose, and finally to his hand. She looked uncomfortable, but absorbing his pain didn't seem like it was too much for her.

When she finished, she gave him a quick peck on the lips. "We'll have to be more careful next time," she said. She put her arm around him and flopped down on the floor. "I thought Porkchop was my friend. I shouldn't have trusted him."

Mardious grabbed her hand and rested his head on her shoulder. He wasn't concerned about the one-sided bounty hauled by Porkchop; he was confident they'd get that money back. Somehow. "We knew it would take some time to make a big difference here," he said. "It was a good start, even if the Tyco got the best of us in the end. Next time, we'll be better."

"Next time, we'll be ruthless," she answered.

CHAPTER 7

And It Goes A Little Something Like This

Mardious wiped the bar top one final time. He made sure the stools were tucked in close, and then stole a final glance around the room. Amelia had done a perfect job cleaning the tables before she went to the backroom to finalize her cash out.

The doors rattled. Gerard was gone, and Mardious had already locked them for the night. He stared at them, thinking his mind was playing tricks. Then came a tap from the outside.

"Sorry, we're closed," Mardious shouted.

"Open up," Porkchop replied.

Mardious sighed. He wasn't in the mood for another argument. He'd been dreaming of his bed his entire shift. After four straight nights of travelling to multiple small towns, he needed a day off.

He unlocked the door and swung it open.

Porkchop was holding a scroll tight to his side, carefully concealing it. A few Tyco members stood behind him. Porkchop stepped inside, but none of his goons followed. It looked like there were a few more of them than usual.

Porkchop placed his tattered scroll on top of the clean bar and unravelled it. He reached into his pockets and pulled out some Aileron. He placed them at the corners to weigh the paper down. There were lines traced all over the parchment, making it look like some kind of map.

"What is it?" Mardious asked.

"It's a blueprint," Porkchop explained. He stood back and admired it.

"What's it for?" Mardious examined it, trying to see if he could figure it out.

"It's for your next job," Porkchop replied. "It's time for you to move away from small houses and into something bigger and better."

The last few nights had not been profitable for Mardious and Amelia. The treasure it had taken them all week to gather was half the amount they'd gotten from their first night. They'd been frustrated, and so had their partner. Porkchop wasn't wasting any more time waiting for their luck to change.

Even though Mardious was exhausted, the new information was exciting. "Tell me more," he said.

Porkchop snorted. "This blueprint shows a building on the east side of the capital city of Kimroad. It used to be a theatre. A few years ago, it was sold to a developer that converted it into four separate shops: a candy store, a grocery, a flower boutique, and a weapons dealer."

Mardious studied the blueprint a little closer. There was a strip of four rooms, with labels on each. Even the entrances were marked. The candy shop was small compared to the grocery, but there was something circled in the corner of it.

"The developer built walls and customized each business accordingly," Porkchop continued. "But some of the old architecture still remains. Specifically, there's a secret underground passage that leads from one end of the complex to the other."

Porkchop pointed to the circle in the candy shop, and then moved his finger to the opposite end, tapping it on the weapons store. "It was used in performances, so actors could get from behind the stage to the front lobby without the crowd noticing; for trickery and showmanship. I want you to use this secret to your advantage."

Porkchop leant back and crossed his arms. "If you enter the candy shop, you can gain access to the office in the weapons store. You can raid it for Aileron, swords, daggers, arrows; whatever you can carry." Porkchop snorted again, waiting for Mardious' response.

Mardious stroked his chin and stared at the paper. It seemed like an easy enough job, but he didn't know how many heavy weapons he could carry. Amelia would end up hauling less.

"Why can't we just go in the back door?" he asked. He pointed to another spot on the blueprint. "Get in and out fast. That way we don't have to drag anything through narrow passageways."

"The doors of the weapons shop rival that of a fortress," Porkchop replied. "They open up instead of out, like the gate of a castle. They're heavy duty, and too loud to bypass without alerting any patrolling Guardians. The candy shop is much easier to get into."

"There are Guardians on patrol?" Mardious asked. He was starting to lose interest.

"I paid a few off, but not all of them." Porkchop sounded frustrated. "There's a bank down the street that's owned by the Triple Crown. They always make sure that someone is watching the area, even if I bought a short window of opportunity tonight."

Mardious shook his head. "Tonight? No, we can't do it tonight. I have to scope the area, ensure that everything you're saying is right, make some more—"

"We don't have time!" Porkchop slammed his fist on the bar. "I've already invested too much into this, and I need more loot to keep things in motion. You don't have an option. I'm telling you the plan, and you're going to get us our bounty."

Mardious stared at Porkchop. He was tired of taking orders from the brute, and knew he could come up with a better plan. It was time for him to start dictating the stakes, rather than following the orders of a thug.

"We'll do it," Amelia said.

Mardious glanced over Porkchop's shoulder. He wondered how long she'd been standing there. "I don't think—" he started.

"Good," Porkchop said. He placed two sacs on the bar beside the blueprint. "I want one of these filled with weapons, the other filled with Aileron. We split the money three ways, but I keep everything else."

"Okay. Now leave," Amelia said sternly.

Porkchop snorted. "So it's like that, then?"

"That's the way it is." Mardious nodded towards Amelia. He didn't agree with the decision, but he'd stand by her no matter what.

Porkchop snorted again. He turned and walked out without looking back.

Mardious stared at the blueprint. It seemed pretty clear, but he felt like he was missing something. "I don't have much Forgetful Medusa potion left," he said. He turned to Amelia. "If we run into any Guardians, I might not have enough. It's too risky."

"We're getting smarter and sneakier with every heist," Amelia reassured him. "We can do this. We need to know what we're capable of if we're going to succeed in the future. If we can pull this one off, we can take some time to plan our next one. Maybe we can even hit that bank next."

Mardious nodded. Her logic was solid, and he agreed that it would be good for them to push their limits a bit, but he was still wary of getting caught. On the other hand, doing what they did, there was always a chance they would get caught.

He liked Amelia's confidence, and was excited to keep their operation evolving. They both deserved to be cunning criminals, and the only way to get more loot was to hit higher-profile places. Pretty soon, they'd be able to go after his dream: the realm, the Triple Crown.

"If you're confident, I am too," he said with a smile.

They locked the pub and left Sugarplum with the blueprints in hand. They rushed home, fleshed out some specifics to their plan, and changed into their black garments. Mardious secured his potions to his belt, while Amelia grabbed some Aileron to finance their journey.

They hustled to the portal gateway, cutting straight through Camptown and across the plain. They were able to calibrate the portal to a spot only ten blocks away from their target in Kimroad. Even though it was late at night, there were a few people still strolling up and down the main streets.

Mardious and Amelia acted casual. She laid her head on his shoulder while they held hands and strolled through the streets. They didn't go out of their way to be pleasant to anyone and fit in with the community, but they didn't look out of place. They had their sacs tucked under their clothes to remain inconspicuous.

Even though Porkchop had warned them about the patrols, they didn't see any Guardians lurking. There were no squads doing rounds, and no warriors on horseback trotting about. The thieving couple made it to their destination undisturbed, rounding the final corner to see the candy shop on the edge of the old theatre.

They hustled to the building's alley. It was nice and quiet as Mardious steadied himself at the back door. He left Amelia at the corner to ensure no one would stumble upon them breaking into the shop.

Mardious picked the lock on his second try and opened the door gently. He mimicked a barn owl's hoot to alert Amelia. She took one last look up and down the street, and then raced over to him. They quickly stepped inside and shut the door quietly, taking a deep breath as their eyes adjusted to the darkness.

They were in a back storage room. Shelves lined the walls around them, with a closed door in the far left corner that hinted at the shop beyond. The moonlight from the tiny window trickled in just enough to make out the shapes of the many jars of ingredients that filled the shelves, similar to Gerard's setup in The Cage. Heavier crates rested on the floor, tucked nicely underneath some of the shelving.

Mardious moved to his right. He remembered the blueprint well, but it was different being in the actual room. He had to move one of the crates to find the small hole he was looking for. It was just big enough to fit an index finger, and wouldn't have been noticeable if he hadn't known it was there.

He stuck his finger in and lifted the panel up and away. A set of stairs led into the depths below. He couldn't see how far down it went; no window's light could sneak in on this path. Beside him, Amelia looked down before pulling a candle from her pocket. She descended a few steps, and then lit the way.

Mardious followed, leaving the trap door open behind him. He had to hunch over; the passageway was lower than he thought. The wooden supports were covered in dirt, so he tried to avoid them as much as possible.

He and Amelia stumbled forwards. It was quiet and peaceful, but their trek took a little longer than he'd thought it would. When they finally made it to the stairwell at the end, Amelia sat down to regain some energy.

"Should we blow the candle out?" she whispered.

"Not yet," Mardious replied. He moved past her and climbed the stairs. He wondered if there was a crate blocking their way, like in the candy store. If he couldn't move the panel, they wouldn't be able to enter.

He put his back against the trap door and tried to lift it. To his relief, the door moved. He peeked through the opening. After being greeted by only more darkness, he slid the trap door to the side and stepped up into the room.

Like the candy store, they were in a separate storage area, but this one had a few chairs, mounds of books, and a desk with papers on it. On one side of the desk was a closed door, but on the other side was a square, black box, nearly as tall as the desk itself.

Mardious was drawn to the mystery of the dark container. It looked like a bigger version of the depository safe that Gerard had at Sugarplum that kept the pub's daily-earned Aileron locked tight. There was no handle or lock on the outside, just a drop drawer on the top that allowed sacs to be deposited without opening the box itself. There was a magic surrounding it; he couldn't see it, but he could feel it.

"Jackpot," Amelia said. She too was fixated on the safebox.

"How are we going to open it?" Mardious replied.

"I thought you'd used Gerard's?" Amelia asked. She held out both sacs in front of her, expecting him to take both.

"Never," Mardious answered. "Have you?"

He grabbed one sac and bent down. There was a ridge around the inside edge of the safe, but nothing else. He pushed on it a few times, but it didn't open. He slapped it harder out of frustration.

"I've used it a few times, but only with Gerard's help," Amelia answered. "He told me what to feel in order to move the magical lock." She knelt down beside him and placed her hand on the front of the safe gently.

Mardious nodded. "Perfect."

"Not really," Amelia whispered. "Every safe is different. Without knowing the proper sequence, I doubt I could crack it."

"If we can't access it, then how are we going to collect any Aileron?" he asked.

Amelia sighed. "We're in a weapons shop. Maybe there's something here that we can use?"

Mardious agreed. He stood up and slid towards the door. He turned the handle and gestured for Amelia to blow out the candle. When they were safely cloaked in darkness, he pulled the door open.

He couldn't see anything. The room was pitch-dark, with no windows to let the moonlight in. He didn't hear anyone else, though, and assumed they were alone in the well-secured room. Amelia helped by relighting her candle without him having to ask.

They both stared at the racks in front of them. Dangling off hooks were axes small enough to carry on the hip, and ones with blades bigger than Mardious' head. He looked left and right, and saw the entire row was much the same.

"I don't like it here," he admitted.

Amelia moved past him. "Let's see what else is around," she said.

He followed her to the left, and then looked down the aisle. There were rows upon rows of racks, like a library of weaponry instead of books. A few had sharp-tipped swords and spears, others held bows and arrows, and even more had thick, unwieldy shields and ominous suits of armour. There were killing tools that Mardious didn't recognize, but he knew they were dangerous just by looking at them. It was the kind of thing worthy of nightmares.

When they got to the front of the store, they saw the giant gate that Porkchop had described. It was like a drawbridge, with chains that dangled on either side of the thick, wooden door. At least they could feel safe knowing that no one could quietly enter while they were there.

Amelia picked up one of the swords on the front rack and held it with both hands. The tip of it extended a foot above her head. "How are we going to fit this in our sac?"

Mardious lifted up his own bag. She was right. Not only were the sacs too small, the sharp blades would slash through the material. Porkchop's plan was flawed.

"How many did he want?" Mardious asked.

"He didn't specify," Amelia answered. She put down the sword and picked up a dagger. "But I don't think I can carry very many."

Mardious shook his head. "Can we use something else?"

"Too bad we don't have a cart," Amelia said with a giggle. "And a team of horses."

Mardious suddenly had an idea. He put his arm around Amelia and hugged her. "You're brilliant, babe," he said.

"I know," she replied. She rested her head on his shoulder.

Mardious rubbed her gently. "We should get a team of horses together."

Amelia stepped away and looked at him with her lips pursed. "What do you mean?"

"We're in the big city," Mardious said with a smile. "I saw a few horse-drawn carts trotting through the streets. All we have to do is borrow one for a while, and use it to haul our bounty. Problem solved!"

Amelia wasn't impressed. "How are we going to get a horse in here? Is it going to come through the secret passageway?"

Mardious frowned. His new plan wasn't perfect after all. He hated having to come up with things on the fly. "We have some time. We can move everything to the candy shop ourselves, then quickly load the cart through the back door."

"What about the Guardians?" Amelia asked.

Mardious grabbed a sword and held it out. "We need cover anyway. We can't really walk around holding large weapons without looking suspicious."

Amelia nodded. "This is getting pretty complicated, babe. I have a bad feeling."

Mardious smiled, and thought about what she'd said earlier. "If we don't push the limits, how will we know what we're capable of?"

Amelia picked up another sword. This one was shorter and had a protective sheath. She put it in her sac. "We need to stick with the original plan this time," she said. "We'll carry what we're able to, and use it to devise a better plan for next time. This place is pretty secure, but easy to get into. We just need to make sure we stay in the shadows."

Mardious nodded. With more planning, they'd be able to do a better job. But that's not what they had been asked to do. As much as he liked their new ideas, they could wait and use them on the next heist. They were evolving, but right here, right now, it wasn't what they needed to do.

He helped Amelia search the room for appropriate weapons to carry. They settled on mostly daggers and small axes that fit easily into the sac. When their first load was full, they returned to the safe in the back of the shop.

Mardious dropped their sac of weapons next to the black box. He pulled out a black dagger from it, removed its leather covering, and tried fitting the blade in the ridge that, to him, looked like the door. The metal blade was too thick, so he searched his sac for another.

"I don't think that's going to work, babe," Amelia said. She put her hand over the front of the safe once again.

"Then it's over," Mardious said. "We'll have to leave the Aileron and load up on more weapons instead."

Amelia ignored him. She pulled her medal out from under her shirt and held it steady. She closed her eyes and concentrated. She clutched the fingers of her free hand, as if she were holding an orb, and then rotated them around, slow as a turtle.

She pulled her hand back, shook it out, and took a deep breath. "Let's try this again."

Mardious held his breath; he wanted to stay as silent as possible, so she wouldn't be distracted.

After a few tries, she pulled her hand back excitedly. "I felt it!" she exclaimed. She shook her hands again, and closed her eyes.

Mardious didn't even try to encourage her—he simply watched in silence. Her tongue peeked out of the corner of her mouth. Her nose was scrunched up just a little bit. He wanted to watch her like this for hours.

Amelia turned her hand to the right, then back to the left, then to the right again. All of a sudden, she stretched her fingers out and yanked her hand back. A click sounded, and the front panel swivelled open. The safe was packed with small sacs of Aileron.

Mardious opened his mouth in astonishment. Even though he'd had no doubt she'd succeed, it was still amazing to see it happen. "How did you do that?"

"I felt the connection," Amelia said proudly. "It was like when I heal you. I absorbed the magic within the safe, and then was able to manipulate it. But instead of identifying the pain and diminishing it, it was like I was in a maze and searching for the right feeling. I just had to stay focused, instead of getting distracted by the other obstacles the magic threw at me."

"You'll have to teach me," Mardious replied happily.

They pulled sacs of coins from the safe and put them in their larger bag. There was more Aileron than they could carry, so they had to leave some behind. Once they had everything they needed, Amelia relocked the safe, and they escaped back down the narrow passageway. Mardious made sure to secure the trap door so that no one would figure out how they had entered.

He followed Amelia's light down the short path. He had the heavier sac of coins slung over his shoulder and could feel the weight pushing down on him. He wondered how Amelia was handling the sac of weapons. He wasn't eager to haul the sac of coins all the way to Camptown, even if it was more money than they could have acquired in weeks of robbing houses.

With a crash, Amelia stumbled to the ground. The light went out, and she screamed.

Mardious dropped his sac and hustled forwards, searching for her in the dark. When he touched her, she screamed again.

"What is it?" he asked frantically.

Amelia laughed. "I'm so stupid," she said. She flicked her fire starter and relit her candle. She lowered it down her body. There was a bloodstain on her right pant leg.

Mardious rolled up her attire and took a closer look. A blade had punctured her calf, but it wasn't fatal. "Looks like you get the souvenir today," he joked.

He helped her to stand. He had to side-step down the narrow passage while they stumbled along together. Amelia had a noticeable limp. They made it to the stairwell, and she sat at the top of it. Blood oozed from her wound.

"I wish I could heal," he said. Healing power was something he could never understand. It wasn't like mixing potions or controlling animals. He just didn't have a feel for it.

"I'll be okay, babe," Amelia replied. "But I don't think I can carry a heavy sac with me."

Mardious removed his handkerchief from around his neck and wiped up the blood. He tied the cloth around her leg and secured it with a knot. He hoped it would buy them some time before returning home, where they could rest and find a healer.

He returned to the passageway. Grabbing the sac of weapons, he noticed a dagger's naked blade sticking out the side. The blade was black, but the tip had a fresh coat of red.

He carried that sac up the stairs of the candy shop first before going back down for the sac full of Aileron. After he put it beside Amelia, he secured the trap door and returned the crate to its original position.

Amelia tried to stand, but she looked weak. She raised her hurt leg, and then tried stretching it out. "I can't do it, babe," she said.

Mardious wrapped his arms around her and held her tight. They'd hit a hiccup in their adventure, but it was far from being over. "I can handle the load," he reassured her. "Let's get out of here together. I'll get you to the portal gateway, and then I'll come back for the loot on my own."

Amelia kissed his cheek, and they exited the candy shop. Thankfully, they were alone in the alley. Mardious closed the door behind them, but didn't lock it. Amelia draped her arm around his shoulders, and hobbled to the edge of the building. They took a look around before continuing to stumble along.

The streets were less crowded now, but there was still the odd person walking about. Mardious preferred the big city to the small towns, because nobody bothered strangers; no one even looked their way.

A block before the portal gateway, there was a park. During the day, it would have been a beautiful place to have a picnic. There was a small lake in the centre, and flowerbeds scattered about. They found a bench and stopped. Amelia took a seat, and Mardious joined her.

"I'll wait for you here while you grab our loot," she instructed.

He felt like resting awhile, but the faster he got their sacs, the quicker they'd get home. He nodded, and then hustled back to the candy shop.

When he arrived, he grabbed the sac of Aileron first; he didn't want to risk the same misfortune as Amelia, and accidentally stab himself in the leg. He closed the door behind him and strutted down the empty alley, returning the way he'd come.

When he had almost reached Amelia's park bench, he turned a corner and froze. A Guardian had dismounted from his horse about half a block down. He wore an oddly-shaped helmet that Mardious recognized: it had the horns of a bull coming out the top. The Guardian was kneeling, studying the ground, and stroking his beard.

Mardious carefully backpedalled and hid back around the corner. He tried to think of another route he could take, but lost his focus: there was a drop of blood on the dirty pavement.

He turned, and saw that the blood trail led around the corner. He didn't have to peek around to know that the Guardian was studying the tracks. He had to move.

As quietly as he could, he left his position and detoured down a different street. He took a few more turns, and then hid in another alley. He stashed the Aileron sac away from the corner, and then re-entered the street.

The Guardian had two directions to go; he'd either follow the trail to the candy shop, or go directly to Amelia. She didn't have anything incriminating on her, but she didn't exactly look innocent. Mardious trusted that Amelia would think of something, and decided to protect their loot first, before they were found out.

He tried to run, but was only able to make it a block before he was sweating and breathing heavily. He pushed onwards, and tried to focus on his goal rather than how much his lungs hurt or how tired his legs were. He made it to the empty alley of the candy shop without alerting any more Guardians.

He pulled the weapon sac outside, closed the door, and used his picks to lock up. He found where the dagger poked through the bag and readjusted its position. Instead of slinging the sac across his back, he gently wrapped his arms around it, like he was carrying a nervous toddler.

For a couple blocks, he focussed on moving away from the crime scene, and only then detoured back to his stash. He placed the bag of weapons in the same alley as the Aileron, and then hustled to Amelia. His route led him past the portals, and then doubled-back to the park where she was.

When he was in view of the bench, he stopped and hid in the shadows. The same Guardian with the horned helmet had again dismounted from his horse, and was studying the bench where Amelia should have been sitting. She was nowhere to be seen.

Mardious wondered where she was hiding. He checked his beltline and grabbed his Forgetful Medusa potion. He didn't have a lot of it left, but he knew it would be enough for one victim. He watched closely, judging the actions of the curious warrior.

The Guardian walked away from the bench, pulling his horse along while he studied the ground. He moved closer and closer to the portal gates, until he finally reached the keystone of the last doorway. He paused for a second, and then looked towards the door.

Mardious closed his eyes and breathed a sigh of relief. Amelia must have used the portal to slip away. He wished he could have been with her, but he was glad she had avoided trouble.

He returned to his stash. He grabbed both sacs, stuck to the back streets, and dragged them back to the portals. His arms were heavy, but he took it slowly and rested when he could. He found solace in the shadows, and wasn't seen by anyone.

It took him longer than it should have, but he finally reached the portal gateway. The Guardian on horseback was nowhere to be found. He must have followed the trail back the other way, towards the candy shop. Mardious didn't waste any time, and calibrated the keystone for the Badlands.

When he went through the portal door, he turned back to watch the reflection of Kimroad. He didn't want anyone to follow, and waited anxiously for the panels to slide closed before doing anything else. When they were secure, he felt two hands wrap themselves around his waist.

"You made it," Amelia said.

Mardious let go of both sacs and closed his eyes. He rubbed the back of her hands, pressing them tightly to him. "I'm glad you're safe," he said.

"I felt like people were eyeballing me, so I decided to get out of there. I knew you'd find me, though." She turned him around and smiled. "We've become a better team the last few nights. It's like you know what I'm thinking without me having to say a word."

Mardious pulled her handkerchief from her face and kissed her passionately. He held her tighter, until his arms gave out from all the work. He broke the kiss and smiled back. "Like that?" he asked.

"Just like that," Amelia replied. She lifted her chin and kissed him again.

CHAPTER 8

Want To Be Ballers? Shot Callers? Brawlers?

A young woman huddled on the corner of the street. A tattered blanket covered her legs in a poor attempt to protect her from the cool night air. She hugged her toddler as they both slept peacefully.

Mardious tiptoed closer and knelt down. He had a few Aileron pinched between his fingers. He didn't want to lift the blanket, or do anything to wake the struggling family. He tucked the coins underneath the woman's boot, hoping she'd see them in the morning.

He crept down the block. Once safely around the corner, he leant against the wall to check his sac. He only had a few coins left. It had been a long night, but he was a little disappointed that it was almost over.

Amelia slithered beside him. She put her head on his shoulder, and took a peek at their bounty. "Is that it?"

"Unless we want to take some out of the shelter donation, that's all we have left," he stated.

"It went pretty fast." She kissed him on the cheek. "We'll have to get more next time."

Mardious and Amelia had decided to distribute their cut of the weapons shop heist before Porkchop had a chance to see it. They didn't want him taking a larger portion for himself again, because it was hurting those in need. Besides, since they took all the risk, and Amelia had gotten hurt in the process, they deserved to call the shots.

Mardious put his arm around Amelia and pulled her close. She leant against him, and they hobbled down the street towards the shelter. Her wound had scabbed up, but they wanted to trade a donation for some healing power. The shelter's headmaster had helped them before, and had always treated them with kindness.

The shelter was a three-storey building that took up a full block. It was made of brick, and had bars on every window. It used to be a prison, but was abandoned when the Triple Crown pulled its funding. Since most of the people who lived in the Badlands were criminals of one sort or another anyway, the government didn't see the sense in wasting money locking up anyone in the area.

Mardious had stashed the rest of their loot at the rear of the building. When they got to it, they took out half the small Aileron sacs and cradled them in their arms. They snuck back to the entrance, and strode in confidently.

The old door creaked as they entered, but the inside of the building smelled fresh. A dozen candles lit the entryway, providing both warmth and comfort. By the time they stepped through and closed the door, a concerned young woman met them. She had dark hair, soft eyes, and clean clothes.

"Welcome," she said with a smile. "I'm Mary Angella. We have a few rooms available, but unfortunately we're out of clean blankets and pillows."

Mardious smiled in return. "We're actually not here to spend the night. We're looking for Mr. Miller. Is he around?"

Mary Angella's smile disappeared. "Unfortunately, he's dealing with …" she sighed. "He's trying to recover from a Rosebud overdose. Like many in Camptown, he is fighting a battle with addiction."

Mardious closed his fist. He wanted to punish the Tyco for inflicting their product on the kind and generous Mr. Miller. It was their fault he was sick and struggling.

"That's okay." Amelia grabbed Mardious' hand, relaxing him a little. "We have a donation for the shelter. Will you accept it on Mr. Miller's behalf?" She proffered the sacs she held.

Mary Angella put her hand over her mouth, her eyes bright. She quickly regained her composure. "Bless your little hearts." She spread her arms out wide and hugged both of them gently.

Mardious felt awkward getting a hug from a stranger, but he noticed Amelia close her eyes and smile. Seeing her joy made him feel good about their donation and their efforts to help those in need.

Mary Angella let go, and then turned to Amelia. Her smile had disappeared. "You're hurt, dear," she said.

"It's just a scratch," Amelia replied. She lifted up her right pant leg to show off her beautiful wound.

Mary Angella bent down and examined the cut. Blood had dried around Amelia's ankle, but the wound had already closed up. There was a little puss, but nothing too extreme.

Without needing an explanation, Mary Angella clutched Amelia's calf. A soft glow surrounded her palm as her healing power came through. Mardious couldn't see what she used as a focus—he wondered if she even needed one. Only the most powerful wizards were able to master their craft without using a crutch like Amelia's medal or his twiddling fingers.

When Mary Angella removed her hand, Amelia's leg was back to normal. Unfortunately, she was too good a healer to leave a beautiful scar.

"I was just about to make some cookies," Mary Angella said. "Would you like to help me?"

Amelia shook out her leg, as if testing the wizard's handiwork. "Thank you, Mary Angella, but we're going to head home. It's been a long night."

"Of course, dear," Mary Angella replied. "But I feel like I owe you something more, in exchange for your generous contribution today."

"Next time," Mardious said with a smile.

"Yes, we'll be back here again with some more donations," Amelia said.

"Bless your souls," Mary Angella replied. "I'll relay the message to Mr. Miller. Who should I say is the contributor?"

Mardious frowned. If their names got out, the Tyco would hunt them down. It was better if they were left anonymous. "Actually—"

"Money Jane," Amelia said, cutting him off. "You can tell him the donation was made by Money Jane."

Amelia was beaming. Mardious could see how proud she was; he was glad she could take a little bit of ownership with the donation. An alias still gave them anonymity, even if it was close to her name. Seeing her joy made it all worthwhile. With these good deeds, he had a feeling that luck would be on their side.

"Thank you, Money Jane," Mary Angella said. Her warm smile returned. "I look forward to seeing you both again."

When they left the shelter, Amelia threw both her arms in the air. She looked up to the night sky and closed her eyes. "Yes!"

Mardious wasn't ready to celebrate just yet. They still had to deliver the rest of their bounty to Porkchop. He wanted to make sure that they fulfilled their duty, but it was more than that: he wanted to keep moving forwards so he could see Amelia this happy all the time.

They didn't know where to look for Porkchop, so they headed for home. Since he had been so anxious about their first job, they knew he'd be even more anxious for this one with its bigger payoff. So when they arrived, they weren't surprised to see D'Angello leaning against their doorframe with his arms crossed.

Mardious didn't say anything. He held out the sac of weapons, expecting D'Angello to take it. Instead, D'Angello walked past them. "Follow me."

"Just take your share," Amelia said. She dropped the sac of Aileron and pushed their door open.

"That's not what this is about," D'Angello replied. "Porkchop wants to show you something."

Mardious sighed. "We're tired, and we—"

D'Angello stopped. He turned around and smiled pleasantly. "It won't take long."

Mardious had never seen the thug smile, but it seemed genuine.

He heard the door close behind him. Amelia clutched his arm. "Let's get this over with," she said, holding Porkchop's cut of the money once more.

They followed D'Angello across Camptown. They avoided the main drag, and instead roamed the backstreets until they found themselves in front of an abandoned building. It was two storeys high and half a block long.

The windows were boarded up, and some street art decorated the sidewall.

D'Angello tapped on the front door three times and waited a few seconds with his fist held high. He then knocked five more times and let his arm drop. The thick door opened, and the sound of chatter escaped as they walked through.

The inside was even uglier than the outside. The walls were worn, the floor had some boards missing, and garbage was piled in the corners. A lone fireplace burnt bright on the sidewall, providing light and warmth for the room. As rough as it looked, it didn't stop the dozens of people in the room from talking, drinking, and laughing. There must have been at least a hundred strangers scattered about, all having a good time.

"There she is," Porkchop said happily from among the partiers. He put his hands high over his head and smiled proudly.

A group followed Porkchop towards Mardious and Amelia. Mardious felt uncomfortable holding a sac filled with weapons in the middle of the room, but he didn't set it down. He gripped it tighter and tried to remain calm.

Porkchop put his arm around Amelia and presented her to his group. "Meet the Saviour of the Badlands," he said proudly. "She's the one who brought us all together, and will lead us into the better life we've been dreaming of."

Amelia reluctantly started shaking hands with the crowd. All of them were thick, strong-looking thugs. Although Mardious couldn't see the mark of the Tyco on all of them, he noticed a few symbols embedded in their skin. He wondered if Amelia had met any of them before, although for now they all acted like strangers.

Porkchop didn't even introduce Mardious before pulling Amelia towards another group. Mardious didn't mind; he wanted to remain distant. He felt like he didn't belong, and was more comfortable in the shadows. He adjusted his grip on the sac of treasure and followed along.

They walked around the entire room. Porkchop was sure to introduce Amelia to everyone, and they all had the same reaction. They were happy, friendly, and respectful. For a second, Mardious thought the drinks must have been the reason everyone was in such a good mood. He wasn't about to trust anyone here. There must be something lurking in the underbelly of this party.

Porkchop finally led them to the back of the giant room, where there was a small hallway and a few closed doors. It was a lot quieter on this end of the building, which Mardious preferred. He would finally be able to drop off the heavy sac that burdened him.

They entered the most central room, but no one followed them in. Porkchop walked behind a desk and pushed away a chair that was too small for him. He steadied his hands, leant over the desk, and snorted. "Let's see what you've brought me."

Mardious swung the sac. He took a deep breath as it landed with a thud. Amelia did the same.

"We already took our share," Amelia said.

Porkchop pulled out a dagger. He brought it up to eye level and studied its edge. He pointed it at Mardious. "That's not how we do things."

Mardious stared right back. "Things have changed."

Porkchop chuckled. "Did you sneak a couple drinks at my party? If you think I'm going to let you take a bigger cut, you're mistaken."

Mardious clenched his fist, but remained calm. "The weapons shop was a good idea, but it was poorly planned. Because we were rushed, we left behind a lot more than we should have. Plus, we almost got caught this time."

He glanced at Amelia, but she kept her head down. She didn't seem to want to be involved in the argument. He turned back to Porkchop, who was smiling wickedly.

"We're going to start calling the shots around here," Mardious continued, pointing to himself and Amelia. "We're going to plan the heists, so that the execution is flawless. If you have a problem with that, then we don't have a partnership anymore."

Porkchop chuckled again. He moved the tip of his blade to the desk, and then twirled the handle. Although playing with his new toy, he was still careful not to damage the surface of the tabletop.

Mardious studied the thug. Was he thinking about the proposition? Was he contemplating his next move? Was he about to use the weapons in the sac? Mardious moved his hand towards his beltline. He still had a little Forgetful

Medusa potion left, and would immobilize Porkchop before he could do any damage with the dagger.

"Do you think all those people out there are going to let you quit?" Porkchop stopped spinning the blade, and looked towards Amelia. "We've paid a high price for their loyalty, and we'll need to pay them even more for their continued silence. If we stop the flow of Aileron into their pockets, then we're all doomed."

Mardious glanced at Amelia again. She was staring at Porkchop with fear in her eyes. "What have you done?" she asked.

Porkchop dropped the blade and started placing the smaller sacs of Aileron on the desk. "You didn't actually think you could just walk around town, giving out Aileron, without anyone noticing what you were doing, did you? You asked me to help protect you, so I'm doing that," he said. "But the problem with making a lot of noise is that someone is likely to hear it, eventually."

He tapped each small sac, counting them with his fingers. "Instead of paying people to ignore what they've heard, I'm simply buying their loyalty. The Tyco is built on respect, but their power comes from Aileron. If we want to challenge that power, we're going to have to be able to pay their members more than they can."

Mardious was reminded of his talk with Gerard. "I thought the Tyco's source of power was Rosebud," he said.

Porkchop snorted. "Power doesn't come from plants," he said. "Power comes from people. The Rosebud that the Tyco sell provides them with income, but if we have more Aileron than they do, then their members will flock to us. We can start our own gang, and take over this part of the realm."

"So you didn't need those weapons for protection," Amelia said. "You needed them to start a war."

Porkchop looked up and smiled. "If everything goes to plan, there won't even be a war."

Mardious rubbed his forehead. Porkchop's plan sounded too simple. If it was anything like the weapons store heist, it probably had some holes in it. That job had been riskier than expected, and now their lives were in even more danger.

"We're not going to be a part of this." Amelia grabbed Mardious' hand and pulled him towards the door.

"Wait," Mardious said.

Amelia raised an eyebrow. She dropped his hand and crossed her arms.

"Our goal is to change the Badlands: to help everyone in this part of the realm have a better life," he said. "The people on the other side of that door are part of that, even if they're not sleeping on the street or scrounging for food. We have an opportunity to make a difference, and if that involves buying loyalty, or tipping the scales of power, then we'll do it."

Amelia's eyes softened. She took a deep breath and nodded.

Mardious smiled, but he felt conflicted. He couldn't believe that he was defending the thugs with the influence to hurt them, especially if they were so easily swayed by Aileron.

"Perfect," Porkchop said. He snorted again.

Mardious whipped his head around and glared at his business partner. "We're not doing it on your terms, though," he said. "We're still going to do it on ours."

Porkchop smiled. "I don't—"

"It's non-negotiable," Mardious said. "We're all in this together, but Amelia and I have to be in control of what happens. You can still distribute the wealth as you see fit, but we're going to call the shots for everything else. We're going to plan the heists. We're going to decide what to steal. We're going to run this operation efficiently and effectively."

"And we're going to do it from the shadows," Amelia added.

Porkchop stared at the two of them, and then smiled. "So you don't want me introducing you as the Saviour of the Badlands anymore?" he asked. "People need to know who the boss is around here in order to keep them honest."

"We'll just use an alias," Mardious said. He gripped Amelia's hand again.

She smiled. "Call us Money Jane."

CHAPTER 9

I'm Not A Businessman. I'm A Business, Man

Mardious held the ring close to his eye. Its setting was shaped like a flower, with petals that were filled with diamonds. They encircled a giant square ruby in the middle, which sparkled in the moonlight.

Amelia brushed his arm, causing him to drop it. He knelt down, removing his gloves to feel around for it in the dim light. When his fingers touched the cold loop, he picked it up gently and held it at eye level again.

"Yes, a million times yes!" Amelia shrieked.

Mardious looked up at her and smiled. She dangled her gloved left hand playfully in front of him where he knelt on bended knee. She twiddled her ring finger.

"I don't think this one's your style," he replied.

"So you don't want to marry me?" she gasped.

His smile disappeared. He'd never thought of it before, but he knew in his heart that she was the only one he wanted to spend the rest of his life with. With everything they had been through lately, he felt a little guilty taking her for granted.

Amelia giggled. "I'm kidding," she said. She held her sac open. "Just put it in with the others."

Mardious stood up. He tossed the ring in her sac, but before she could close it, he grabbed her wrist. He pulled his handkerchief down to his chin and smiled. "I do want to marry you," he said. "Someday."

Amelia pulled her handkerchief down too. Her smile was wicked and beautiful. "You'd better plan your proposal well, because I'm not sure I'll say yes so easily next time." She closed her eyes and kissed him deeply.

Mardious was up to the challenge, but he wasn't in a rush. They were already building their dream life together; they would have a chance to relax and celebrate soon enough.

For the last few months, Mardious and Amelia had been flawless with the implementation of their—now well-planned—heists. They'd both quit their jobs at Sugarplum in order to become full-time criminals, and could use all hours of the day to their advantage. As much as Gerard was disappointed to see them go, and to lose Mardious' potential in The Cage, they hadn't given him a choice. There was nothing he could do to keep them.

They used some of their stolen Aileron to purchase more supplies. They bought clothes so they could fit in with the locals in the cities they visited. They shopped for ingredients so that they always had ample potions made. They even spent nights at a local inn so they didn't have to travel back to Camptown as frequently.

Mardious and Amelia were blending in well with the people in the rich cities and towns. Amelia excelled at this—of the two, she was certainly the more social butterfly. Through her efforts, they met storeowners and learned about their businesses within the pleasantries of shopping. They talked with local Guardian patrols in order to see what safety measures were being taken. They even made friends with a couple of disgruntled security guards in a few of the high-end shops.

"We'd better hurry up," Amelia said. "The sun is rising."

Mardious glanced out the window. Daybreak was upon them, and he wanted nothing more than to watch the sunrise with the future Mrs. Hood. He hustled around the jewellery shop to shovel more bounty into his sac.

Amelia punched through the last glass case in the shop. Her leather gloves had held together well, and were a great purchase. Her hands were not only protected from the impact, but they made picking up the jewellery easier, too. Mardious didn't like his, though. He felt like they restricted his fingers, and thus disrupted his power.

They tossed the last collection of rings and necklaces into their sacs and headed for the back entrance. They closed the door behind them and hustled to the end of the alley. As planned, there was a horse-drawn cart waiting for them.

Amelia tossed the driver a sac of Aileron. He tucked the coins into his pocket, but kept his eyes on the road ahead. "Thank you, Money Jane," he said.

"You're welcome, Nightrider." Amelia had taken to the idea of aliases, and liked using them with their hired help.

Mardious and Amelia crawled into the back of the cart. A leather cover rested on top of the crates that their driver was transporting. There was an empty spot down the middle that they slithered into. When they were secure, the driver made a clicking sound and the cart rolled into motion.

Mardious held Amelia tight. He rubbed her arms gently and kissed the top of her head. She was facing away from him, but he heard her giggle with delight.

They had to take extra precautions moving around the city. Since they had been so successful with their latest robberies, word had spread of their criminal activity. There were wanted posters plastered on billboards, more Guardians on patrol, and a reward was being offered for information leading to their capture.

None of the wanted posters had details of what they looked like, or any distinguishing facts. Only a single silhouette with a hood and a dark mask was ever shown, with the name 'Money Jane' sprawled across it. Amelia was the face of their organization, but her true identity was still protected.

It felt a little exhilarating for her to be a celebrity, but they had to be careful to remain hidden. Those they trusted had to pass a background check. Each phase of their plans were detailed and calculated, with contingencies in case of emergency. All it took was one mistake for everything to unravel.

The cart made another turn, but then started to slow down. "Whoa," the driver said before coming to a full stop.

The sound of hooves hitting the brick road came at them from the left. "It's pretty late. Where are you headed?" a voice said.

"I have a sunrise delivery to make, Mr. Guardian," Nightrider replied. "Early bird gets the worm and all that."

Mardious' heart pounded. Was the Guardian alone? How many others were there? There wasn't enough room in their hiding spot to move his arms and grab his potion sacs without making any noise. He was frustrated that he'd missed that detail.

"What kind of delivery?" a new voice said from the other side.

So there were at least two of them. Mardious tilted his head up, and noticed a gap between the leather cover and the base of the cart. He stared at the cover's edge, getting ready to move if it was pulled back at all. He'd have to be quick, but he was confident they could avoid trouble.

"Fruits and vegetables, mostly," Nightrider said. "Some restaurants in Kimroad pay top Aileron for fresh produce."

The sound of hooves got a little louder, and then stopped. "Show us," the Guardian said.

"Look, gentlemen," Nightrider pleaded, "I'm already running late this morning. This isn't even my cart; it's my neighbour's. His wife's sick, and I don't want to inconvenience them any longer than I should. I actually need to—"

"Enough," the Guardian said. He must have been tired of all the excuses. "Just show us."

"I really don't think—"

"We could just arrest you," the other Guardian said. "How would you like to spend the morning in a cell, rather than making your deliveries?"

"That's a little extreme," Nightrider muttered. There was a rustling at the front, and then a soft grunt as his feet hit the ground. "Guilty until proven innocent. Stupid Guardians."

"What was that?" the Guardian said.

Nightrider didn't respond. He hated the High Guardians, and blamed them for the hardships in his past. It was one of the reasons Amelia believed they could count on him.

Mardious still hadn't moved. He stared at the edge where the leather cover met the wooden panels of the carriage. Sweat dripped from his brow, and the air seemed heavy. He took a few deep, calming breaths to try and focus. He needed to be ready to spring into action.

A horn sounded in the distance.

"That's close to us," the Guardian said.

"Do you really think someone saw her?" the other asked.

"Let's go find out!" the first Guardian answered.

The rustling of hooves were loud at first, but quickly got softer. Mardious kept staring straight ahead. Why would the Guardians have sped off so fast?

"Hmm, that was close," said Nightrider. He tapped the side of the cart with his fist, and then hopped back up into his seat. He made a clicking sound, and they were moving again.

After the next turn, Amelia shifted. "That was new."

Mardious had relaxed, but sweat still dripped from his forehead. He didn't wipe it. "There's too much heat on us. I think we need to cool off for a while."

"I agree. We need a vacation," Amelia replied.

"Somewhere quiet," Mardious agreed. "Maybe find a beach, or a lake."

"A place we don't have to hide," Amelia said.

The cart made a few more turns before coming to a stop, this time at their designated location. Nightrider dismounted, and then finally removed the leather cover. Mardious and Amelia slipped out of the back and took some fresh breaths. They had arrived at the front of their inn.

"Here's the other half," Amelia said, tossing the small sac of Aileron to the driver.

Nightrider smiled, nodded, and headed back to his cart. He didn't talk about their short delay, or ask any questions. He was a professional. With a few clicks, he was off.

The inn reminded Mardious of their place in Camptown. It was a single-storey building with about fifteen rooms. Each unit had access from the outside, with a secure entrance door. Amelia took the key out of her pocket and led the way.

They had requested for the room to not be disturbed, so there were linens all over the place, dirty towels in the corner, and a garbage pile of half-eaten food. More importantly, there were sacs of treasure beside their bed, ready to be hauled off to the Badlands.

Before they could relax, there was a knock at the door.

Mardious leant against the entrance. "We requested—" he shouted.

"Open the door," Porkchop replied calmly.

Mardious let his business partner into the room. He looked around to see if anyone would follow, but it appeared that Porkchop was alone.

"You're hurt," Amelia said.

Mardious closed the door. Porkchop sat on the edge of the bed. He had a cut above his right eye, but it had scabbed up already. There was a little bit of dry blood on his cheek, but he didn't look like he was in any pain.

Porkchop snorted. "We have a problem."

Mardious leant against the door and crossed his arms. "What is it this time? Do you need more weapons? Are you not happy with your percentage of the loot?"

"You've been more than generous to me," Porkchop said. His humbleness seemed out-of-place to Mardious. "But we might need a bigger score to set things right," he added.

"Of course," Mardious said, rolling his eyes.

Amelia put a hand on Porkchop's shoulder. "Maybe we all need to take a break for a while," she said. "Mardious and I were thinking of going on a vacation. Maybe you could use one, too."

"Gerard ratted us out," Porkchop said bluntly.

Mardious dropped his arms. He met Amelia's fearful stare. They hadn't told Gerard what they were up to, but there was a chance he'd heard about it. Despite his hatred of them, he kept the Tyco close, and it wasn't surprising that he'd have an angle.

"What happened?" Mardious asked.

"The increase in riches throughout the Badlands has led to more sales of Rosebud," Porkchop explained. "All members of the Tyco, not just the ones we've paid off, have been deepening their pockets. But instead of celebrating this new wealth, the inner circle started to ask questions."

"The inner circle?" Amelia asked.

"That's what we call the leaders of the Tyco." Porkchop rolled up his sleeve and traced the gang symbol that was branded on his skin. It was a circle with a line down the middle. "The inner circle protects our one true leader, Ravon Tyco. Even though he died centuries ago, the current leaders of the Tyco embody his essence by supporting each other. The idea is that they create an impenetrable seal, so that their vision remains pure."

Mardious nodded. He knew the Tyco members were all branded with the same mark, but he'd never known what it meant. "Aren't you part of the inner circle?"

Porkchop laughed. "They're all a bunch of stubborn, lame, old men. They're too busy living in the past to get excited about the bright future."

"So we can't just pay them off?" Amelia asked. "We can't buy their loyalty, like you originally planned?"

"They don't negotiate," Porkchop replied. "They've already killed off a few members whom they thought were involved, including Gerard."

Amelia put her hand over her mouth. "He's dead?"

Mardious felt suddenly short of breath.

Porkchop snorted and nodded. "When you two quit, he tried tracking you down to see if you would reconsider. Because you haven't been around town, he started to put two and two together. He took inventory of that secret room of his below the bar, and concluded that you two were using it to your advantage."

Mardious shook his head in disbelief. "How do you know about The Cage?"

Porkchop sighed. "Once Gerard started talking, the Tyco made sure he told them everything. They tortured him, so he gave in. He led them back to Sugarplum, showed off his collection of potion ingredients ..." he bowed his head respectfully to Amelia. "And then was left to die as Sugarplum burnt down."

"No," Amelia whispered. She covered her face with her hands, but a shuddering sob still escaped between them. "It's all my fault."

Mardious rushed to the bed and put his arm around her. He pulled her close and rubbed her gently. He felt tears in his eyes too, but tried to remain strong. "No. No, it's not. It's the Tyco's fault," he said.

"If you two were to return to Camptown tonight like we'd planned, you'd likely suffer the same fate." Porkchop snorted again. "I have an idea, though."

Amelia tried to collect herself, but instead she curled deeper into Mardious' embrace.

Mardious looked up at Porkchop over Amelia's head. "What is it?" he asked.

"The inner circle isn't perfect. Even though they don't normally negotiate, I'm confident that a few members have a price," Porkchop said. "If we can get a couple of them to break away, then the rest of them become vulnerable. We can take them down, piece by piece. It's just ... not going to be cheap."

Mardious rubbed Amelia's shoulder again, but looked over beside the bed. "Will that do?" he asked.

Porkchop checked the sacs of treasure, but shook his head. "Not quite," he said. "I think it's time you go for the big one."

Mardious' stomach sank. "I don't think we can," he said. Porkchop had been pushing them to rob The Bank of the Triple Crown. The government's riches were stored in the basement of their prized bank, and even a small portion of it would rival the richest merchant in the realm. The only problem was that it was heavily guarded.

"I'm sure you'll figure it out," Porkchop said. "We don't really have another option. You two have become a big deal in the Badlands, and the fact that the Tyco leaders see you as a threat is proof that you're becoming bigger than their institution. If we fail to buy off more of their leadership, and soon, people will suffer. Gerard won't be the only one lying in a grave."

Amelia lifted her head and stared at Porkchop. Her eyes were filled with tears, but her face was set. "We'll do it," she said. "But when we succeed, you'd better fix everything. No one else can die because of us."

Porkchop snorted. "Of course," he said with a smile. "I believe in the two of you. I know you can do it, and save us all."

Mardious and Amelia gathered some of their clothes, potions, and enough Aileron to help them on their biggest heist yet. They left Porkchop alone at the inn—he could haul their bounty to the Badlands on his own.

They had to escape into the shadows. This time, they weren't just avoiding the Guardians around Kimroad, but now the members of the Tyco that wanted to hunt them down. They were in deep, and couldn't afford to get caught. Porkchop, the shelter, and the people of the Badlands were counting on them.

Mardious knew how difficult the challenges of their final heist would be, but he felt confident. They had the experience, knowledge, and skill to push the stakes a little higher. He knew they'd succeed; they had to.

The fate of the Badlands was in their hands.

CHAPTER 10

Would You Capture It, Or Just Let It Slip?

Mardious tiptoed down the stairs of the bank. He was careful not to make a sound, but he wanted to hurry back to Amelia. They'd split up so he could take care of the perimeter.

Thus far everything had gone as planned, but he was concerned about how much Forgetful Medusa he had left. The Guardians had added extras to their patrols, but Amelia had had the brilliant idea of drawing some away by using the horn call they'd heard the other day in the cart. It had saved them from using the entire potion to get in, but hopefully there was enough to get them out.

On the bank's lower level, a light flickered from inside a vault halfway down the hall on his left.

"Freeze!" A deep voice echoed.

Mardious stopped moving. Even his heart skipped a beat. He gently grabbed his pouch, which was three-quarters empty, and measured another dose into his palm. He had walked the whole of the bank—both outside and in. Had he missed one?

"Anything else?" Amelia said. "Would you like me to dance, or sing perhaps?"

Mardious exhaled in relief. Amelia sounded calm, in control. He had time. His breath sent the powdered contents through the air. He twiddled his fingertips hurriedly, and followed the dust to the edge of the vault entrance. He peeked around the corner to survey the scene.

"Drop the jewels." A lone Guardian was pointing his blade towards Amelia threateningly. His arms were the size of tree trunks, and he held the heavy sword as if it were as light as a stick. Mardious stiffened when he recognized the bull-shaped helmet on the man's head.

Amelia laughed. "What if I don't? What are you going to do?" It seemed like she was enjoying herself a little too much.

"Keep your hands where I can see them," the Guardian commanded. He levelled his sword, resting it on Amelia's shoulder, pressing it lightly against her neck.

Mardious stopped playing his imaginary piano when the warrior inhaled the potion. He didn't put the Forgetful Medusa away just yet. He contemplated whether a man that size needed a bigger dose.

Amelia closed her eyes. "Do it," she whispered.

Mardious leant his head against the frame of the vault entrance. He could tell that the potion was in full effect; the Guardian didn't react to her surprising request.

Amelia never ceased to amaze him. She looked so strong, standing up to a man twice her size, all the while laughing in the face of sure doom. She was wicked, beautiful, and perfect. He wanted to remember the moment forever.

"He's the last one," Mardious said, his voice breaking the spell of the perfect scene in front of him. He moved into the room and looked down at the sac that Amelia had been filling. There were two others beside it of different sizes.

"Good job, babe," she said, opening her eyes and spinning towards him. "I have to finish filling the third sac, and then we can get out of here."

"So this one's for the shelter." He pointed at the medium-sized sac. "And this one is for distributing throughout the Badlands?"

"No," Amelia replied. "That one is for Porkchop and his thugs. This big one is for the shelter." She rattled the sac in her hands.

Mardious smiled. He was happy that Amelia's priorities had remained the same; her heart was still with helping the shelter and the people of Camptown. However, as desperate as he'd been at their last meeting, he wasn't sure Porkchop would see it the same way.

"I wish we didn't have to pay them," he muttered. So much trouble had occurred because of the rumblings in the underbelly of the Badlands. The scheming, the murder of Gerard, and the destruction of Sugarplum shouldn't result in a reward for those responsible, but that was precisely Porkchop's plan.

"They're ruthless, but he and his little gang protect us from the Tyco. And we can always come back for more." She pointed at Mardious' waist. "What's that?"

She never missed anything. Mardious turned with a smile, dropping his hand to hide his prize. "I don't know what you're referring to," he drawled.

Amelia laughed. "It looks like something special. Maybe we can replace some of Porkchop's loot with it so we have more to distribute to others." He let her pull the green-handled knife from his beltline.

"I got it off one of the Guardians," he said. "I was hoping to keep it as a souvenir."

Amelia caressed the sharp dagger seductively. "Babe, we don't need any treasure." She stared at him and smiled. "I know of a better souvenir for you, though. Lift your hand up."

Mardious matched her smile. It had been a while since he and Amelia had created a beautiful scar to remember their adventures. It would be the perfect end to this perfect heist.

Amelia held his hand steady. She placed the tip of the blade on the centre of his upraised palm and slowly spun it. Their eyes met again. "Are you ready?"

Mardious nodded, his heart pounding with anticipation. He trusted her.

Amelia stopped twirling the dagger and put her weight into it. The blade entered his hand, and she pulled it towards his fingertips. He tried to be strong, but his body couldn't help but tremble.

He couldn't take it any longer. The pain seared his hand, filling him like fire. He yanked his hand away, clenching his wrist. He stumbled around the room, trying to clear his head. Amelia's musical laughter filled his ears.

He screamed, but it felt like he had no voice. He kicked their piles of treasure to release some of his emotion, but it didn't help. He almost lost his balance, tripping on the jewels that covered the floor.

"Babe," Amelia said calmly. She pulled out her medal. "Let me heal you."

As always, her voice cut through his haze. The relief that could be found at her healing hands drew him back to her. He stumbled towards her. She clutched her medal with one hand, and held his palm in the other.

A warm glow shone from her healing touch, and her head tilted back. She screamed and trembled like he had. Then laughter mixed in with her painful screams. She threw her arms up in the air and collapsed.

Mardious didn't feel any more pain. He studied his souvenir, and traced it with his fingers. "You're getting better at this," he said. Her handiwork was faster than before, but the result was still the same. "All that's left is a beautiful scar."

Amelia placed her hand on her chest; she was breathing hard. "Now we'll remember this day forever," she panted.

"Like this one?" Mardious lifted up his shirt. He loved reminiscing. Now they could look back on this day fondly, too.

"Exactly," Amelia said with a laugh. "That's what you get for teasing me." She reached down to her left pant leg. "Or like this one," she said as she rolled up the edge. She showed off her favourite, arrow-head shaped scar.

"We almost got caught that day." Mardious checked their bounty. They almost had enough, but he wasn't sure how far he wanted to push their luck. "We should probably get out of here."

Amelia nodded and stood tall. They quietly gathered the scattered Aileron, added some more jewels to their bounty, and then tied the sacs tight.

Mardious grabbed the largest one. He was about to leave, but he saw Amelia admiring a tiara. Maybe it made her think of their old escapades together, when it was just about the two of them having fun.

"Do you think that will fit on your apple-sized head?" he teased. "You'd look like a princess. Princess Money Jane!"

"Don't call me that." Amelia laughed. As much as her celebrity had grown with the name, Mardious knew she liked that he still knew the real version of her. "It sure is pretty, though." She looked over at the Guardian and got one of her wicked smiles. "I think it would look better on him."

Mardious didn't agree, but he followed her to their frozen prisoner. Amelia tried to reach the horn, but she was too short. Mardious grabbed it instead, lifting the helmet off. It reeked with the need to be cleaned. Did Guardians not keep more than one helmet?

"Hardly impressive—just gross and sweaty," he muttered. He dropped the helmet and watched it bounce off the stone floor.

Amelia wasn't paying attention to him; she was focused on the Guardian's face. She brushed his long hair away from his forehead.

"Look at him," she mumbled. "He looks so ..."

"Angry?" Mardious answered. The warrior's eyebrows were furrowed above his swirling eyes. Mardious was glad the effects of the potion were still strong.

"Honest." Amelia sighed. "I can tell that he's gentle and kind. He's not corrupt like the warriors we know." She positioned the tiara in place of his helmet.

Mardious suppressed a scoff. The man had threatened her at sword-point, even though he was more than twice her size. "All Guardians are the same," Mardious replied. He slung the large sac over his shoulder and got ready to leave.

"Not this one," Amelia said. "This one is a true warrior. He fights for what he believes in."

Mardious didn't care about the warrior now that he was dealt with. He sauntered towards the entrance. "Time to go," he suggested pointedly.

"I'm a fighter too," Amelia whispered. "You're not going to remember me, but I'll remember you. Until next time, princess." She hustled to the final two sacs, tossed one over each shoulder, and then followed Mardious out of the vault.

They rushed up the stairs to the main floor of the bank. There, passing two more guards that were as still as statues, they made their way to the front entrance. Mardious opened the door just a little bit and peered out into the open street.

There were Guardians that were still statuesque, but a few new ones stood with them. He saw two of them talking, and wondered how many others were reinforcements that had arrived during the time that he and Amelia were inside the vault. He gently placed his sac of treasure on the ground and reached for his Forgetful Medusa potion. "We have more company, but I can't see how many are out there," he whispered to Amelia. He emptied the rest of the contents onto his palm.

"If I cause a distraction, can you identify who needs more potion?" Amelia whispered back.

"What did you have in mind?" he asked. They were at the only known entrance to the bank, and he needed a better view of the entire street in order to succeed.

"You're not going to like it," she answered. "It's wild and crazy."

Mardious smiled. "I love wild and crazy."

Amelia giggled. She kissed him softly on the cheek without removing her mask. Her eyes twinkled, and then she pulled the door wide open.

Mardious covered his potion with his free hand so that none of the dust would blow away. Amelia stepped through the entrance with her hands raised and strutted out of the bank. "You got me!" she yelled. "I surrender."

Although he remained in the shadows, Mardious could see the entire fleet of Guardians that stood outside the bank entrance now that the door was wide open. Some of them had their backs turned, and didn't react to Amelia's confession. All of the others either drew their swords or bows. Amelia had made it extremely easy for him to identify where his potion was needed.

He played his imaginary piano as fast as he could. There was no time to waste.

"Get down on the ground!" one of the warriors shouted.

Amelia's shoulders shook. Mardious could tell she was enjoying herself. She sat on the ground and straightened her legs. She leant back on her hands, as if she were sunbathing. She gently tapped the toes of her boots together.

"Face down!" another shouted, but it didn't matter. His lungs were already filled with Forgetful Medusa.

Mardious slung his large sac of treasure over his shoulder, and then grabbed Amelia's two with his free hand. He dragged them out of the bank to where she sat. He looked around at all the Guardians staring at her, unable to do anything else.

A barricade had been set up by the Triple Crown to try and prevent thievery within their most prized vault, but now it worked in Mardious' and Amelia's favour. They were protected from being discovered by any witnesses, and with the setting sun the cover of darkness would be with them.

They slithered along the wall of the bank, keeping to the shadows. Once past the barricade, they found their escape chariot.

"Any trouble, Nightrider?" Amelia asked. She tossed him a small pouch filled with Aileron.

"Quiet as a mouse, Money Jane," Nightrider answered. "Hopefully it stays that way."

Mardious helped Amelia into their hiding spot in the back of the carriage. This time, they had a little more wiggle room. He pulled the leather cover down and breathed a sigh of relief. A soft clicking sound started their journey, and the horse and cart moved them away from their crime scene.

Their trip through Kimroad was uneventful. No one stopped their carriage as they travelled the streets at a brisk trot. Mardious expected to hear horns sound in the distance, signalling their latest heist. He was relieved that there wasn't; it meant they had more time to get away.

When they arrived at their destination, Amelia tossed Nightrider another pouch, this one a little bigger than the last. He gave them a nod and casually continued on his journey, leaving them in the back alley alone. When he was out of view, Porkchop and D'Angello appeared from the shadows.

Porkchop snorted, and rubbed his hands together. "How much did you get?"

Mardious opened the second-biggest sac. "It's by far our greatest haul yet," he said proudly. "Some of the jewels in here are so big, they have to be worth—"

"Do you think it's enough?" Amelia interrupted.

Porkchop dipped his hand into the bag. He picked up the green dagger and studied it. "It's perfect." He snorted again and looked at Amelia. "Who are the other sacs for?"

"This one is for the shelter," Amelia said. She was standing in front of the biggest sac, guarding it with a pure heart. “The other is for those around the Badlands that need it most. Don’t worry about that though; we can take care of it.”

Porkchop’s smile disappeared. “It may take some time for us to make peace with the leaders of the Tyco. Until then, you won’t be able to show your faces in Camptown. How long can you carry those sacs for?”

“As long as it takes,” Mardious said confidently.

Porkchop snorted. “We can take the sac to the shelter for you. We don’t want to be involved in giving individual donations around town, but a drop at an institution is easy for us to do without being recognized.”

Mardious glanced at Amelia. She raised her eyebrow and shrugged her shoulders. “It *would* make it easier for us,” she said.

Mardious still didn’t trust Porkchop completely. But if they wanted to return home, believing that Porkchop was capable of doing the right thing was necessary. He smiled back and nodded to her.

Amelia stepped back, and let D’Angello take the sac. He didn’t even look inside before he swung it over his shoulder. “I’ll personally ensure this gets to the shelter. You have my word.” His smile for Amelia was genuine, which made Mardious feel better about their decision.

“We’ll meet back here in four weeks,” Porkchop instructed. “If we don’t have a solution in place at that time, it just means you’ll get an extended holiday.”

Mardious breathed another sigh. It had been a long time since he’d been relieved of the pressure of masterminding criminal activity for the benefit of others. He was already looking forward to spending time being free, with the person that meant the world to him.

“Thank you, Pollock,” Amelia said, calling Porkchop by his real name. “We appreciate everything you and D’Angello have done for us already. The next few weeks will be the most difficult, so stay safe.”

“Enjoy your well-deserved rest,” Porkchop said with a smile. He nodded towards D’Angello, and they left the alleyway.

Before they were out of view, Amelia wrapped her arms around Mardious. “So, are you going to tell me where we’re going?” she asked.

Mardious squeezed her gently. “Do you really want me to ruin the surprise?”

Amelia giggled. “How about a hint?”

“It’s west of here,” Mardious answered. “If we hurry, we might still be able to see the sunset in that part of the realm.”

Amelia pulled down his mask and kissed him. She dragged her teeth over his lower lip. “Let’s get going then,” she said.

Mardious grabbed their remaining sac and pulled her down the alley. He had their route planned perfectly. They were a short block from a portal gateway station, so it was easy for them to reach their final destination. They walked to the first portal door and stopped in front of the keystone.

Mardious reached into the sac and pulled out the Aileron needed for travel. He set the location, hiding it from Amelia, and watched as the calibration light pulsated twelve times before the doors ground open. Through the glimmer of the portal, the fading sun bounced off distant, rolling hills and a lake.

“It’s beautiful,” Amelia said. “The sunlight makes the lakes look pink.”

Mardious smiled. “They’re pink all the time,” he said. “Some special property in the water. But it’s still nicer to look at during dusk.” He swung the sac over his shoulder and grabbed her hand.

Before they stepped through the portal, a horse snorted from behind them. Mardious casually glanced backwards, and met the gaze of a Guardian on horseback, readying his bow. A chill shuddered through Mardious. He had a bull-horned helmet.

“Run,” he said, pushing Amelia forwards.

Amelia stumbled through the portal while Mardious twiddled his fingers as fast as humanly possible. He felt the connection he was searching for, and made his move.

As the Guardian pulled back on his bowstring, his horse whinnied and lifted its front legs. The startled warrior released his arrow, sending it flying high into the sky. He was bucked off the horse and landed hard on the ground.

The edges of the door started to reappear, so Mardious jumped through the portal. He grabbed Amelia’s hand and sprinted up the grassy hill in front of them. He focused on the pink lake beyond and the freedom it represented.

Mardious and Amelia were both gasping. They slowed their pace and strode to the top. Mardious dropped the sac onto the ground and looked back. The doors of the portal gateway were closed, and no one else had followed them through. Hopefully, the Guardian hadn't been able to see their destination.

"I knew there was something different about that one," Amelia said. She removed her hood and handkerchief. She took a few more breaths. "He's relentless."

"Even if he was able to shake off the effects of the potion ..." Mardious rested his hand on his heart, and felt it pound through his chest. "How did he find us?"

Amelia looked back at the gateway. A look of fear crossed her face.

Mardious turned. A light shone through the crack in the doorway. Slowly, the panels separated.

Amelia started running towards the beach of the pink lake. Mardious snatched up the sac and followed her.

"There's a boat on the shore." Mardious pointed ahead, even though Amelia wasn't looking back at him. "If we can get to the water, he won't be able to follow us."

His legs felt strong. The only thing Mardious had to concentrate on was not tripping on his own feet. Once he got to the sand though, it was a different story.

Amelia slowed. Sand flew from her footsteps. Mardious moved even slower with the weight of the treasure holding him back. He tried to stay focused on the boat that was pulled up on shore. It was about a hundred yards down the shoreline, but the way they were moving, it felt like it was miles away.

Sweat dripped down Mardious' forehead. He could hardly breathe. He tried to remain focused on his destination, and not turn to see how many Guardians were following them.

He heard a thud directly behind him and looked back.

An arrow stuck out of the sac. Coins and jewels leaked out and fell to the sand. Mardious dropped it and tried to run faster.

Amelia was a few steps ahead. He wanted to shout a warning, but he couldn't find his voice. He was breathing too hard. He looked back again.

The lone, bull-horned Guardian was on the top of the short hill, holding his bow firmly. He reached back and pulled an arrow from his quiver.

Mardious' toe caught on something, and he fell to the ground. He tried to stretch his hands out to break his fall, but he still ate sand. He blinked a few times to clear his vision. Amelia skidded to a stop. Her ocean blue eyes stared at him. She looked worried.

An arrowhead pierced her neck. She reached for her throat and collapsed.

Mardious finally found his voice. "No!" He pushed himself up, but his legs weren't working. He stumbled forwards a few feet, and knelt beside her. Blood flowed from her neck like a tiny waterfall. Already it clumped the sand around his knees. "Amelia!" he screamed.

He placed his hand behind her head and held her in his lap. Her eyes were watering as she struggled for air. She was choking on her own blood, spraying it as she coughed.

Mardious put his left hand on her wound to apply pressure. If only he could stop the bleeding. He reached into her shirt and grabbed her medal. He held it tight and tried to focus. He needed to summon her healing power.

He closed his eyes. Tears ran down his cheeks. He didn't know how to heal; he had no idea where to even start. He searched for any kind of sign. He tried to reach deep inside himself, and deep inside her. He could feel her slipping away.

He felt her hand on top of his. He opened his eyes and stared into hers. She didn't look panicked anymore. She didn't seem hurt or in any pain. He tried to tell her that everything was going to be okay, to not give up the fight, but his throat had closed up.

Amelia choked one more time, and then stopped struggling. Her hand went limp and fell to her side.

Mardious pulled her close. He'd failed her.

To him, everything went silent. He threw back his head and screamed. He didn't hear his voice, or the soft, crashing waves on the shoreline. The cool breeze didn't register on his skin; neither did the soft sand under his knees.

An overwhelming hole gaped in his chest. It felt like something had escaped his body, and his emotions were trying to fill the void. Rage, sadness, and loss all rushed in.

Then a sharp blow to the back of his head brought darkness.

CHAPTER 11

Give Anything To Hear Half Your Breath

The air was still. Only a slow drip echoed down the hall: the sound of water forming a puddle somewhere on the prison floor. Mardious' own cell was dark and smelled of mould. But none of it mattered.

Mardious had curled into a ball, finding refuge in the corner. The cold walls collected his tears. He cradled his head as he relived the moments in his mind. The arrow. The blood. The death.

It should have been him. If he hadn't fallen, the arrow never would have reached her. He'd have sacrificed himself a thousand times if it meant Amelia could still be alive. She was gone because he had failed to stand up in time. It was his fault.

He could have surrendered at the top of the hill instead of running away with her, staying behind while she escaped. He'd still be imprisoned, and his doom would be sealed, but at least she'd be breathing. At least she'd be able to laugh, be wild, be free.

He closed his eyes. The hole inside his chest expanded. More tears escaped.

There were other cells in the block, but Mardious was alone. No other criminals were locked up with him, which made it eerily quiet. The block was underground, on the bottom floor of the jailhouse. Isolated from everyone and everything.

A flicker of light in the hallway joined him in his despair.

Only rats would venture this far below ground, but the pitter-patter of rodents wasn't the noise that Mardious heard from the stairwell. The footsteps were lighter, more elegant, but equally as sly. They got louder as they made their way towards his cell, and then stopped.

Mardious didn't move from where he faced the wall. He didn't acknowledge his captor. As painful as his thoughts of Amelia were, remembering her was the only thing he could do.

"What's your name?" The strange voice was deep, soft, and friendly.

Mardious didn't respond. He didn't want to talk to anyone. He didn't want to give the guard any information. He only wanted to be left alone.

"My name is Zuke," the visitor said candidly. "I have some food and water for you." The sound of metal hitting the floor echoed through the small, stone cell.

Mardious' mouth felt drier. He didn't know how long it had been since he'd woken up—time stretched on without Amelia—but he hadn't been brought anything to drink, let alone eat. Still, he didn't want to give in.

"It was quite an impressive bounty you took from The Bank of the Triple Crown," another male voice said. "All the Guardians were shocked when they found the open vault and missing jewels. How did you sneak by without alerting them to your presence?"

Two captors were worse than one. Mardious wished harder for the peace of loneliness.

"I don't think he's going to tell you," Zuke said. "There's a reason he's pulled off some of the greatest heists in history without getting caught. Being behind bars must be a lot to take in."

"Then he can starve to death," the other man snapped.

"Hey," Zuke yelled. It sounded like a hand or arm got slapped. "Don't touch his soup. It took me hours to prepare."

Someone sighed.

"It's okay," Zuke said softly. "We don't need him to talk right now. We just need him to listen."

"You're right." The other man chuckled. "You know, you're pretty wise for a wizard."

"Just because you're a scholar doesn't mean you know everything." Both men laughed. "Let's start over."

"Agreed," the other man said. He cleared his throat. "I apologize. My name is Sheese, and Zuke and I aren't here to interrogate you. We've come to ask for your help."

Mardious' wish had almost come true—they had almost left—but now even that hope was taken away from him.

"We know you have the skills to get into places others can't," Sheese continued. "In fact, we're quite impressed with your talents. However, we're not interested in robbing banks, or businesses. And I think someone of your sensibilities would be interested in a much higher payoff."

Mardious didn't want to get involved in another heist. What was the point?

"There are a few hidden caches throughout the realm that hold vast amounts of treasure," Zuke explained. "There's more gold and jewels in these secret locations than in any bank in the realm. Legend has it that there are enough riches to build three kingdoms."

"Not to mention the lost history and magical texts that historians would beg for," Sheese added.

"That's not really important," Zuke whispered.

"It's important to me," Sheese replied.

Mardious wished he had some of his potions with him. He'd move the particles to his captors' noses, freeze them like statues, and hope they'd never talk to him again.

"Ultimately, just a fraction of this treasure would make you the most powerful person in the realm." Sheese continued. "Since money is power, you could use your share to accomplish whatever you desire. You are from the Pink Lakes, correct? That's why you had the Aileron with you—because you have family there that you are providing for?"

Mardious was getting angry. Zuke and Sheese didn't know him. They didn't understand where he was from. They didn't know the sacrifices he'd made to bring his home to a level of prosperity. He felt like yelling at them to go away.

The silence lingered.

"I don't think he was motivated by Aileron after all," Zuke said softly. "We assumed that he was Money Jane's accomplice, but maybe she was more than that."

Hearing them use her alias was like a knife cutting through his heart. Mardious felt a lump in his throat, replacing the dryness that had arisen from thirst.

"Like family?" Sheese asked. "I saw her body. They're similar in age, but they don't really look alike."

"No, not family. I think he did it because he loved her," Zuke said. "And now she's gone."

Mardious dipped his head closer to the corner of the cell, and turned his shoulder further away from his captors. He tried to curl up deeper into the comfort of the cold walls to escape their torment.

"Well, if he's not motivated by money, then he might be more aligned with our own goals," Sheese said. "He's a more perfect candidate than I thought."

"I'm sorry for your loss," Zuke added.

Mardious' lower lip quivered. He let his tears fall freely, and the warm liquid streamed down his cool cheeks.

"There's something else in these treasure chambers that we haven't mentioned," Zuke said. "Pieces of an ancient, magical doorway. It's a portal that gives the user the special power to bring people back from the dead. To resurrect those we've lost."

Mardious opened his eyes. He didn't think he'd heard Zuke correctly. Did he just say there was a doorway of life? That there was a way to get Amelia back?

"I thought it was a myth at first," Sheese admitted. "Until I saw a portion of it with my own eyes. We have one piece in our possession, but we need three more to complete the doorway. If you help us obtain the ancient relics, we'll help reunite you with the one you just lost."

Mardious brushed his cheek against his shoulder, wiping the tears from his eyes in the process. He peered across the cell, studying his captors through the steel bars.

They were both dressed in extravagant robes. One of them was well-groomed, with a perfectly trimmed beard. He had purple garments with a golden cape and matching golden gloves.

The other was paler, and a little taller. He had blue and silver garments, and a square hat that looked neither stylish nor practical. He was holding a torch in one hand, and a rope ... no, a noose, in the other.

"You got his attention," Zuke said. He knelt and grabbed the spoon, holding it steady with his golden glove. "Come have something to eat," he added with a smile.

Mardious took a deep breath. It seemed too good to be true. The smell of the meal made his stomach grumble, and he decided that a quick bite wouldn't hurt. It would give him more energy to dream about Amelia.

He leant against the wall, using it as support as he stood. He felt weak, and his legs were stiff from sitting in the same position for hours. He stumbled to the front of the cell and bent down.

He accepted the spoon from Zuke, but didn't look up at him. He picked up the tray, returned to his comfortable spot against the wall, and sat back down. He took a sip of water, and then dipped his spoon into the soup.

"I think he likes it," Sheese said after Mardious had slurped half the bowl.

Mardious took the piece of bread on the tray and dipped it into the broth. It was easier for him to chew, and he quickly devoured it.

"We need your help getting past the creatures that guard the treasure and ancient relics," Zuke said. "You have gotten past many in your heists with no one any the wiser, and if you can do the same with dragons and—"

Sheese held up his index finger. "Hold on," he interrupted. "We can't just give him all our information. I've spent years researching this, and I'm not going to divulge it all to someone who won't even tell us his name."

Mardious stared at his captors. It seemed like they were waiting for him to respond, but he didn't feel like talking yet. Something in his gut told him not to get his hopes up. He lifted the spoon back to his mouth and took another slurp of his soup.

"He's a stubborn one." Zuke smiled. "I like him already."

Sheese shook his head. "There are only two ways out of your cell," he said to Mardious. He tossed the rope he'd been holding. The noose landed square in the middle of the floor. "The first is easy. It requires no effort, and you won't have to talk to us at all. You'll be sent to prison without trial, and then placed on death row."

Mardious stared at the noose. He didn't see a reason to live in the world without Amelia, and a quick death would join them eternally.

"The other is so difficult, it's nearly impossible." Sheese put his free hand on the bars of the cell, as if slightly adjusting his position would help him study Mardious further. "It requires patience, strength, and determination. It will take months of planning, years of service, and every ounce of energy you have to even have a shot at success. However, high stakes mean high rewards: you'll be compensated with money, power, and a reunion with the one you've lost."

Mardious looked down at his hands. He slowly caressed the last scar Amelia had given him.

"First, I would train you," Zuke said. "Judging by the potions we found on your belt, I'd say you're already quite the wizard, but I want you to be the best. You'd be my new aide at the castle of the Triple Crown. That way I can ensure you'll be ready for the incredible tasks at hand. We'll also incorporate you into the political lifestyle, so that you're prepared after we obtain the doorway of life."

Mardious looked back up at Zuke and Sheese. He raised an eyebrow in confusion.

"Our end goal is not to bring someone specific back to life," Sheese explained. "We want to change the world: to build a realm of equality and peace. A realm where no one *has* to die. We can reward those that share our vision and create a utopia. We'll become the most beloved rulers in history."

Mardious wasn't interested in their end goals. He'd wanted to improve the Badlands, and knew that changing the whole realm wasn't as easy as they were making it out to be. No ancient relic could bring peace and tranquility.

He removed the tray from his lap, curled back into his corner, and closed his eyes.

"I have something else for you," Sheese said. "It was the only item of value we found on Money Jane. I thought it would be worth something to those closest to her, and now, I'm guessing that's you."

Again, the sound of metal hitting the floor echoed through the cell. Mardious glanced over. A shiny object rested beside the noose. He turned his head and opened his eyes wide. Amelia's medal was almost within his reach.

He felt frozen. Seeing a piece of her made him sad, angry, and helpless all at the same time. Thoughts of failure flooded his mind, and as much as he wanted to turn away, he needed to hold it. He needed to hold her.

"This is your reason," Sheese said. "It represents the light at the end of the tunnel. But if you choose to accept your new journey, then it starts in complete darkness. You must choose whether or not you want to succeed, and what you're willing to do to get there. Are you prepared to sacrifice everything you have? Can you follow our plans for as long as it takes? Will you die for the cause? Are you willing to kill for it?"

It felt like Mardious was under his own Medusa spell. He wanted to grab the medal. He wanted to answer Sheese's questions. He wanted to ask even more. But he couldn't move.

"Take some time to think about your future," Sheese said. "We'll come back with more food tomorrow. If you want to help us, we'll show you the next step. But only after you tell us your name."

The light slowly faded away, leaving Mardious alone in the dark again.

Mardious closed his eyes. A single tear dripped down his cheek. He felt guilty for Amelia's death, but now he had a slim chance of rectifying it. He didn't know if he was strong enough to accomplish the impossible. He didn't know if he should even try.

His body finally felt like it was working again. He crawled to the middle of the room. He tapped about with his fingertips until his hand brushed the thick rope. He felt around a little more and found Amelia's cool medal.

He lay down, bringing the medal close to his heart. He wished he could hold her. He didn't want to believe that there was a light at the end of the tunnel—he didn't deserve it—but he couldn't help feeling a little excited.

He wanted to hear more from Zuke and Sheese. Would their plan make any sense?

All he had to do was wait one more day. Then he'd decide if he'd accept imprisonment and death, or give it everything he had to bring Amelia back.

CHAPTER 12

You Tried Everything, But You Don't Give Up

Mardious sped up his fingers. They moved faster and faster, but it didn't make a difference. The flame remained flickering on the candle.

"Fire is the most difficult element to control." Zuke patted Mardious' arm. "It's not like manipulating physical things, like droplets or dust, because fire depends on fuel as its source. The trick is to expand and contract the flame by using your emotions."

Zuke tugged on the cuff of his right glove, and then extended his palm. The small fire grew, and then quickly diminished. It became five times as large, and then blossomed like a flower. The tips twirled together like a braid, before returning to the original shape. Zuke brought his arm back down.

"Show off," Mardious mumbled.

"Don't worry." Zuke clapped Mardious hard on the shoulder. "You'll get there."

Mardious took a deep breath and closed his eyes. He needed to impress Zuke so that he could help Amelia. He kept his arms low, playing his imaginary piano under the tabletop. He searched for any feeling he could embrace, from uncertainty to sadness. His concentration was broken by a knock at the door.

"Come in," Zuke instructed.

A man wearing black robes and a white apron pushed a cart into the room. There were two silver platters with matching lids sitting on a lace cloth. The man placed each platter on the table and lifted the lids.

"Today I have prepared a roasted chicken, slathered in garlic-herb-lemon butter," he said. "Accompaniments include mashed potatoes and a roasted vegetable medley. For dessert, I've prepared a gentle apple crisp with a touch of extra cinnamon. Enjoy."

Mardious' stomach instantly growled. He hadn't eaten since he'd entered the castle of the Triple Crown earlier today, and the delicious aroma made him salivate. As much as he wanted to shovel mashed potatoes into his mouth, he stayed respectful. He didn't want to look like an outsider.

"Thank you, Chadwick," Zuke replied. He sat down beside Mardious.

Chadwick placed some drinks beside each plate before exiting the room.

Zuke picked up his glass. "Cheers," he said with a smile.

Mardious held the stem of the glass as Zuke did and tipped the rim to make contact. He wanted to mimic Zuke's actions precisely, so he wouldn't look out of place at the castle. He took a sip and thought about how much Amelia would enjoy the delicious wine.

"Do you dine like this every day?" Mardious asked to distract himself.

Zuke nodded. He carefully cut his roast chicken. "It's one of the perks of working for the Triple Crown."

Mardious nodded, watching how properly Zuke held his utensils. He could believe it. Even he'd spent the day getting pampered. He was able to wash up, get a haircut, and select his robes from a full rack of options. He'd gotten a tour of the castle of the Triple Crown, and then started working with Zuke on a series of tests to determine his level of wizardry.

They were currently in a room as big as all of Sugarplum, sitting at a table that could fit twelve. There was a fireplace on one side and open windows on the other. Rich tapestries hung on the walls, along with candles that lit the room perfectly for their work this evening.

After potion making and some animal control, they had moved on to elements. Mardious showed off his liquid and powder control, but struggled with air and fire. He stared at the candle in front of him as he devoured one of the best meals he'd ever had.

When his dessert plate was so shiny it looked clean, Mardious pulled the candle back towards himself. If he was going to be useful to Amelia, he had to get this right. He started twiddling his fingers, but Zuke leant over and blew out the flame.

"I admire your work ethic," he said. "But there's something I want to show you."

They left their dinnerware on the table and exited the room. Zuke led the way down a few flights of stairs to the main level. Mardious noticed that the halls of the castle weren't nearly as busy in the evening. He wondered if they were late to an event or something.

These main-level halls were much larger than those in other parts of the castle. Thick arches crested the entrances, and circular stone pillars reached up to ceilings two storeys high. Tapestries hung down the walls, statues were on display, and chandeliers filled with candles made the castle the most extravagant place Mardious had ever been. He couldn't stop swivelling his head to take in all the glamour.

Zuke opened a large steel door at what Mardious assumed was their destination. The way he struggled with it made it look heavy. The thick smell of hay, animals, and a hint of manure made Mardious wrinkle his nose.

"Hi, Zuke," a female warrior said. She stood up from her stool that was nestled just inside the doorway. Beside it was a small table with a stack of books and papers. "Who's your friend?"

The warrior wasn't wearing a bull-horned helmet, but Mardious felt rage course through his veins nonetheless. He thought about grabbing her sword, swinging it at her neck, and standing over her corpse. He wanted to make every warrior pay for Amelia's death.

"This is my apprentice, Mardious," Zuke replied.

"I'm Jules," she said. "Were you also the top wizard in your class from The Academy?" She stuck out her hand.

Mardious didn't shake it. Her hands were bigger than his. He was less confident he'd be able to take her sword and attack her so easily.

"He's talented, but a little shy," Zuke said.

"Cute and mysterious," Jules said with a smile. "Just like his master."

Jules had a dagger tucked into the front of her beltline. Mardious could grab it and stab her in the midsection; it didn't look like she had any armour there.

"We're here to see stable eight," Zuke said, changing the subject. "Do you mind?"

"There's no ..." Jules started. "Oh, of course." She winked at Mardious.

Zuke put his hand on the back of Mardious' shoulder and led him away.

Mardious was impressed with how pristine the stables looked. Each one was bigger than the room that he and Amelia had shared over the years. The hay was stacked neatly, the water troughs were filled, and tools hung perfectly from their hooks. The horses were living a life of luxury.

Zuke pointed out that the High Guardians used these stables exclusively. Their steeds were the most majestic in the realm, and went through rigorous training to be the strongest, fastest, and most obedient. The animals deserved the care and attention they needed to perform at their best.

"This one is extra special, though," Zuke said, stopping his lecture. "Her name is Brooke, and she is by far my favourite." He tugged on the cuffs of his gloves, and then opened the gate.

Mardious covered his mouth. The dark eyes of a white unicorn stared back at him. Her horn was coloured like a rainbow. Her mane sparkled in the low light of the stable torches. A yellow glow surrounded her coat, as if the sun had been brought down from the sky and was hiding behind it.

"You have unicorns here?" Mardious asked in awe.

"It's pretty impressive," Jules said from behind them. "You're getting better at that."

"Thanks," Zuke said. He brought his arms down, and the unicorn disappeared.

Mardious looked around frantically. "Where'd she go?"

"She was an illusion," Zuke explained. "She lives only in my imagination. I actually haven't even seen a unicorn before, to be honest."

"I wish she was real," Jules said. She closed her eyes and clasped her hands together. "I'd ride her around the realm, patrol the streets, and wear a rainbow uniform to match her horn. I'd be the greatest Guardian ever!"

Mardious ignored his dislike for the warrior and tried to wrap his mind around Zuke's demonstration. "You created an illusion?" It had looked so real.

"Illusions are my specialty," Zuke said. "We'll work on them together, but I just wanted to show you what's possible. Most wizards create illusions based on what they've seen, or something they've connected with. I like to expand on that a little bit. In this case, I used a horse as a base, and then added to it. The surrounding stables help make the experience more realistic."

Mardious' heart fluttered. "Can you make an illusion of someone who's passed away?"

"People are difficult," Zuke warned. "There are too many details and idiosyncrasies. The facial features must be perfect. The voice must be clear and unwavering. Gestures and habits need to be imitated with ease. Even those we are most intimate with are challenging to recreate."

Mardious smiled. He couldn't wait to try his hand at illusions. He knew he'd be able make one of Amelia. He was ready to see her again.

"Do you not know how to create an illusion?" Jules asked. "I thought all wizards knew how."

"It wasn't part of his curriculum," Zuke said quickly. "Every wizard specializes in an area of expertise. Mardious is extraordinarily talented, but even the best of us struggle with something."

He pulled Jules away, and led her back to the entrance to the castle. He whispered something to her, which made her toss her head back in laughter.

Mardious was about to follow, but he stopped when the main gate opened on the other end of the stable yard. Two High Guardians entered on horseback. They both wore shiny armour, but only one of them held a torch to light the way. The other was wearing a distinct helmet. It had horns on it, like a bull.

Mardious forgot where he was. He clenched his teeth and took a few heaving breaths. He marched towards the mounted Guardians, searching for a weapon along the way. A pitchfork hanging on a post seemed too bulky. Beside it was a stack of horseshoes, some nails, and a farrier's hammer.

He gripped the hammer tightly. If he could get the bull-horned Guardian on the ground, he could bash his face in with a few quick strikes.

He wouldn't stop swinging until Amelia's killer was unrecognizable.

He extended his hand and fervently started playing his imaginary piano. If he could connect with the horse, he could get it to buck the Guardian off at the right moment. He needed to let him come closer for an attack, to take down the warrior before he had a chance to draw his weapon. He waited a little longer, flicking his fingertips ever so slightly.

He leant against the stable wall to remain in the shadows. Just a few more seconds, and then he'd be in range.

Someone grabbed his robes and pulled him backwards. He stumbled back into an open stable and fell to the ground. He hit his head on the wooden wall, which caused him to drop his weapon. He blinked a few times to escape his daze.

Zuke carefully closed the gate and leant against it. He glared at Mardious and put his index finger over his lips.

Mardious clenched his fists. His breathing got heavier. How could Zuke deny him this moment? How could he betray him? After he was done bashing the Guardian's face in, he'd kill Zuke, too.

Mardious searched desperately for his hammer, and saw the edge sticking out of the straw. He bent to pick it up, but Zuke tackled him. Before he could get up again, Zuke knelt on his back. Mardious' arm twisted, and his head was pinned to the ground.

"Get off!" Mardious grunted.

"Be quiet," Zuke said. "They'll hear you."

Mardious tried to wriggle free. He didn't stand a chance against a skilled, strong warrior in direct combat without a plan, but he didn't care. He wanted revenge for Amelia's death. He needed to honour her with retribution.

Zuke leant harder and put his hand over Mardious' mouth. Mardious breathed hard through his nose, but there wasn't much else he could do. He was at the mercy of his captor. He decided to save his energy for one last push.

A few minutes passed. Then the heavy footsteps of warrior boots got louder.

"I'm honoured to have served with you on your final night of patrol, Roman," a man said.

"Thank you, Benji," Roman replied, "but I don't plan on staying cooped up in the castle. Someone has to make sure you don't slack off, right?"

Both men laughed.

Mardious tried to push himself up with his free hand. He turned his shoulder, but Zuke's whole weight rested on him, and he was too heavy. He thought about biting Zuke's hand, but he didn't know if his teeth would even get through the other wizard's golden leather gloves.

"We're almost in the clear," Zuke whispered.

The warriors' voices were already too low to hear. After a few more minutes, Zuke let go of Mardious' arm. He stood up and brushed off some hay.

Mardious rolled over. He clutched his arm, and then rotated his shoulder to make sure it wasn't injured. A tear slid down his cheek, but it wasn't because his body was hurt. "Why did you stop me?"

"You're not ready yet," Zuke peeked through the gate, and then seemed to relax. He turned back to Mardious and sighed.

"If I were in your shoes, I'd want to kill him too," he said. "But there is a better time and place for the murder of Roman Garrick. He's about to become the High Warrior of the realm, and his death would be more impactful at the right moment."

"I don't care," Mardious said. He wiped the tear from his face and stood up. "Whether he's the High Warrior or not, he deserves to die."

Zuke nodded. "I'm not arguing with you on that, but there are other steps we need to take on our journey towards ultimate power. Sheese wants to become the High Scholar of the realm, and I the High Wizard, but we're not going to reach those positions if we're involved in slaughtering officials. We need to be smart about it, or we're all doomed."

Mardious looked down. Their plans didn't matter to him. All he wanted to do was escape the stable. He'd hunt down the High Warrior himself if he didn't have the support of his new friends.

"I promise you'll get the chance to avenge Money Jane's death," Zuke said. "But you have to trust me. Your goal shouldn't be to do just one thing to help her, but to do it *all*. If you kill Roman Garrick tonight, you won't have a chance to bring her back. You'll die a villain, and you'll lose the opportunity to change the world. You'll lose the opportunity to give her the life she deserves."

Mardious took a deep breath. Zuke was right. He'd already decided not to take the easy way out. Killing Roman Garrick would be satisfying, but it wouldn't help bring Amelia back.

If Zuke was willing to put his own life on the line to ensure Mardious got his revenge, then the ultimate plan must be better than anything Mardious could do on his own. He would need to stick with what was logical, instead of acting on pure anger and emotion.

"Her name is Amelia." Mardious took another deep breath and stared at Zuke. "Don't call her Money Jane anymore."

"Very well," Zuke said with a smile. "Let's do it all for Amelia."

CHAPTER 13

Stay Scheming

Sheese set his quill on his desk and closed his notebook. He grabbed a small stack of papers and quickly fanned through them. He grabbed a second stack, but didn't take any time to look through its contents.

"How was your sleep?" he asked.

Mardious took a sip of his tea. "It was very comfortable," he lied. As much as he enjoyed not having to spend the night on the cold, stone floor of a cell, he didn't get much rest. He stayed on his side of the bed, wishing that Amelia were beside him.

"Excellent," Sheese answered pleasantly. "I like your new outfit. It appears to be a perfect fit."

Mardious faked a smile. After his practice dealing with customers at Sugarplum, he was accustomed to pushing his emotions aside in order to engage in small talk. As tired and sad as he felt on the inside, he didn't want Sheese to see his pain.

"Luckily, Zuke and I are the same size," Mardious said. He'd picked out some purple and black robes that were fancier than anything he'd ever worn before. "He has a really nice place. How long am I going to be staying with him?"

Sheese raised his eyebrow and tilted his head. "It depends," he said slyly. He looked at each stack of paper. "I have two reports here, but I'll only be giving one to my superiors. I'm hoping that you can help me decide which one I'm going to turn in."

Mardious rested his mug on the coaster Sheese had provided. He would help if he could. The only way he could recover what he'd lost was through the deal they'd made. He forced another smile and nodded.

"My job at the castle of the Triple Crown is Advisor to the High Scholar," Sheese continued. "My projects include ensuring policies are written correctly, communication between political members remains clear, and important information is accurately delivered to the public. The reports I have here outline what happened to Amelia Jane."

Mardious couldn't draw a breath, like he'd just been punched in the stomach.

Sheese waved the papers in his right hand. "In this one, I give an accurate description of the events you're familiar with. The bank heist, how you fled to the Pink Lakes, Amelia's death, and your capture. It also explains the heroic efforts of the warrior who tracked you down, and how he deserves to be rewarded for his efforts."

Mardious clenched his fists. The man in the bull-horned helmet was a murderer, not a hero.

"This other one is slightly different." Sheese waved his left hand. "It bends the truth just a little. It still explains your bank heist and Amelia's death, but it leaves you out. No one will ever know that she had an accomplice, and she will live on in history as one of the most feared criminals of our time."

"Bending the truth?" Mardious asked. He was starting to like Sheese. The advisory role was just a front, like Mardious' smile as a bartender. He could relate to what was beneath Sheese's mask. "So, you're a liar."

Sheese laughed. "I just want to demonstrate how powerful information can be. Haven't you heard that the quill is mightier than the sword? If I know all the facts, I can manipulate the narrative in order to produce something that is even stronger than the original story. Like me, you hold information that's powerful, even if you don't realize it yet."

Mardious raised his eyebrow. "Like what?"

"Tell me something I don't know about you," Sheese replied. "Something worthy of bartering. If your answer is valuable to me, I'll submit the report that keeps you anonymous." He waved both stacks in the air again.

Mardious didn't know what to say. He never knew that information could be traded. The only bartering system he was familiar with was on the main strip of Camptown. He remembered an experience he'd had there, where he traded something else intangible for a meal.

"I used to play the piano in exchange for food," he admitted. "I started at a shelter, found a few other venues that had one, and then worked my way into playing at a bar on the edge of Camptown. The owner was so impressed, he offered me a job as a bartender. That's how I met Amelia."

"Camptown?" Sheese asked. "You're from the Badlands?"

Mardious nodded.

Sheese put the second stack down and stood up. He pulled out a fire starter from the top drawer of his desk and ignited the sheets of paper that outlined the truth. He placed the burning papers on a metal plate on the windowsill of his office so the smoke escaped from the room.

"I've made my decision," Sheese said happily. "No one at the Triple Crown will ever know of your criminal past. They will only know you as the young wizard apprentice, Mardious Hood."

Mardious was confused by the theatrics. "What about the High Warrior?" he asked. "Is he not going to tell everyone that he caught me?"

"Zuke told me you saw him," Sheese said. He sat back down, clasped his hands, and leant forwards on his desk. "High Warrior Roman is under the impression that you were already sent to prison. We had another detainee take your place, and I provided the paperwork to match him to your description. As for the High Warrior's reliability, he has his reasons to not contradict the official report that I'm going to hand in."

Mardious was starting to understand. Sheese had everything planned already, and merely used his theatrics to get a confession. It was a cunning move, but it worked. It seemed like everyone had motives and secrets, and Mardious was now part of the scheming. He knew he had a lot more to learn, though. "Bending the truth," he said with a nod.

"If we can control the narrative, we can use it to our advantage," Sheese said. "We can eventually rise through the ranks, eliminate those in charge, and lead the people in the realm to greater prosperity. We can build a better world for all."

Mardious thought about his and Amelia's plans. They seemed to align with Sheese's goals, but she needed to be a part of it, too. "And find the doorway of life," he added.

Sheese smiled. "That is already in motion," he said. "You've started your training with Zuke, and you'll become powerful enough to help him on his mission. Meanwhile, you can help me in a different way; not by using magic, but by using knowledge."

Sheese leant back and stretched his arms high. "How many books in my office do you think have information about the Badlands?"

Mardious looked around. Bookcases lined the wall behind Sheese's desk. Low shelves were built under the window. A small table was pushed into the corner, with stacks of paper occupying the entire surface. Even more bookcases stood beside the table. There must have been thousands of documents in the tiny room.

Mardious thought it must be a trick question. Surely most of the books at least mentioned the Badlands. "Half?"

Sheese smiled. "Optimistic, but wrong," he said. "The correct answer is zero. Oh, I've seen a few books at the library that have history dating back a few hundred years, but I've been searching for something a little more current. You're exactly what I've been looking for, and now destiny has smiled upon me. You can tell me all about the activity in the Badlands." He reached into the top drawer of his desk and pulled out a notebook and quill.

Mardious felt uneasy. As much as he didn't like some of the people in his hometown, he wasn't about to admit to any other criminal activity. He wasn't going to be the reason they got arrested. "Like a rat?" He crossed his arms and leant back in his chair.

"No, not like a rat." Sheese huffed, like he was getting impatient. "I want to help the people in the Badlands, and the only way I can do that is to understand their way of life. The Triple Crown ignores what's going on out there because they're afraid. They don't want a segregated part of the realm to mix with their privileged world, because they believe it will throw off the balance. It will cause chaos."

Sheese's smile returned. "But I like chaos. I believe that embracing it is the only way to change the present into a brighter future. The leaders of the Triple Crown are too narrow-minded. They were threatened by you and Amelia, and I think that we can use that fear to our advantage."

Mardious smoothed the arms of his new robes. Even though he'd seen wanted posters of Money Jane around Kimroad, he didn't think that they'd made that much of an impact on the rest of the realm. "The leaders of the Triple Crown were threatened by us?" he asked.

Sheese nodded. "High Scholar Robert held daily strategy meetings with the High Warrior, specifically about how to capture you. Everyone thought Money Jane was a ghost! High Wizard Jolene was tasked with trying to figure out what kind of magic you were using to slip through walls, but she was obsessed with her own theories. She thought you could fly like birds."

Mardious raised his eyebrows. Flying or being a ghost would have been a lot easier than making his special potions and sneaking around.

"The reason they were threatened by you was because of the amount of Aileron and weapons you were stealing," Sheese continued. "They were afraid you were building an army with the intention of starting a revolt against them. They wanted to avoid losing their control over the realm, starting a war, and putting innocent citizens in harm's way."

Mardious tried not to laugh. He thought about how Porkchop was trying to destroy the Tyco, not lead an army to battle the Triple Crown. Going after the government seemed like a ridiculous idea. "So, you want me to tell you about the Badlands to make sure that we aren't a threat?" Mardious asked.

Sheese shook his head. "I want to know everything that you know," he answered. "Then we can come up with a plan. I want everyone to have the equal opportunity to work together to create a better world, and that includes those who have been segregated from it."

Mardious thought about Amelia. He imagined how happy she'd be when he brought her back from the dead, and they could live in an entire world that was like the Badlands. They could go anywhere they wanted to, and it would feel like home. They wouldn't have to hide from the Tyco or escape the Triple Crown. They could be free together.

It sounded too good to be true. He didn't know if he could trust someone who admitted to being a liar. On the other hand, what did he have to lose?

"Where should I start?" he asked.

Sheese opened his notebook to the first page. He grabbed his quill and steadied his hand. "Let's work backwards," he said. "Reverse chronology often encourages story tellers to focus on the how and why, rather than working towards an ending. Tell me: why did you choose to rob the largest bank of the Triple Crown?"

Mardious grabbed his mug of tea and got comfortable. "We needed a big score," he said.

He outlined the heat that he and Amelia had been feeling from the Tyco. He explained Porkchop's plan to buy their freedom, but was careful to leave out names. He wanted to protect his partners as much as he could, in case Sheese were to double-cross him.

He relayed the information that Porkchop had given him about the inner circle of the Tyco. He also confessed to giving Porkchop the sacs of jewels from the heist: both the one that was going towards their plan, and the other that went to the shelter to provide care for the less fortunate. He talked about the idea that he and Amelia could change the Badlands for the better, and make everyone prosperous.

None of his comments earned a response from Sheese. The scholar didn't look up from his notebook once: he just kept scribbling things down with his quill.

Mardious hesitated before talking more about Amelia, but as soon as he started to share more personal details about her, he felt better. He spoke about her generosity, how excited she was to hand out Aileron to the less fortunate, and the impact she made on everyone she touched. She was the face of their Money Jane operation, and deserved all the praise.

He described their living situation, and their full-time jobs at Sugarplum. He explained how welcoming Amelia was towards travellers, members of the Tyco, and local Guardians. He talked about how upsetting it was for her to hear of Gerard's death, and the destruction of The Cage.

He also provided details about their minor heists. Working backwards, he started with the jewellery shops and weapon stores, and ended with the small-town homes. He talked about how easy it was for them to break in, and how good it felt for them to do bad things. Thinking about Amelia's laughter and smile made him laugh and smile in turn.

Sheese finally put his quill down. He rubbed his writing hand. "I can see why you loved her," he said solemnly.

Mardious choked up. All the reasons he loved her flooded his memory. His good mood instantly flipped, and he succumbed to the emptiness that had opened inside his chest. He set his mug down, brought his hand to his forehead, and wept uncontrollably.

A drawer opened. He peeked through his fingers. Sheese held out a white handkerchief. Mardious accepted the soft cloth and dabbed his eyes.

"I think that's enough for today," Sheese said, closing his book. "I have a lot to study, and I'm going to revisit the history books. With the information you've given me about the Tyco, I'm interested to learn of the gang's origins."

Mardious used the handkerchief to blow his nose. "You're welcome," he said.

Sheese smiled. "Thank you," he said. "I should have said that first. This is a great start in the development of our plan, and I want to continue to build this relationship. It's important for me to know more about the Badlands, but it's also important to relay information to the people there when the time is right. Is there any way you can get a message to the Tyco members that were helping you and Amelia?"

Mardious sniffled. "What kind of message?"

"That Amelia is still alive in all of us," Sheese said. "That her actions will never be forgotten, and that we will continue to do the work for her."

Mardious sniffled again. "That's a nice sentiment, but ... I don't think I can do this without her. She was the face of Money Jane, and the peacemaker between those involved. Why can't we just focus on the doorway of life, and bring her back?"

Sheese leant forwards on his desk. "You *can* do it," he answered, "and she'll be back soon enough. But until then, we can continue to help everyone between now and when she's able to return. If I could get some resources together to accompany your message, would that help?"

Mardious sighed. He didn't want to argue anymore. "Resources?"

"A man in my position has access to the treasure in the bank of the Triple Crown," Sheese said. "All I have to do is fill out the right paperwork, use my connections, and make a withdrawal. It will be completely legal, and no one will come chasing after us."

Mardious shook his head. "I'll believe it when I see it," he muttered.

"If I give you a sac of Aileron to continue with your plan of causing turmoil in the inner circle, can you get it to your friends?" Sheese asked again.

Mardious ignored the reference to Porkchop being a friend and focused on the desperation in Sheese's eyes. He knew he could take advantage of the situation. He tried to think about how Amelia would respond.

She'd do something wicked, selfless, and ruthless.

"The plan after the bank heist was to meet our friends in four weeks," Mardious said. "If I had some Aileron to give them, they might be receptive to hearing what you have to say."

Sheese smiled and bumped his fist on the desk. He grabbed his quill and scribbled something into his notebook. "I will get you whatever you need," he said excitedly.

Mardious was happy to help Sheese, but he still felt a little underwhelmed. If he was going to continue to do good things for the people of the Badlands, he wanted to find a way to do something good for Amelia, too. He needed to make it feel like she was alive.

"One more thing," Mardious said. Sheese stopped writing and stared at him. "Can you make sure that Amelia's name is recognized by the entire realm? She deserves to be remembered as a noble figure, instead of as a feared criminal. She deserves to be known because of her kind heart. That way, when she returns, she can be embraced by everyone."

Sheese smiled. "Of course," he said. "It's what I do."

Mardious grabbed his tea and leant back in his chair. He breathed a sigh of relief. He felt Amelia's calming presence within him. It might have been a small gesture, but knowing that everyone would learn who the real she was gave him a little peace.

He imagined her smiling face, and how appreciative she'd be that he was carrying on her legacy. He promised himself that he'd find more ways for her to live on until he could see her passionate blue eyes again.

"Thank you, babe." Her voice was clear in his mind.

"I hope you know that you deserve just as much recognition as she does," Sheese said. "When our plan is implemented, you'll be just as big an icon as she. You'll be a leader to the people of the Badlands, as well as to the rest of the realm."

Mardious hadn't thought about it that way before, but he liked what Sheese was saying. If Amelia were the queen, then he'd gladly be the king.

"We'll see." He smiled, but this time it wasn't fake.

CHAPTER 14

It's Been Too Long And I'm Lost Without You

Mardious walked a coin along his knuckles. Zuke believed it was the way he focused his power, and Mardious hadn't seen a reason to correct him. As a result, Zuke taught him to use an actual coin in an effort to improve his dexterity and focus. Mardious was a little surprised by how much he enjoyed the trick. He tucked his thumb underneath the coin, and brought it back to his index finger.

The sound of hooves from the end of the alley broke his concentration.

Mardious leant back, slipping deeper into the shadows. A horse-drawn carriage clattered down the road, but the driver wasn't paying attention to the side streets. Mardious shook off his disappointment—it wasn't the person he was waiting for.

It had been four weeks since Porkchop had left for Camptown with the loot from the bank heist. Although Sheese was adamant that no news travelled to the Badlands, Mardious wondered if Porkchop had heard of Amelia's death. If he had, he might have assumed there wasn't a reason to meet.

Mardious continued to play with his Aileron. It was too dark to see his hand clearly, but he felt like his other senses were heightened. Feeling the motion of the coin was calming. Boots scuffed the alley street.

"You're alive," Porkchop grumbled.

His stocky silhouette stood tall in the darkness of the alley. He appeared alone, but others could be lurking in the shadows. The moonlight offered little luminosity, and all the businesses on the street were closed, which were some of the reasons why Mardious had chosen this spot.

Mardious didn't know what to expect. Was Porkchop still having trouble with the Tyco? Was he on the run? Or was he looking for more funding for his cause?

"You are too," Mardious said with a fake smile. He stood up, brushing the dust from his clean robes. He was becoming accustomed to wearing clothes that fit in with the Triple Crown and the locals of Kimroad.

Porkchop stepped forwards. Mardious bent over to grab the sac of Aileron Sheese had given him. A hard blow to the cheek stopped him. He fell to the ground in pain.

"Coward!" Porkchop yelled.

Mardious tasted blood. He shook his head to get rid of the stars he was seeing, but before his vision cleared he felt a yank on his collar. Porkchop tossed him to the other side of the alleyway like a ragdoll, slamming him hard against the wall.

"She's dead because of you!" Porkchop screamed.

Mardious keeled over. He didn't think he had any broken bones, but his whole body felt numb. He tried to speak, but he struggled to breathe. A kick to the stomach made him gasp.

"You show up in your fancy clothes ..." Porkchop kicked Mardious again. "You probably sold her out the first chance you got."

"It's not what you think," Mardious finally said. He'd curled into a ball to protect his face and midsection.

Porkchop grabbed him by the neck and pulled him up. He squeezed his fingers around Mardious' throat, crushing his windpipe.

"Then how come she's gone, and you're still here?" Porkchop snarled. "If you had any honour, you would have died for her. Or at least died with her."

Mardious was choking. He didn't think Porkchop would let go. He deserved to die instead of Amelia, that much he agreed with, but Porkchop wasn't going to be the one to do it now. He twiddled his fingers twice as fast as he did when walking the Aileron coin and focused.

"Let go, Pollock," Amelia's voice said. "It's not his fault."

Porkchop abruptly let Mardious go and spun around. Mardious crashed to the ground, gasping for air as he fell. He was careful to concentrate on his illusion and remain in control.

A black hooded figure stood strong in the darkness. A light blue glow shone from behind her, illuminating her silhouette, but the light wasn't strong enough to show her face. Mardious was still struggling to put all her facial features together in his illusion.

"I can't believe it!" Porkchop exclaimed. "I thought I'd lost you." He rushed to Amelia, arms wide for a hug. All he grabbed was air, and the illusion disappeared.

Porkchop stumbled, and then fell to the ground. He knelt in the dirt and crumpled over. His shoulders shook as he sobbed.

Mardious sat up against the wall. He touched his puffy lip, smearing blood across his chin in the process. "We were ambushed."

Porkchop continued to sob. Mardious spat some blood from his mouth.

"When I close my eyes, I can still see the arrow strike her neck," Mardious admitted. "I couldn't save her. Every day, I wish I could have been the one to take the hit; that it had been me that was murdered. Unfortunately, I'm still here."

Porkchop wiped his eyes and sniffled. It wasn't his usual snort. He crawled to the wall opposite Mardious and sat with his back to it. He took a few deep breaths.

"I miss her more knowing for sure that she's gone," Porkchop said. "It must be hard for you, too."

Mardious nodded slightly, but stopped when he felt a sharp pain jolted up his neck. He decided not to move. Porkchop had done a number on him.

"Whenever I ordered finger food at Sugarplum, she'd bring me some hot water with lemon to clean my hands," Porkchop said. "Each time, I'd make the same joke. 'Lemon soup!' I'd say. She'd always laugh, as lame as it was. It made me feel good to make her smile."

Mardious chuckled, but held his stomach. The pain was too much. He'd never heard her retell the joke, probably because it wasn't funny. Making all of the guests at Sugarplum feel welcome was definitely something she'd do without expecting praise.

"On one of my first shifts," Mardious said, "I poured a couple of ales. I set them on the bar for Amelia to take away, but one was too close to the edge. It fell behind the bar and shattered everywhere. I was embarrassed, but she didn't make me feel guilty. Instead, she took the full ale, held it over the floor on her side of the bar, and dropped it. Hearing the glass break made me feel better."

Porkchop laughed. "That sounds like something she'd do," he said. He snorted and laughed again. "Rules didn't apply to her."

"She made me clean up both messes, too," Mardious added. They both laughed through the pain.

Porkchop and Mardious shared a few more stories. It felt good to think about Amelia's impact on each of them. Every time Mardious laughed, it was as if his body was healing. The more he remembered her, the less he hurt.

"Everyone loved her," Porkchop said. "It's a shame she can't see what's happening in the Badlands now. The bounty from your last heist has already sparked change."

Mardious felt sad again. "What do you mean?" he forced himself to ask.

"I was able to buy off two members of the Tyco's inner circle," Porkchop said. "Now it's chaos. There are trust issues between the remaining members, and the ripple effect has forced panic. Alliances are being formed, groups are declaring war on each other, and mayhem is ensuing. It's like watching a beautiful thunderstorm."

Mardious couldn't believe it. Porkchop's plan had actually worked. He wondered if Sheese would be delighted with the news, and how it would fit into his schemes. "What do we do next?" he asked.

"We don't have to do anything," Porkchop said confidently. "It's become survival of the fittest. We wait in the shadows while the rest of the Badlands goes to war. When the bloodbath is over, we form a new, single group that we control."

"What do you mean by 'wait in the shadows'?" Mardious asked.

"With the Aileron that everyone received, some of us have relocated for the time being," Porkchop said. "Even those people of yours at the shelter invested in some property here in Kimroad. Their new location is a refuge for those who want to escape the madness of Camptown."

Mardious gritted his teeth. "That's not what the money was meant for," he said.

"What *was* it meant for then?" Porkchop shot back. "If it was meant to help the people of the Badlands, it's doing just that. It's expanded the reach of the shelter, and they're helping the citizens of Camptown stay safe, fed, and warm. You should have seen Mary Angella's face when she bought the building. She was so happy."

Mardious didn't care, but he knew that Amelia would have been pleased. He wished she could have been a part of it.

"I guess you don't need that sac then," Mardious said, pointing to Porkchop's right.

Porkchop felt around in the dark until he touched the treasure that Sheese had legally taken from the bank of the Triple Crown. There was also a little bit extra in there. Mardious hadn't planned on stealing anything while he lived with Zuke, but he just couldn't help himself.

"Silverware and coins," Porkchop said, staring up from the open sac. "You've been busy robbing houses again?"

"Not exactly," Mardious admitted. He told Porkchop of his capture and the deal he'd made. He left out the part about the doorway of life. He didn't want to get Porkchop's hopes up yet, probably because he didn't want his own dreams to overwhelm him.

He also shared the conversation he'd had with Sheese. He didn't divulge the whole plan, but stressed the importance of relaying information between the Triple Crown and the Badlands. Porkchop was impressed by how much Mardious had learned.

"It's been four weeks of rigorous wizard training, and my skills have already improved," Mardious said. "I don't know what lies ahead in their quest for power, though."

"I can't believe you've infiltrated the Triple Crown." Porkchop shook his head. "If your friends are scheming to be the High Authority leaders, you're in a position to change the entire realm!"

"We'll see," Mardious said. He still didn't know how it would all play out. He just wanted to keep working to obtain the doorway of life and get Amelia back.

Porkchop snorted. "Why were you and Amelia stealing all that Aileron?" he asked. "Besides helping people in Camptown get enough to eat and shelter to sleep."

Mardious tried not to laugh. Porkchop was sounding a lot like Sheese. "We were just trying to balance the scales," he said. "We want the people of the Badlands to have the same chances as the rest of the realm."

"Exactly." Porkchop snorted again. "And now you're in a position to balance the scales more by working with influencers at the Triple Crown. You're a genius."

Mardious remained silent. He didn't want to take credit for the plan, but he also didn't want to say anything to make Porkchop second-guess it. This meeting was already a success.

"Creating a life for the people of the Badlands that's as prosperous as the rest of the realm." Porkchop shook his head. "But what happens after that? Once your friends are in power, are you going to take it away from them?"

Mardious perked up. He hadn't really thought about removing them from power. If Amelia were queen, and he the king, then there wouldn't be a need for Zuke and Sheese. He was impressed that Porkchop had come up with the idea so quickly.

"How do we do that?" Mardious asked.

Porkchop snorted. "You keep doing what you're doing. You learn from your friends at the Triple Crown. You help them reach their goals of becoming the High Authority. Then you either bend them to your will, or end their short reign."

Mardious smiled. He was worried about being double-crossed by Sheese and Zuke, but what if he were the one taking advantage of them in the end? He and Amelia would control everything. "Amelia would love this idea."

"Of course she would," Porkchop said. "And so will everyone else. You can take the man out of the Badlands, but you can't take the Badlands out of the man. The people need a leader; since she isn't with us anymore, you'll be the one they follow. You will be the new Money Jane."

The nickname made Mardious shudder. He didn't think anyone should have that name except Amelia. He was glad to have Porkchop's support, but he didn't know if he was the leader they deserved. "I don't think it will be that easy," he admitted.

Porkchop laughed. "Trust me, I used to *hate* you." He snorted again. "I hated that Amelia loved you more than anyone else, and I couldn't stand to look at the stupid grin you'd get whenever she made you laugh."

Porkchop wasn't doing a good job of improving his confidence.

"But now," he continued, "I can see how much she lives on in you. I know how much you loved her, and I respect that. I know you can lead our people, because I believe in you. Instead of an enemy to me, you're now like a brother."

Mardious smiled. He hated Porkchop too, but now he respected him more. "She lives on in us," Mardious said. "Your support means a lot to me, though."

"Of course," Porkchop replied. He looked up and down their quiet alley. "But there's one thing I need you to do for me."

Mardious nodded. "What is it?"

"Can you ... can you make an illusion of Amelia again?" Porkchop asked. "I want to see her one last time."

Mardious smiled. "I'll try. I can't really do her face yet, but her body and voice are pretty good."

Porkchop snorted. "Hearing her will be good enough."

Mardious closed his eyes, his fingers moving as if he were playing a slow song for Amelia to dance to. He imagined her wearing a red dress, and white gloves that were too big for her. A red-jewelled tiara sat atop her apple-sized head.

"Thank you, Pollock, for everything you've done," Amelia said. Porkchop sobbed instantly. "Take care of your brother for me. He might be a pain sometimes, but he means well."

Porkchop chuckled and wiped his cheek.

"I love you both very much," Amelia said. "Never forget me, because I'll never forget you."

The illusion disappeared. Porkchop cried some more; Mardious felt tears streak down his face, too. They both sat silently with their tears in the alley for some time.

"Again," Porkchop finally whispered. He cleared his throat. "Can you do it again?"

"Of course." Mardious' voice cracked a little, but he forced the words out. He'd recreate that illusion for eternity if he could.

CHAPTER 15

You All Know Me

Mardious hit the low key with his pinkie, completing the chord. His fingers slithered along the keyboard, providing accompaniment to his masterful illusion. The tiny dragon danced to the music.

"Once we uncover the secret portal door underneath the cavern floor, I'll use my magic to influence the dragon," Mardious explained. "It will heat up the stone, causing the doors to open."

Mardious hit the keys harder as the little beast blew fire. The flame covered a grey portal frame, and then intensified to encompass the entire illusion. He ended his magical presentation and the song at the same time.

Zuke gave him a standing ovation. "Well done. I liked your choice of red for the dragon. A suitably scary guardian." Although it was his plan, he always appeared to enjoy Mardious' performances, and this presentation was no different.

Sheese remained seated. He tapped his chin a few times. "You're sure this will work?"

Zuke's smile disappeared. "It has to," he said. He put his gloved hand on Sheese's shoulder. "We're running out of willing recruits. This is our best chance of retrieving another piece of the puzzle, and continuing our righteous quest."

"We have already lost numerous good men simply by mapping out the safest path through Skyland to the cache," Sheese said, shaking his head. "I don't need to lose my best." He put his hand on Zuke's.

Zuke beamed with pride. "Maybe the best is what we need to finally bring it home," he replied.

Mardious cared little about the danger; he was finally going to get a shot at obtaining a piece of the doorway of life.

It had been nine long months of training with Zuke in their shared quarters at the castle of the Triple Crown, but Mardious felt stronger than ever. His relentless magical studies had made him a powerful and competent wizard. He was able to add illusions, basic healing, and pyrokinesis to his list of abilities. He improved his animal control, potion making, and element manipulation skills, too. He was a fully-trained wizard. He had even done some studying, like a scholar, under the guidance of Sheese on the history and policies of the Triple Crown.

Amelia had been with him the whole time. He cherished the time he had to talk to her alone, reflecting on his life in the capital city of Kimroad. He'd give her updates on his plans, and she'd help him focus on his end goals. Knowing that they were moving forwards gave him hope that he would achieve everything they ever wanted.

"We're ready," he heard Amelia whisper.

"I'm ready," he said.

Zuke smiled proudly. "I'm confident that our plan is foolproof."

Sheese stood and smiled. "I trust you," he said. "But if you die, I'm going to kill you when I bring you back to life."

Zuke and Mardious laughed. "You're merciless," Zuke said.

"I have some assignments I need to complete for High Scholar Robert," Sheese said. "Let me know if you require anything else from me before you set off on your adventure." He left the room, closing the door softly behind him.

Mardious rested his hands on the keyboard. "Want to hear another song?" he asked.

Zuke smiled. "I always love hearing you play, but first there's something I need to show you. It will help you prepare for our mission."

Mardious nodded. He obediently followed Zuke's orders, as he had been doing for months. He never asked unnecessary questions, always trusting that the path Zuke laid out for him was correct. He worked diligently, knowing that the process was necessary for his end goals.

They left their secluded piano room and swiftly crossed the grand hallways of the castle of the Triple Crown. At this time of night, hardly anyone was scurrying about. They made a few turns and then climbed the steps to the top floor.

They walked past rooms that Mardious didn't recognize or care for, until they reached a small door that marked the end of their journey. Without a word, Zuke opened it slowly, revealing a few brooms and some cobwebs.

"You want me to sweep this floor, too?" Mardious asked. He wasn't thrilled with another chore, especially after a long day of work.

Zuke smiled. "This isn't what it seems." He leant over and put his hand on the left side of the wall. "See this mark?"

Mardious had to bend down to see what Zuke was referring to. A five-sided star was etched into the stone. "What does it mean?"

"It's a pentagram," Zuke said. "It's the sign of the Chosen. Now, watch carefully."

Zuke counted bricks along the wall, and placed both hands carefully against the spots he'd chosen. He applied pressure at the same time, until the two bricks moved a finger width into the surface.

"Now wait until you hear a click," he whispered.

After a few seconds, Mardious heard a sound from the other side. Zuke moved his right hand to another brick on the wall, and pressed it in like he had the others. Another moment passed, and then the entire wall slid upwards.

"You have a secret lair?" Mardious whispered back.

"*We* have a secret lair," Zuke replied. He pulled a fire starter out of his pocket and stepped into the darkness. "Close the door behind you."

Mardious followed Zuke into the room. Zuke lit a torch on the sidewall, and then pulled a lever beside it. The wall slid back down into its original position. With a tug on his gloves and a wave of his arms, all the torches in the room ignited.

Mardious' head swivelled as he checked out the secret lair. A few bookshelves rested against one wall, but only a couple books stood on each shelf. A map of the realm was tacked up on another wall, next to a single curtain that blocked any outside light from entering.

In the centre of the room was a large table with wooden chairs all around. A few neatly stacked piles of papers rested in the middle with a quill placed parallel to them. Mardious tried to see what was written on the top sheets, but found it difficult to read the poor handwriting upside down.

"Come this way." Zuke headed straight for the curtain, eager to show off the room. Mardious followed closely behind.

When Zuke pulled the cloth back, Mardious expected to see a glamorous view of the city, but what the curtain actually hid was much more beautiful. Instead of a window, it concealed a golden stone artefact, etched with ancient symbols and hieroglyphs. Its presence felt bold and powerful.

"Can I touch it?" Mardious asked.

Zuke chuckled. "It's nothing special ... yet." He walked to the middle of one side of the table, and took a seat in front of the paper stack.

Mardious ran his fingers along the stone edge. It was a six-inch wide by six-inch deep oblong column. The top of the column came to a sharp edge above his head, and then bent at a right angle at his feet. The intricacies of the detail were so mesmerizing. It felt magical.

"That piece of the doorway comes from an ancient vault, hidden by the Eidola," Zuke said. "Centuries ago, the Chosen trusted the Eidola to keep it safe. Now, we must do the same."

Mardious could hear Amelia's voice whisper in his ear, "It will soon be ours."

"Who were the Chosen and the Eidola?" Mardious asked. He reluctantly moved away from the artefact and sat down beside Zuke.

Zuke cleared his throat. "Before the realm was united, the Eidola ruled the western desert. At the time, they were the most knowledgeable, wealthy, and respected scholars in the entire world."

Mardious tried not to roll his eyes. "The realm is hardly united," Amelia whispered.

"The Chosen were the wizards who controlled the doorway of life," Zuke continued. "They became worried about the power of the doorway falling into the wrong hands, so they separated it into pieces; they entrusted the Eidola with guarding one of them. We now know the Eidola were one of four guardians that protected the artefact from the rest of the realm."

"So how did you get it?" Mardious asked. "Are you a descendant of the Eidola or something?"

Zuke laughed. "No. Sheese and I discovered it while exploring some of the treasures that the Triple Crown keeps hidden in the underground vaults of the castle. He's always had an interest in history, and uncovering this artefact sparked a new obsession for him."

"So none of the other pieces were in the vaults?" Mardious asked.

"No." Zuke's smile faded. "That's where it gets tricky. The scholars of the Eidola helped the wizards of the Chosen build three other safe havens for the pieces of the doorway of life. We only know where one of them is, but we're confident that buried with the artefact is information that will lead us to the next."

"And treasure," Amelia whispered to him.

"And treasure," Mardious said aloud.

"Right," Zuke confirmed. "We'll need the doorway piece, clues on the other locations, and gold to fund our future endeavours. We have a lot riding on this mission."

He slid one of the stacks of papers in Mardious' direction. 'Final Recruits' was written on the top page.

"I want you to read all of these," Zuke said. "Sheese had to hire warriors to help us with our journey. They don't know our plan yet, but they'll help us along the dangerous path and haul our spoils back. Within these pages is everything that Sheese has gathered on them."

"We have to work with warriors?" Mardious still hated anyone in uniform, not just the one in the bull-horned helmet.

"I don't like it either," Zuke said, "but we don't really have a choice. They're all serviceable in their own way. However, we can't afford to overlook anything or be surprised, and I value your opinion. I want you to study their profiles so you know what to expect from each of them."

Zuke stood from his chair and patted Mardious on the back. "I'll go get us some food. Then we can talk more about our team and go over our plan once more. This is what we've been working so hard for over the last few months; just a little more effort, and I know we'll be successful."

Zuke pulled the lever beside the room's entrance. The wall opened up, and he stepped through. When he closed the door to the broom closet, the wall returned to normal.

Mardious calmly twitched his fingers, and Amelia appeared across from him at the table. She wore a beautiful green gown, white silk gloves, and, of course, her golden medal. Her hair was perfectly combed, her skin was soft, and her eyes were sparkling. She looked around, crossing her arms in disgust. "This room is hideous."

"For a secret lair, it's pretty lame," agreed Mardious.

Amelia stood and studied the bookcases carefully. "We could store so many potions in here," she said. "It could be our new and improved Cage."

"We could get rid of this bulky table," Mardious said, tapping its surface. "It takes up too much room."

Amelia spun around, a wicked smile curling her lips. "We'd have room for a bed," she said. "We could lie around all day, and no one would bother us."

"Or hear us." Mardious looked up to the roof. "We could put a window up there, and stare at the night sky together. We'd make plans that will keep the people of the entire realm happy and prosperous forever. We'll be the greatest rulers the world has ever seen."

Amelia giggled, and then skipped to where Mardious sat. She leant on the chair next to him. "First things first, babe," she said.

Mardious was always more disciplined with Amelia around: she helped him study. He was able to stay focused on the tasks at hand, whether it was practicing magic, or learning the policies of the Triple Crown. He knew that getting her back required him to be at his best, and her presence made him feel more powerful.

"These warriors are all so old," Amelia said. Mardious read the sheets in the first stack, and then moved to the next one. He memorized their names, qualities, and skills. They were all former Guardians who had been caught breaking the law on duty.

"They're just as crooked as the Guardians we knew in the Badlands," Mardious said. "They're strong, useful, and disposable. They're perfect."

"Don't you think they'll try to keep the treasure for themselves?" Amelia asked.

Mardious sighed. "If they do, I'll know where to find it." He tapped where the profile pages listed their addresses and location in the realm. He'd be able to sneak into their homes and steal back any extra Aileron that the warriors kept. "I'll make sure to get it all. It will allow Porkchop to buy more property in Kimroad; with it, we can move more people from the Badlands here."

"I love how you're already making this city a better place, babe," Amelia said. "I can't wait to visit it soon." She leant over and puckered her lips.

Mardious closed his eyes. He imagined his mouth on hers. She'd bite his lip, and they'd ravage each other for hours. They'd mess up all the papers on the table, and probably break a few chairs in the process. The room would barely be able to contain their passion.

When he opened his eyes, she wasn't in front of him any longer. His hands were steady, resting softly on the table. He took a deep breath and returned to studying.

He read both stacks over and over. He had to make sure he didn't miss anything. He needed the plan to succeed—not just for Zuke and Sheese, but for Amelia too. It was one step closer to seeing her for real. It didn't matter how much time had passed since the last time he'd held her: only how much closer he was to holding her again.

"I love you, babe," she whispered.

CHAPTER 16

What It Is, What It Isn't

Mardious was calm now that they were under the cover of darkness. The rivers of lava that cut through these upper regions of Skyland created a warm glow that provided just enough light to see, which was comforting. Although the looming threat of dragons above them concerned the rest of the team, he was excited for the opportunity to use his animal control techniques on them when the time came. Wearing Amelia's medal on his journey helped him feel invincible.

Zuke, on the other hand, wasn't even pretending to be calm. He kept nervously looking up, shifting his head from side to side, and jumping at random noises. Mardious even noticed Zuke's hands trembling from time to time. He wanted to help his friend stay focused.

"Look, a scorpion." Mardious pointed to the left of the path, trying to get Zuke's attention away from the sky.

The captain of the warriors spun around. "Quiet," Richard said. He jabbed his index finger towards the sky and tapped his helmet. He shook his head, and then resumed leading the group deeper towards the caverns of Skyland.

Mardious rolled his eyes. He'd just met Richard, and already hated him. Richard was a typical warrior: arrogant, self-righteous, and brash.

"I wish *he'd* stay quiet," Amelia whispered.

Although he continued walking with the rest of the task force, Mardious let his left arm dangle at his side and stretched his fingers. He closed his eyes, and tried to link with the little beast he'd just spotted.

The cold-blooded creature was as still as a statue, now behind the group.

It wanted to remain hidden, but Mardious was about to change that. He could feel the tiny tremors of the arachnid slow down to match his heartbeat. Smaller creatures were always easier for him to control. He continued to play his imaginary piano.

The scorpion's legs shuffled forwards, climbing over the warm rocks it was perched on, and down the uneven path. It weaved around Aaron and Jesse at the back, sped past Mardious and Zuke, and scurried ahead of Scott, Nate, and Timo before slowing just behind Richard's foot.

Mardious wondered how best to strike. What would hurt Richard the most? The scorpion's claws looked too small to penetrate through a boot. Its stinger would be more effective, but how long would it reach? Could the scorpion climb to a vulnerable chink in Richard's armour? He was about to make a move when he felt someone grip his forearm.

He froze. He'd been caught.

If he hadn't respected Zuke so much, he would have done it anyway without a moment of regret. He didn't even glance in his friend's direction, but felt Zuke's hand release.

"At least his hands aren't trembling anymore," Amelia said in support.

He fluttered his fingers some more, and the scorpion scurried away from the path. He'd get Richard another time.

They continued down the rugged trail. The area was a garden of cavernous hillsides and small, active volcanoes that provided both warmth and light. The uneven terrain made their journey difficult, but it also gave them plenty of spots to hide and rest as necessary. There had only been two occasions so far where they had spotted a dragon flying above them, but unfortunately, Mardious hadn't been able to connect with any of them yet.

Richard raised his closed fist, and everyone stopped. They'd arrived.

Across a stream of lava was a field of brittle shale. A single cave stood in the very centre of the area. The entrance was broad enough for a giant, and although Mardious couldn't see in, he knew that the mark of the Chosen would be etched into the wall somewhere.

Richard drew his sword and hunched over. He used his weapon to sketch an outline of the territory in the loose, rocky path. Everyone else huddled around.

"Once we get to the cave entrance, we'll search for the mark of the Chosen," he said. They all nodded in agreement. "Once we find it, I'll be able to mark the spot where the relic is buried, and we'll all dig together."

"Dragoon," the warriors rumbled. Their trademark salute made Mardious shudder.

Richard made two circles, one on each side of the cave entrance. "I want you two to be our eyes," he said, pointing to Mardious and Zuke. "If you give us the signal, we all take cover until the danger passes. We'll only engage as a last resort."

Mardious nodded along with Zuke. He was growing tired of all the instructions. This was *their* plan. He'd gone over it countless times, but here Richard was, treating him like a dumb warrior. He wished the rest of the task force were as prepared as he was.

The group cautiously crossed the narrow bridge over the stream of lava. Once on the other side, they quickened their pace. Even though many of the warriors were twice the age of the wizards, they were much stronger, and ran a lot faster.

Mardious was instantly tired. He thought it would be more strategic for them to take their time, but that wasn't the route the warriors were taking, and he didn't need to get left out in the open. So he sprinted as fast as his legs would carry him—and still fell behind. He watched as the warriors rushed into the cave. He slowed his pace and jogged into position on the right side of the cave entrance. He leant over in exhaustion and tried to catch his breath.

"Looks like I won," Amelia whispered. "I'm still faster than you."

"Clear," Timo said.

"Clear," echoed Aaron.

"There are some bones here. They still have meat on them," Richard said.

Mardious stood tall, looked up to the sky, and focused on his task. He didn't see any dragons flying about, but he heard a few roars. He absently twiddled his fingers in hopes of connecting with one, but he didn't feel anything. They must have been too far away.

Mardious glanced over at Zuke, who was whipping his head about frantically again. He looked more worried than usual. Their eyes met, and they both shrugged.

"Found it," said Jesse.

Mardious and Zuke both glanced back. Richard whispered something to the other warriors, and then stood tall. He counted out twelve steps from the cavern wall, and then checked his original position. He took six wide steps to his left, and pointed at the ground.

Scott rushed over and dropped a sac, spilling shovels to the dirt. Each of the warriors grabbed one and broke ground. They worked hard and fast, and dust flew everywhere.

"I hope they uncover it soon," Amelia whispered. "We have so much more to do."

Mardious checked the sky again. He played his imaginary piano, but he still didn't feel anything. He wanted to tell Amelia that everything would be okay, but he kept quiet.

A loud clang echoed throughout the cave, but Mardious ignored it for something more exciting: a dark shadow was approaching from beyond the bridge they'd crossed. Its body was massive, but the slender, flapping wings were clearly visible. His fingers moved faster.

Light from the lava reflected off the golden scales of the three-headed dragon as it descended. There was a darker figure in its clutches, but Mardious didn't recognize it until the dragon landed with a thunderous crash. It was a giant dead hog covered in blood.

"You can't feel anything," Amelia reminded him.

The dragon's wings were spread so wide they blocked all the light from the volcanic surroundings. Two of the dragon's heads were looking off to the sides, but the centre one was sniffing the air curiously. The plan assumed that dragons had one head, not three. Maybe that was why he couldn't control it?

"Don't let it see you," Amelia said.

Mardious retreated into the cave. "Hide," he said to Zuke, who was standing awestruck in his path. He rushed past Richard and hid behind a boulder at the back of the cave. The rest of the warriors joined him after a few moments.

Richard pulled Zuke behind the boulder and shoved him angrily. "Do something."

Zuke looked worried. When he met Mardious' eyes, he snapped out of his panicked state. His face softened, and he nodded to signal the first phase of their contingency plan.

Mardious closed his eyes and leant his head on the hard surface of the boulder. He tried fluttering his fingers more gently this time, and searched for the three-headed dragon. His breathing slowed as his power heightened, but he couldn't feel the beast anywhere.

"I think it's gone," Mardious whispered confidently. He opened his eyes, and saw Richard relax.

Richard carefully looked around the boulder, and then ducked back quickly. His eyebrows furrowed in anger. "Try again," he said.

Mardious peeked around the boulder. The dragon had entered the cave, and was sniffing around. Something was wrong. Why couldn't he connect with it? He had never had this much trouble controlling an animal before, let alone not even being able to feel its presence.

He turned to Zuke. "I can't do it," he whispered.

"Your turn, Beardy." Richard shoved Zuke, out of frustration. Mardious' anger with the warrior grew. Yes, he and Zuke looked similar, but could he really only tell them apart by Zuke's facial hair? He hadn't once used either of their names. Mardious wanted to stand up for his friend and throw Richard into the dragon's path.

"Not yet, babe," Amelia warned.

Zuke stretched out his arms and pulled at the cuffs of his golden leather gloves. He peered around the other side of the boulder and went to work.

A loud screeching noise echoed from the cave entrance. When Mardious looked around the boulder, the dragon had spun to face a giant black scorpion outside the cave. It looked exactly like the one they had seen earlier, but its size matched that of the dragon. Mardious was impressed that Zuke could make such a detailed illusion based on a creature they had only seen once.

The dragon roared. All three heads swam in the air like sea serpents, each trying to study the scorpion from a different angle. The central head leant back, and blew fire towards the threat. But Zuke had foreseen this, and the illusion backed away from the cave entrance, out of the dragon's range.

The dragon chased after the scorpion, into the open field of shale. Zuke moved to the entrance so the rest of the group could focus on their plan of escape.

"Nice work," Richard said. "Grab your shovels, we're almost done."

"Dragoon," the warriors responded. They returned to the relic beneath the surface, which glowed white. Mardious had assumed that the portal leading to the ancient relic would look like a regular gateway, but he was wrong.

"You need to escape from the dragon, babe," Amelia whispered.

There were more important things than studying the magical doorway. "Are you crazy?" Mardious scolded. "We don't have enough time. We need to get out of here before that thing comes back."

"Get back to your post," Richard commanded. He continued to throw dirt and rocks in the air with his reckless shovelling.

Mardious rushed back to the front of the cave, keeping one hand on the rocky wall. He watched as the dragon chased the scorpion around. It seemed to be well-distracted, until a loud clang echoed through the cave.

The dragon stopped moving. All three heads turned to face its den curiously. One of the heads looked back at the scorpion, which moved back and forth as if taunting the dragon.

"It knows," Zuke said.

All three heads started barking. Mardious didn't think dragons could communicate with each other, but it looked like this one was having a conversation amongst itself. Instead of continuing the chase, the dragon scraped at some of the loose shale and kicked it towards the scorpion. The stones flew right through the arachnid and bounced on the ground. The illusion disappeared.

Zuke brought his arms down and stared straight ahead. The dragon was now peering at the front of the cave. The middle head leant back and then shot forwards as it let loose a crippling roar. The other two joined in to create a threatening cacophony.

Mardious and Zuke shared a glance and retreated. They ran past the digging warriors to hide behind the boulder. They peered back around the edge as the dragon charged the cave. Instead of hiding, the warriors stood strong.

"Get ..." Zuke started, but Mardious reached out and grabbed his arm. He shook his head; their pleas wouldn't matter. The warriors were going to face the danger head-on, and the wise warnings of wizards were not going to deter them.

"I can't wait to see the dragon destroy them," Amelia said.

Timo, Scott, Nate, and Jesse held their shields in front of them, while Richard and Aaron grabbed their bows. They all huddled together, guarding the precious white treasure.

The dragon slowed as it reached the cave entrance. Its heads darted low, and all six eyes stared straight ahead. It growled, analyzing its enemy.

"Hold," said Richard.

The middle head lifted high, while the others slithered around maniacally.

"Hold!" Richard yelled louder.

The dragon stopped moving. The middle head opened its mouth. An orange glow formed in the back of its mouth.

"Now!" Richard commanded.

The two archers fired their arrows at the dragon. The dragon closed its eyes and mouth, and then barked at itself again. None of the arrows penetrated its scales.

"They're doomed," Amelia whispered eagerly.

The front four lowered their shields, drew their swords, and rushed the dragon.

They had only taken a few steps before the dragon decided to go on the offensive. Its right head leant down and blew a stream of fire across the warriors.

While the warriors used their shields to block the incoming flame, the dragon head on the other side made its move. Its sharp teeth grabbed Timo and threw him against the wall. His painful scream was brought to a sickening halt by the impact of his head against the cavern.

Mardious turned away and hid behind the boulder. He looked down at the scar on his palm. Seeing someone else lose their life made him think about Amelia's death: the smell of the pink lakes, the heavy sand under his feet, and the splattered blood across her neck.

"We're dead." Zuke clutched Mardious' arm.

Hearing Zuke panic instantly made Mardious doubt their mission. They had a plan in place, and even though the warriors were trying their best, Mardious knew it would fail. The only course of action left was to escape—while they still could.

"Leave him," Amelia whispered.

"Get ready to move," Mardious said. His eyes remained closed, but he tilted his head from side to side as his power flowed through his entire body. His fingers quickly went to work on their imaginary piano.

He focused his power on the surrounding air. The dirt and rock that the warriors had carelessly tossed about was now broken up and easier to control. A small, black cloud covered the lower half of the cave. Screams still rang through the area. Mardious grabbed Zuke's hand and led him away from the danger.

He slithered along the cave wall until he found the exit. He didn't see the dragon through the dust cover, which meant that the dragon couldn't see them. Before he knew it, they were back in the barren, open terrain of Skyland.

Mardious let go of Zuke and ran as fast as he could. His legs felt stronger than they had on the way over. Zuke started to pull away. The fear must have helped him run faster, too.

A roar escaped the cave. Mardious turned, hoping the dragon wasn't already chasing them. Richard had emerged from the darkness, and was now retreating like the wizards had. Soon after, a second roar sounded from behind the cloud of dust.

Mardious turned, and stared at the bridge that marked their escape route. They weren't even close. There had to be a place for them to hide, but he didn't see anything. He remembered caves labelled on Richard's map, but he didn't know exactly where they were.

Zuke checked back on him. "C'mon," he said. "We're almost there."

"I … can't …" Mardious panted. He was struggling to keep up.

"There's a small cave just beyond the bridge." Richard had outpaced them, and now ran on Zuke's other side. He didn't look tired at all. "The dragon won't be able to reach us in there."

Another roar sounded from behind them. Mardious looked back, and saw the dragon emerge. It barked a few orders to itself, and then spread its wings wide.

Mardious turned back to the bridge, but they were still too far away. It felt like he was getting slower, trudging through sand instead of on top of loose shale. It was impossible for him to outrun the dragon; it would only be a matter of time before he was caught and killed.

Mardious closed his eyes and thought about Amelia. It would be wonderful to finally join her in death. He wondered if he'd be able to hold her again, instead of seeing her illusion disappear.

A scream broke through his thoughts.

His eyes flew open just in time to see Zuke stumble. He looked back. Richard had fallen to the ground.

"Stupid, clumsy warrior," Amelia said.

Mardious was grateful for the diversion. He refocused on reaching the bridge. A roar came from the dragon's direction, followed by a thundering crash. Another faint scream pleased Mardious; Richard had finally gotten what he deserved.

Mardious and Zuke crossed the short bridge over the lava stream and entered their cave of refuge. Mardious went in first, looking for a spot far enough away from the entrance. They didn't need the dragon to reach them with its teeth, claws, or fire.

He felt along the wall on his right, until he came to a noticeable gap. "Over here." He grabbed Zuke's arm and dragged him into the small nook.

They both slunk to the ground. The dragon landed with a crash in front of the cave, and then barked to itself. Its low rumblings were amplified as they echoed down the cavern.

A second later, the walls to their left glowed orange, and a burst of fire went rushing past. They sat comfortably in their nook, finally out of danger.

"That was close," Amelia whispered.

Mardious rubbed the scar on his hand. Amelia was wrong: they weren't close to obtaining their goal of ancient relics, riches, and information. They had failed. Zuke's great plan had been a disaster. He had claimed it was foolproof, but Mardious couldn't even control the dragon, which was their first, biggest step. He felt in that instant that their mission was impossible.

"I'm sorry," Zuke whispered. He touched Mardious' arm.

"You did all you could," Mardious replied. He wore a fake smile in the darkness, and pretended to be strong and confident. "Next time we'll be better," he lied.

"Don't let him off the hook," Amelia whispered. "His plan was terrible."

The dragon screamed again. Another pulse of flame shot past them, followed by two more. It was so hot, Zuke had to turn away from the blaze.

"Next time we'll be better." Zuke leant back against the wall and closed his eyes.

Mardious didn't know if there would be a next time with Zuke. Although the scorpion illusion was impressive, it hadn't accomplished much. The team he'd put together was useless. The warriors were stupid and arrogant.

It felt like the semi-failed heist at the weapons shop. Poor planning had caused injury to Amelia, led to riches being left behind, and ended with them almost being caught. This time, mistakes had led to death. It wasn't a good plan, and Mardious wasn't confident that Zuke could come up with a better one.

"We can do this on our own, babe," Amelia said confidently. "And next time, we'll be ruthless."

Mardious was pleased Amelia still supported him, but if he couldn't control the dragon, how were they supposed to open the portal? How were they going to haul all their spoils back through Skyland? How would they know where to look for the next pieces of the doorway of life?

"We'll figure it out," Amelia reassured him. "We always do."

Zuke was a failure. Mardious looked over at him. He trembled as another burst of fire shot past them, gently rocking back and forth. He looked weak. He would have never survived the violence that Mardious had grown up in. At this point, he might not even make it back to the castle of the Triple Crown.

Mardious knew he only had one option left. He was a powerful wizard, and could create illusions of his own. He was smart enough to come up with a better plan. He would use his skills to build up enough resources to do the job right. He would be the one in control.

He closed his eyes. He reached into his collar and held Amelia's medal with his scarred hand. He was the only one who could bring Amelia back. He was powerful enough to do it. He was done with Zuke, Sheese, and any warriors they had convinced to help.

He felt angry. He felt determined. It was his time to take over.

CHAPTER 17

Six Million Ways To Die: Choose One

Mardious peeked around the corner of the hallway. Sheese's office door was still closed. He wondered why Zuke and Sheese hadn't left for their meeting with the High Wizard yet. The way Zuke had been talking about it, it seemed urgent.

Then again, Zuke often played up the importance of his tasks. In Mardious' months of working with him, he had realized that Zuke wasn't as influential, recognized, or respected as he thought he was. He was highly skilled, but his superiors often silenced him before he could speak, his proposals were shelved in favour of more popular ones, and he was consistently left out of social events with other wizards. One of his colleagues had even mistaken Mardious for Zuke one time. What if the meeting was cancelled, or they didn't have to attend?

"Patience, babe," Amelia whispered.

Patience wasn't needed. The door opened, and the duo exited. Sheese locked the door, while Zuke, holding their books, waited obediently. The two left without a backwards glance.

As soon as they were out of sight, Mardious made his move, staying close to the wall out of habit. When he stopped in front of the door, he looked over his shoulder to make sure there was no one else in the hallway. He inserted his tension wrench into the keyhole, and used his pick for entry.

A couple light dabs and a flick of the wrist, and he was in. He slipped into the room and locked the door behind him.

"Where do we begin?" Amelia asked.

Mardious tried to put himself in Sheese's shoes. He thought about where he'd keep the special documents that could withdraw Aileron from the bank of the Triple Crown. Was there a hidden book on the highest shelf? Were there stacks of paper that acted as camouflage? If he pulled one of the books from its resting place, would a secret door or safe appear?

"It's going to take too long to search every book," Amelia said. "Try the desk."

Mardious took a seat in Sheese's chair. It was made of thick wood, and the padding was hardly comfortable. He put his hands on the surface and tapped it a few times in thought. He noticed how precisely the quill was placed beside the blank notebook in front of him.

"Don't make too much of a mess, babe," Amelia said. "He probably knows where everything is supposed to go."

Mardious pulled the top right drawer open. He carefully removed a notebook and opened it. The first page had a date in the corner, and then a list of duties. It looked like a daily journal. He fanned through the pages, but nothing indicated where he might find what he was looking for. He sighed, placed the book carefully on the desk, and reached for the next one.

"We'll find it," Amelia said. "Don't worry."

The sound of keys rattling made him release the second book. By the time the key hit the lock, there was nothing else Mardious could do except find a hiding place. He dipped under the desk and pulled his legs in as tight as he could.

"Sloppy, babe," Amelia whispered. "Not a good start to your devious plan."

The desk drawer was still open. The first notebook was exposed on the desktop. The chair was pushed away. Mardious thought about why he was hiding; he was clearly in trouble.

The door opened. A couple of footsteps shuffled across the stone floor, but they were soon followed by silence. A dark shadow loomed closer until it covered Mardious' boots. He wasn't so much disappointed that he was caught as he was embarrassed about how it happened.

“Did you find what you were looking for?” Sheese asked.

Mardious crawled out from his hiding place. He kept his fists clenched as he stood up. He locked eyes with Sheese, intent on forcing the weak scholar into giving him what he wanted. “Where’s the paperwork for a Bank of the Triple Crown withdrawal,” he said in a low voice.

Sheese raised his left eyebrow. “I thought we paid your friends a few weeks ago.” He reached into the left drawer of his desk, tiptoed his fingers to the edge of a stack of paper, and pulled out a sheet.

Mardious snatched it out of Sheese’s hand and marched to the door, bumping into the scholar on the way out. Before he exited, he noticed that most of the sheet was blank. He turned around to a smiling Sheese.

“Don’t know how to fill it out?” Sheese asked slyly. He paused, staring at Mardious intently. The silence in the room felt heavy. “I might be able to help you.”

Mardious didn’t break eye contact.

“Maybe you should play nice, babe,” Amelia suggested.

Mardious put on a fake smile, stepped back towards the desk, and held the sheet out. “That would be greatly appreciated,” he said politely.

Sheese sat down and grabbed his quill. “How much would you like?”

“Twenty thousand,” Mardious replied. It was ten times the amount they usually withdrew.

“Hm,” Sheese said. He wrote the notation clearly on the sheet. “Do you think you can carry all of that?”

“I have a cart lined up,” Mardious lied. He hadn’t asked Nightrider yet, but he remembered how to track him down.

Sheese nodded, and sat down to fill in the rest of the form. He stopped when he got to the last line.

“This is where we need High Scholar Robert’s signature,” he said. “I normally forge it, but I’m not going to do that until you tell me what you’re going to use the Aileron for.”

Mardious clenched his fist. He should have known Sheese wouldn’t make it easy. "Don't make me hurt you," he threatened.

Sheese put his quill down. He clasped his fingers behind his head as he leant back in his chair. "Hurting me won't solve your problems."

"Hurt him slowly," Amelia whispered.

Mardious leant on the desk, searching for something sharp. It wouldn't take much to pin Sheese down, seeing as he didn't look threatened.

"Making a withdrawal takes a lot more than a signed document from the High Scholar, anyway," Sheese added. "You don't even know which banker to go to. I've spent a lot of time building relationships with a few of them. Picking the wrong one might get you arrested."

It seemed like Sheese was having fun now, which only made Mardious angrier. Since Sheese was the one to handle the money every time, Mardious didn't know exactly what the process was. But it couldn't be that difficult to figure out what to do.

"Do you really want to take that risk?" Amelia asked. "You have a lot of other things to worry about."

Mardious took a deep breath. He was tired of playing Sheese's game. "I'm not using the money for the Badlands," he admitted. "I'm going after the doorway of life on my own."

"Interesting." Sheese smiled and signed the High Scholar's name on the form. He handed it to Mardious. "Make sure you ask for Tenille. She's dedicated to our cause."

Mardious smiled politely and took the sheet of paper, but Sheese kept hold of it.

"You know, I could save you a lot of time by giving you the locations to the other pieces." Sheese let go of the paper. "If that's something you might be interested in."

"Leave, babe," Amelia whispered. "You've got what you need."

"Zuke said you only know about one location," Mardious replied.

Sheese smiled. "Zuke knows what I want him to know. He needs to stay focused on one task at a time, or else he misses important details. I think you've noticed this."

Mardious had thought that Zuke and Sheese were making plans together, but now it seemed like Zuke was just a pawn in the grand scheme. He needed to uncover more. “I’m not going to fail again because of his mistakes.”

Sheese got comfortable behind his desk. “Sit down. Maybe I can give you more than just Aileron today.”

“I don’t like this,” Amelia said. “But I trust you.”

Mardious took a seat. Sheese turned around and grabbed a notebook from the bottom of his bookcase. When he opened it, Mardious read the title upside down: The Tyco.

“I thought we were going to talk about the doorway of life,” Mardious said.

“We’ll get there,” Sheese said.

Mardious rolled his eyes. He put his hands on the arms of the chair and went to stand, but Sheese put his arm out.

“Fine,” Sheese said. “One of the pieces is on the island of the Giants, while the other is in the ocean. I have maps, strategies, and information about certain obstacles, but I will only give them to you if you listen to what I have to say.”

Mardious relaxed. “Just listen?”

“Well …” Sheese cleared his throat. “I’m also hoping you might do something for me.”

“Unbelievable.” Mardious shook his head. He stood from his seat and turned to the door.

“It involves killing High Warrior Roman,” Sheese said.

Mardious froze. It had been a while since he had thought about getting revenge on Amelia’s murderer. Instead, he preferred to remain focused on bringing Amelia back. To do so, he avoided any contact with the High Warrior. Just the thought of him made his blood bubble.

“Sit back down,” Amelia ordered.

Mardious turned back to the desk again and took a seat. He folded his arms, and then rolled his hand forwards in a gesture for Sheese to proceed.

“It starts with the Tyco,” Sheese explained. “I was able to dig up some history about their leader, based on what you’d given me. It turns out that Ravon Tyco was an idealist, with just as much vision as you or I.”

Mardious didn't appreciate being put in a group with Sheese and the original leader of the Tyco.

"He lived in a time where the leaders of the Triple Crown were failing their people. Drought, starvation, and a lack of shelter caused the people of the realm strife, yet the richest in the realm still thrived. The Triple Crown wasn't looking after the majority of the realm, and Ravon wanted to balance the scales."

"I like him," Amelia whispered.

"He was known as an honourable Guardian, but claimed he had studied as a scholar and a wizard. He displayed his magic in a heroic fashion when he single-handedly saved a family from their burning home. He gained the attention of the struggling communities, and demanded the political court represent them as opposition to the Triple Crown."

Mardious liked Ravon Tyco too, but how had this idealist become the leader of a violent gang?

"After months of improving his voice around the realm, the Triple Crown granted him his wish. They had a formal election where voters could pick their favourite candidate, and the winner would be granted political title."

Mardious unfolded his arms and leant forwards in his chair.

"Although Ravon had a lot of followers throughout the realm, he didn't have enough to win the election. With only twenty percent of votes going his way, he lost in a landslide."

Mardious fell back into his chair. He didn't know why he thought the story would have a good ending.

"It was at this point that the Triple Crown made a ruthless decision. They arrested Ravon on charges of treason and publicly hung him without a trial. Since they had the names of all the voters, they banished them, his supporters, to the Badlands.

"Without any aid to set up a community, the new inhabitants of the Badlands were left to fend for themselves. They had no shelter, no food, and they couldn't even fight back against the government, because they were outnumbered."

"I hate the Triple Crown," Amelia said.

“However,” Sheese continued, “On the other side, the population dip left fewer mouths to feed throughout the rest of the realm. The starvation issue lessened, land titles were distributed to families that supported the Triple Crown, and the majority of the people began to prosper again. By segregating part of the population, the Triple Crown not only found a solution for the struggling citizens, but gained more loyalty from them in the process. It was a brilliant move.”

Mardious clenched his fists. “I wouldn’t call them brilliant.”

“You’re right,” Sheese said. “But that’s not the point of the story. The part I’m interested in is how Ravon Tyco was able to drive fear into the rich and powerful. He was able to become an extraordinary being, and instigate a movement that upset the balance of power of the Triple Crown. They were able to stop his reign before it gained any traction, but he was a viable threat. I think we can do the same thing with you and your friends in the Badlands.”

Mardious folded his arms again. “I thought you wanted me to kill High Warrior Roman.”

“Yes, but in order to get to him, a few actions are required first.” Sheese answered. “My plan is simple, but the execution requires a lot on your part. I need you to create fear, insecurity, and hatred throughout the realm so that the leaders start to worry. So much so that the public will demand new representation.”

“It doesn’t sound simple,” Mardious quipped. “I’ve already wasted too much time training to be a wizard, working with Zuke, and failing at your other plans. I’m not going to waste years petitioning to become a leader, or the next Ravon Tyco.”

“Well, I’ll help you speed it up this time.” Sheese leant back and tapped his chin. “I can spread rumours, give the Triple Crown false information about how you’re both a wizard and a scholar, and create panic in a matter of weeks. All I need you to do is make one good threat, go back to the Badlands, and do what you do best: steal from the rich and create havoc.”

Mardious chuckled. “And that will get me close enough to kill the High Warrior?”

Sheese smiled. "We're starting a war. The only thing that will end it is if one of you wins. I'm betting that it won't be Roman Garrick."

"I like his confidence," Amelia added.

"And after I do this for you, I'll get the details on the rest of the doorway of life?" Mardious asked.

Sheese stood and reached for a book on the top shelf. He tossed it on his desk and sat back down. "This is all the information I have on the piece located in the ocean. If you succeed in spreading panic, I'll give everything else you need, including ships, money, and resources. You don't have to work for the Triple Crown. I'll let you choose your own personnel; you can even be Zuke's boss if you want."

Mardious flipped the cover and read the title: *The Leviathan Triangle.*

"You wouldn't be the only one benefitting from our arrangement," Sheese added. "All of the people from the Badlands have something to gain from your actions. Your name and Amelia's will echo through the ages."

"It sounds perfect," Amelia whispered.

"What's next?" Mardious asked.

Sheese cleared his throat. "I see it proceeding in three stages. First, you administer a verbal challenge to the High Warrior. Somewhere that's public enough for other leaders to hear, but with an easy escape route. You threaten the realm with carnage and death, and then disappear into the Badlands."

"Creating panic," Amelia added. "I like it."

"Second, you get a small gang together in Camptown. You pull off a few minor jobs, similar to what you and Amelia used to accomplish. I will exaggerate the narrative, causing a public uproar and forcing action from the leaders of the realm."

Mardious nodded.

"We can do that," Amelia whispered.

"Finally, you get into a standoff with High Warrior Roman. You'll fight him to the death. If you succeed, we will continue our partnership. If you get captured, we'll try again. If you die ..."

"You'll bring me back when you piece the doorway of life together,"

Mardious agreed.

Sheese reached out and put his hand on Mardious' arm. "You have the passion of a wizard, and are prone to making decisions with your heart. But I know that part of you is as logical as a scholar, and a good plan goes a long way."

Mardious raised an eyebrow. "What about Zuke?"

Sheese laughed. "I told you, I only tell Zuke what he needs to hear. He will continue to pursue the doorway piece that the dragons guard in Skyland. If he succeeds, that's one less trip you have to make. If he fails, you'll be up next."

"He's cunning," Amelia whispered. "I never trusted him, but I do now."

"So he won't be involved in our plans?" Mardious asked.

"As long as you don't tell, I won't," Sheese said. "I need his reaction to your fight against the Triple Crown to be real. I'd advise not telling anyone."

Mardious smiled. He enjoyed having a plan that might actually work this time.

"I'm in." Mardious extended his hand.

"We don't have to be so formal." Sheese grabbed a book from his desk, and walked to the door. "Zuke is going to wonder what took me so long. I'll be sure to tell him something convincing." He laughed and exited the room.

Mardious looked at his palm. He rubbed his scar and smiled.

"We have a lot of work to do," Amelia said.

Although the specifics of their plans had changed dramatically, he felt good about it. Sheese had given him a brief outline, but this mission was his. He'd be the one calling the shots, evaluating the strategies, and making sure that every angle was considered.

He was happy to be both a scholar and a wizard.

CHAPTER 18

You Can Hate Me Now, But I Won't Stop Now

The dining hall was fit for celebration with its glorious décor. Golden chandeliers hung from the high ceiling. Impressive statues stood on pedestals. Fresh flowers, artfully placed around the room, provided both a beautiful backdrop and pleasant aroma.

There were thirty people seated at the long table in the middle of the room. All of them were dressed in expensive robes, except for one, who wore armour. High Scholar Robert and High Warrior Roman were seated near the head of the table, laughing and drinking together.

Although Mardious didn't recognize anyone else, he knew they were all important political figures. Sheese had targeted this event because of all the rich, high-profile scholars and strategists in attendance. There were no wizards invited at all. It was the perfect event for them to put their plan into motion.

The event wasn't heavily guarded: only four High Guardians stood tall in the corners of the room. Sheese had paid one of them so that Mardious could stand in his place. Mardious was dressed in shiny green, gold, and silver armour that made him look thicker. The outfit was complete with sword, shield, and open-faced helmet. He gave himself a beard using his illusion magic to add to his disguise.

"It's time," Amelia whispered.

With the main course having been consumed, and plenty of wine now added to the mix, it was the moment Mardious had been waiting for. He set his shield down, took a deep breath, and started to inconspicuously play his imaginary piano. He needed to be patient, focused, and precise.

The candles in the room flickered. A strong breeze appeared to rush through the curtains framing the open windows, and a swirl of black dust appeared at the back end of the table.

Some conversations stopped, but not all of them. Mardious had hoped for a better reaction; clearly his display was a little too subtle. He sped up his fingers and the dust settled, revealing an illusion of him dressed in a long, black cloak. His hood was up and a handkerchief was secured over his mouth.

"It's Money Jane!" A shocked scholar slid his chair back, away from the illusion.

"That's better," Amelia whispered.

"Roman Garrick!" the illusion yelled. Mardious had made his illusionary voice lower for effect. The tip of a gleaming sword was aimed at the High Warrior. "I have come to deliver a message to you."

Roman stood up from his seat. "Dragoon!" Roman yelled back.

The other High Guardians took a step forwards, but Mardious had predicted that. Before the dinner, he had spread a clear potion around the table. With a flick of his wrist, he moved the flame from a candle to the floor, and ignited the volatile liquid. A ring of fire encompassed the room, trapping the guests in the middle and keeping the guards away.

"For too long, my people have sat idly by," his illusion said in a commanding voice. "You've forced us to live in the outskirts of the realm, preventing us from improving our lives. We have no land to prosper from, and no wealth to validate our people."

"Benji, go get the High Wizard," Roman shouted. He drew his sword.

One of the High Guardians rushed out the door.

"We don't have much time," Amelia whispered.

Roman walked slowly around the table, staying close to the scared guests and away from the crackling wall of flame. Mardious moved his illusion in the opposite direction, keeping distance between it and the High Warrior.

"The time has come for our rebellion!" the illusion shouted. "We will flood the cities and take back what is rightfully ours. We will march upon the castle of the Triple Crown, and reclaim the lands that you control. We will become the true power of the realm, and there is nothing you can do to stop it!"

High Warrior Roman showed no emotion. "That's a serious threat," he said. "But the Tyco are no match for the High Guardians. There is no power in the Badlands strong enough to defeat us."

"I don't represent the Tyco." The illusion pulled back his hood and mask. Mardious had spent time practicing in the mirror to get every detail correct. "My name is Mardious Hood, and I am the leader of a new power. Mark my words, Roman Garrick. You will pay for our deprivation, and we will take what we want with blood and death."

The illusion looked up to the sky and laughed maniacally. Roman put his hands on the shoulders of two of the guests and stepped onto the table. The illusionary Mardious lifted his sword above his head, and a bright light flared from the tip. Everyone shielded their eyes, even the High Warrior.

Mardious concentrated on the fire and dust in the room, bringing the flames down and spreading the dust over his potion to help smother them. In the same instant, he stopped his illusion and extinguished the fire. He quickly drew his sword to look like a High Guardian.

Roman Garrick surveyed the room. Everyone remained silent.

The door burst open, and Benji led High Wizard Jolene into the silence, along with a few more High Guardians. She looked around at all the stunned faces. "Is it over?" she asked.

"Perfect timing," Amelia whispered.

Roman nodded. "I want him found," he growled. "Benji, I want this castle put on lockdown. No one goes in or out until we deal with this madman."

Mardious smiled. He hadn't thought his enemy would flatter him, but he did.

"Hold on," High Scholar Robert said. "Are we even sure this threat is real? When did we start caring about the Badlands? Has anyone even heard of this Mardious Hood character?"

"Mardious Hood?" High Wizard Jolene looked shocked. "He's one of our most promising researchers here at the Triple Crown. He's worked here for years as a specialist on dangerous animals. He's a powerful wizard and talented pianist."

Mardious had just met the High Wizard a few days prior. Sheese had made sure to introduce them without Zuke's knowledge. Even though Mardious hadn't done much work, Sheese had already spread the word about his fake background. Information truly was a powerful tool.

"Take me to his quarters," High Warrior Roman commanded. He jumped off the table and hustled to the door. "Benji, you'll come with me." He pointed to the rest of the High Guardians with his sword, including Mardious. "The rest of you stay here and make sure the room is secure."

"Dragoon!" They all shouted. Mardious hated saying it more than he hated hearing it, but he had to play the part.

"Dragoon," Amelia mocked. He had to stop himself from laughing.

Mardious turned his attention to the other High Guardians. There were now six of them in the room. They looked composed and confident, standing firm with their chests puffed out. Mardious tried to imitate them, so he wouldn't stand out.

"How did this happen?" High Scholar Robert asked. "I thought we had the Badlands under control."

"We've never had it under control," one of the advisors said. "But it's never been a problem."

"It used to be structured chaos," another chimed in. "Maybe now, the chaos simply has a new face. We should find out everything there is to know about Mardious Hood. That way we can decide if there's any merit to his warning."

"I want your best analysts and archivists on this," High Scholar Robert commanded. "Get all the information you have on him tonight, and bring it to my chambers. I need to think."

"Sheese will be ready for them," Amelia whispered.

The High Scholar strode to the door, but was met by the outstretched hand of a High Guardian. "We should stay here, sir," she said.

"I'm not going to sit here and do nothing," the High Scholar said. "Half of you come with me; the other half can keep this room on lockdown."

This was Mardious' chance to escape. He rushed through the door after the High Scholar. The murmurs and worried conversations of the advisors and strategists proved that no one suspected him as one of the protective Guardians. He snuck out the door with High Scholar Robert and three other warriors.

As they walked down the halls, he slowed his pace. There were High Guardians all over the place. Some searched rooms, while others shouted orders. With the High Scholar in the lead, they didn't even pause to question his group's march. It couldn't have worked out better.

They reached a stairway, and the High Scholar hustled down. While the three other High Guardians followed closely, Mardious held back. He hugged the wall, completely out of sight from the u-shaped stairwell. He waited a few moments to make sure he had lost them.

"They're gone," whispered Amelia.

Mardious strode away in the opposite direction. He turned a few corners, rushed past other High Guardians, and arrived at a different stairwell. He climbed to the top floor and hustled to the secret lair.

Before he opened the door to the broom closet, he looked back. He hadn't seen anyone searching this floor, but he still felt the need to be careful. He pushed the bricks in the correct pattern, and watched the wall lift. When he stepped in, the room was already lit. The disappointed eyes of Zuke greeted him.

"This is unexpected," Amelia said.

Zuke sat at the table across from the entrance. He tugged on the cuffs of his golden leather gloves, but then he placed his hands gently on the surface. Mardious closed the broom closet door and pulled the lever to seal them inside the secret room.

He stared at Zuke, waiting for the lecture. His illusionary beard disappeared.

"What have you done?" The strain in Zuke's voice was mirrored by the stiffness in his shoulders.

"I'm seeing what it's like to be a High Guardian." Mardious smiled and brushed the shoulder of his fancy armour. "I impressed the High Warrior with my strength, combat skills, and bravery."

Amelia laughed, but Zuke didn't.

"Don't lie to me." Zuke's voice quivered. "High Wizard Jolene and High Warrior Roman are hunting you down as we speak. They came looking for you, saying you're a threat to the realm. What have you done?"

Mardious removed his helmet, and placed it gently on the table. "Things have changed," he said. "It's time for me to move on."

Zuke shook his head. "Just like that?" Tears welled up in his dark brown eyes.

Mardious nodded. He wondered why Zuke was getting so emotional. It's not like he was an innocent wizard, obeying all the laws of the realm. Their schemes involved taking control of life and death, no matter who was at risk.

"I thought you were my brother," Zuke said, his voice now steady. "We were going to do so many great things together, like bring Amelia back."

Mardious glared at him.

"How dare he," Amelia whispered.

"You don't know me," Mardious replied. "You don't know what I'm capable of. Do you really think we're cut from the same cloth? Did you grow up in a world of poverty and violence? Do you know what it's like to lose everything you've ever loved?"

"I won't pretend to know everything about your past," Zuke said. "But I know your future. We could've had it all together, but now you've made a huge mess. I might be exposed."

"I'm just getting started," Mardious threatened.

"Not if I turn you in." Zuke tugged on the cuffs of his golden leather gloves again.

"Don't!" Mardious warned. He drew his sword and pointed it at Zuke.

"Don't what?" Zuke said with a smirk. He snapped his fingers, and all the torches in the room went out. They were in complete darkness.

Mardious pulled back and squatted against the wall. He was comfortable in the shadows. Even though his eyes couldn't see, his ears would pick up any sound. He waited in silence for Zuke to do something.

He didn't hear any movement from Zuke. Was there powder floating in the air? Was their first encounter an illusion? Was Zuke concentrating on something else? Mardious tried to think of what he'd do if he were in Zuke's shoes.

He finally heard the chair slide. "I'm not going to let them hurt you." Zuke's voice carried across the table. "But I'm also not going to let you hurt anyone. Especially me."

Mardious didn't respond. He heard something hit the wall beside him. Was Zuke throwing something his way? Was it an illusion? He didn't want to use his magic, and accidentally give his location away. He concentrated on Zuke's footsteps, listening for the sound of boots hitting the floor.

Zuke couldn't hurt Mardious unless he was able to find him. Would Zuke use magic or weapons? Mardious didn't want to hurt Zuke, but he'd defend himself if he had to. He gripped his sword a little tighter.

"The Stone-Cold potion," Amelia whispered.

Mardious had stashed his dark cloak on one of the bookcase's lower shelves. He'd been able to experiment with a few supplies that he'd collected during his tenure, and made a concoction similar to the Medusa mixture Gerard had used, only longer-lasting. Unlike the mixture from his and Amelia's heists, there was no memory loss component.

If he could get to it, he could use it on Zuke. The potion would work for a few hours, so it would buy him the time he needed to escape. He had initially planned to remain in the room until the lockdown was lifted, but now he'd have to improvise.

"If you give up now, I'll make sure you get a lighter sentence," Zuke said. He was still across the table, but a little closer to the bookshelves.

Mardious had to make his move.

He placed the sword gently on the floor. His fingertips touched the stone, and he slunk forwards one leg at a time. He was as cautious as a lone wolf hunting its prey, making sure that his boots didn't make a sound while he crept along the floor. He was careful to feel for any obstacles first before moving forwards.

"I have a lot of connections with the prison," Zuke said. He was getting closer to Mardious. "They can either make your stay comfortable or terribly unpleasant; it's up to you."

Mardious just needed a few more steps to reach his goal. His cloak was on the lowest shelf, tucked into the corner. He lunged forwards and pivoted on his right foot, still keeping one hand on the floor for balance.

The torches in the room ignited. Mardious was at the end of the room, an arm's length away from his target. Zuke stood in the corner, just a few feet away. Mardious looked up, and met Zuke's gaze. For a second they both froze.

Zuke took two steps forwards while Mardious dove for his cloak. He was able to grab it before Zuke tackled him flat.

Zuke wrapped his arm around Mardious' neck and held tight. He rolled onto his back, wrapping his legs around Mardious' midsection. He pulled harder, choking Mardious in the process.

"I learned this move from a Guardian friend of mine," Zuke said. "Sometimes it pays to be friends with warriors, and not just imitate them."

As Zuke gloated, Mardious frantically searched his robes for the potion. First he grabbed a handkerchief, and moved it up to his face. He bit the cloth, hoping it would block anything from entering his nose and mouth. He couldn't breathe anyway, but he didn't need to be turned to stone while being choked.

He found his belt, which had five potion bags strung to it. The Stone-Cold potion was in the middle, so he counted to three and yanked it off. He dumped some out onto his open palm. Tucking his head in, he tossed the powder over his shoulder.

Zuke coughed and loosened his grip. Mardious pushed Zuke away and escaped his clutches. Zuke's hands twitched a few times, and then they became rigid. He looked like a dead cat that had keeled over with its claws up.

Mardious held the handkerchief to his face and crawled away. When he felt like he was out of range of any stray powder, he finally took a few deep breaths. He leant against the wall while he regained his composure.

"What now, babe?" Amelia asked.

Mardious flicked his fingers on his right hand rapidly. He searched for any airborne powder, and found some around Zuke's face. He collected it into a pile, and then brought it back to his potion sac. He tied the strings tight, and then removed his handkerchief from his mouth. He took some more deep breaths before grabbing his sword.

He stood up and walked towards Zuke, dragging the sword with him. The tip of the blade scraped along the stone. He lifted it to Zuke's chin.

"You were a good friend," Mardious said. "I'm grateful for the new life you've given me, and for teaching me everything you know. That's why I'm sparing your life today."

He placed his sword back in its sheath. "But I have a new plan. It doesn't involve waiting for things to fall into place, or searching for answers in secret rooms. I'm going to take action now, and fulfill my own destiny. I'm going to seize what's rightfully mine, and no one's going to stop me."

Mardious stood tall, grabbed his robes and potions, and put his High Guardian helmet back on his head. He recreated his illusionary beard, and then exited the room.

He was confident that he could sneak around the castle as a High Guardian, and use his potions if he ran into any trouble. He'd get through the castle and make it back to the Badlands. He wasn't going to risk being stopped by Zuke, Roman Garrick, or any wizards at the castle.

His plans were changing, but his goal remained the same. Phase one was complete, and now it was time for phase two: to become the true leader of the Badlands.

CHAPTER 19

We Came Too Far To Turn Back

"Remember what you told yourself, babe," Amelia whispered.Mardious nodded. Despite her reassurances, he couldn't shake his nervousness. He'd stopped to take a deep breath and prepare himself for the next part of his quest. It had been a longer journey than he thought, but the outskirts of Camptown were a welcoming sight. He flipped the reins.

After fleeing the castle, he'd had to wait until the lockdown was over before making his next move. Since he was wearing the armour of a High Guardian, he was able to go about as he pleased. Rather than hiding in the shadows of the night, he decided to enjoy the capital city one last time.

He broke into a deli and ate some meat and cheese. He picked the lock of a bakery to enjoy some dessert, and brewed some coffee for his trip. He sat on a park bench across from the Bank of the Triple Crown, and reminisced about his last heist with Amelia. The darkness of the night was comforting.

Finally, just after midnight, he met with Sheese in their prearranged spot. They didn't even speak; Sheese simply handed him the reins of a single horse-drawn cart filled with enough gold to start a war. Mardious wanted to ask if he'd done well with the first part of their plan, but as long as things were still moving forwards, he knew it must have been a success. He wondered if Sheese knew about his confrontation with Zuke.

Instead of travelling directly to the Badlands through the portals, Mardious took an alternative route to slip by any Guardians that might have been watching the passage. When he was far enough from the city, he changed out of his armour and into his own black robe.

He'd worked on this escape route with Sheese, picking a path that wouldn't have any trouble. He rode all through the night, reaching a seldom-used portal door in the small town of Tinselton. He used it to get as close to home as possible without using the portal next to Camptown, since Sheese had warned him that it would likely be watched. The others in the area were clear, however; the main goal of the High Warrior was to protect the Triple Crown, not go headhunting through the Badlands.

He reached the edge of the main strip by late afternoon. He was exhausted, but he had to keep reminding himself how important it was to succeed.

"Remember what you told yourself, babe," Amelia whispered again.

"I'm doing this for you," Mardious answered, trying to gain confidence. Threatening a group of strangers was a lot easier than speaking in front of a crowd of his peers. "I'm doing this for everyone."

He closed his eyes and took another deep breath. He let go of the reins, connecting with the horse to keep it moving calmly. While focusing on the road ahead, he thought about his High Guardian uniform. The way the armour had fit around his body, and how stylish it would look if it were black.

When he opened his eyes, his cart was surrounded by foot soldiers in dark armour. They marched in unison, their heavy boots beating like a drum. Their uniforms were complete with full-masked helmets, and they held black scythes instead of swords. Mardious thought the curved blades were more menacing than traditional battle weapons.

He could tell the moment he was noticed: everyone went quiet. Instead of arguing or bartering, traders stood frozen with their mouths agape. Crowds huddled against nearby walls, avoiding the spectacle marching down the street. Some patrons disappeared around street corners, only to return with more people.

"You have their attention, babe," Amelia whispered. "It's time."

Mardious spotted Porkchop in the middle of the street, staring at him. Even though he hadn't told his friend of his new plan, he knew he'd have his support. He stopped the cart and his marching soldiers, turning them to face outwards. He cleared his throat and tried to embrace the moment.

"Ladies and gentlemen," Mardious shouted. His hood was drawn back, his handkerchief pulled down around his neck. "My name is Mardious Hood. I have returned to the Badlands bearing gifts. In exchange for a moment of your time, I will make sure that everyone gets their fair share."

He reached behind his seat, grabbing a small sac of Aileron. He tossed the sac as far as he could into the crowd. A few coins spewed out while it was in the air, and they sprayed everywhere when they hit the outstretched arms of his audience.

His foot soldiers grunted, lowered their weapons to a battle stance, and stomped their front feet. Mardious didn't need anyone to get the wrong idea and challenge his illusion.

"For years, Camptown was my home." He kept pivoting so everyone could hear him. "I grew up working the streets, peddling for food and shelter. I picked up odd jobs here and there to make a little extra Aileron. Many of you might recognize me as a bartender from Sugarplum."

He noticed D'Angello standing on the opposite side of the cart from where Porkchop was. They were never far from each other, and Mardious questioned the distance between them.

"Although I loved living in the shadows, I always wondered what life was like away from home. Were territories as barren as the Badlands? Were cities as rough and rugged? Would I fit in if I lived in another town? It was only when I saw the outside world with my own eyes that I realized how unfair our reality was."

"You're doing it, babe," Amelia encouraged. "Now, bring it home."

"With my partner, Money Jane, we set out on a mission to balance the scales." The mention of her name drew murmurs from the crowd. "We provided you with weapons, jewels, and Aileron. She gave her life trying to make us as rich as the rest of the realm. With one final heist, we were able to get a little closer to our goal."

Mardious reached back and flung the cover open. The cart was piled with sacs of Aileron from The Bank of the Triple Crown. He hadn't counted it, but he assumed that there was at least twenty thousand there.

"Follow me, and we can become even wealthier. We can become a legitimate community, like the cities in the rest of the realm. If two people from the Badlands can make this much money, imagine what all of us can do together!"

The crowd rustled a little more. Their whispers felt negative and insincere. Mardious felt his nervousness creep in again. Had he said something wrong? Why wasn't anyone excited about his revelation?

Amelia didn't say anything to encourage him.

"Don't follow him. Follow us!"

Mardious looked to his left and saw a man holding an axe high. The weapon looked rusty. "The Gam Gang has the courage, strategy, and steel needed to take over the realm. We can lead you to more wealth than Mardious Hood."

The crowd started to rumble a little more.

"Shut your mouth, Devon," D'Angello said. He raised a short sword. "Money Jane was my cousin. If anyone can lead us to victory, it's my crew: The Posse Killers."

"He's not my cousin," Amelia said. "And you're losing them."

"The Posse Killers can't do anything right," Porkchop shouted. His snort couldn't be heard over the crowd, but Mardious saw it. "The Posse has the numbers to get things done. Follow us, and we'll give you more riches than these posers combined."

The crowd grew louder. Mardious just stared at the mob. There wasn't a lot of movement, just more shouting. A few more gang names were hollered, with higher goals and loftier promises. No one was rushing the cart—yet—but at this point Mardious didn't even care.

How quickly he'd forgotten the ruthlessness of the Badlands. It was a land of violence: a land of toughness and posturing. A person couldn't ask politely for anything, or beg for loyalty. There were no politics to play, even with a cart full of Aileron and the illusions of power.

If Mardious wanted the support of his people, he'd have to take it. He shouldn't have asked for it, but rather told them they had no choice. There was no more debate to be had, no matter how loudly the crowd shouted.

Calm rushed over him. He knew of only one person who could stand beside him and unite everyone in his favour.

He cupped his hands, and created an illusion of a crystal ball. He moved his fingers faster, and the orb floated into the sky. The higher it rose, the larger it became. Its colour changed from blue, to yellow, to green, and finally to red. The flashing light caught the attention of the crowd and they quieted down.

A final light shone so bright that everyone shielded their eyes. When the light disappeared, an illusion of Amelia dressed as Money Jane flew in the sky, courtesy of her matching black wings. She was so high up that Mardious didn't need to focus on the details of her new accessories too much. The crowd went completely silent.

"Why are we fighting?" she asked. "When did we become so selfish? When did we fill our hearts with so much hate?"

She pointed at Porkchop. "When did our friends become our enemies, Pollock?" She waved her other hand and pointed to D'Angello. "When did we want to kill those who were once close to us?"

She brought her hands together. "I've been watching you all for months now, fighting for power in the Badlands. Your aggression, your greed has poisoned you. Before, at least you were organized by the rule of the Tyco. But even then your purpose was the promise of a man who lived centuries ago."

She floated down and hovered over the cart close to Mardious. He was careful not to touch her.

"The ways of the Tyco are ancient and out-dated. They have failed you in the long-term. But you live in a time where a historic figure is right in front of you. His ideas, his magic, and his leadership are trailblazing. He is my partner and my love: Mardious Hood."

The crowd rumbled again, but this time they weren't arguing. They weren't holding their weapons high, or threatening one another. Amelia was turning them around.

"Together, he and I fought against the injustices that the rest of the realm has dealt us. We brought in the wealth that our community deserves. We tried desperately to have our voices heard by those in power, so they could show respect to the Badlands and our people. We succeeded only by striking fear into the hearts of the powerful, even though I paid the ultimate price for it."

She flapped her wings and rose up again. "But all is not lost. You will continue to grow and prosper. You will find new opportunities to bring money to Camptown, and invest in lands elsewhere. Instead of being imprisoned by a government that has separated you from the rest of the realm, you will have the freedom to live as you like, wealthy enough to support your children, and your children's children."

Amelia clenched her fist and raised it high. "We are strong. We are fierce. We are the people of the Badlands. We will not be the victims of an unjust system any longer. We will unite to fight for what is rightfully ours. We will build a new world and become more powerful together."

She waved her other hand at Mardious. It was time to tell them how to act. "Break free from your petty gangs. Follow the one true leader: Mardious Hood. He knows the enemy, owns the resources to battle their platoons, and has the determination to rise up against the Triple Crown. He is more than just a head of state; he is your family. He is my one true love. He is your brother."

Amelia flapped her wings one last time, and then disappeared.

Mardious stared at the mob again. No one spoke. Some searched for where Amelia might have flown to, while others just looked at each other. No one moved.

After an eternity of silence, one man spoke up from the crowd. "I will follow you, brother Hood," Porkchop shouted.

"And I," a fellow said behind him, followed by a few more.

"I will follow you, too," D'Angello shouted.

The crowd started to murmur again. Heads nodded. Weapons lowered.

"And I," yelled Devon, along with his cohorts.

"To our brother Hood!" Porkchop raised a dagger in the air, a gesture that was quickly followed by his posse.

Chants of "brother Hood" rang through the street as the crowd pumped their fists and waved their weapons in the air.

Mardious finally smiled. It felt good to have his people support him:

more so than he had anticipated. Amelia had done it. She had been able to complete phase two of his plan, and persuade the people of the Badlands to join him in his quest.

"You're welcome, babe," Amelia whispered. "Now for the next phase of our plan."

Mardious picked up a few sacs of Aileron and tossed them into the street. As the crowd rushed towards the money, he let his illusionary soldiers disappear.

He paused to look at the scar across his palm. He was confident that his plan would succeed. He was one step closer to reaching their dream.

"We did it," he whispered.

CHAPTER 20

I Bomb Atomically

Mardious screamed as loud as he could.

He dug his heels into the mud, driving with as much force as he could muster. The power of the twelve Brotherhood members behind him pushed the battering ram forwards. The head of the ram hit the bricks once more, finally causing the wall to collapse.

They all cheered in victory.

Four members rushed to the front to squeeze through the new opening. Mardious walked back to his team who watched over the Guardians. All six warriors were still gagged, restrained, and kneeling in the mud. One of them had a gash on his cheek.

"What happened?" He pointed to the wounded warrior.

Daryn laughed. "This fool was moaning, so I shut him up."

Marc and Bobbie joined in on the laughter. The warriors stared at the ground in silence.

Mardious glared at Daryn. "I told you not to touch them," he snarled.

The Brotherhood members stopped laughing. "Sorry, boss," Daryn said. "I—"

"Do you know why?" Mardious cut him off.

Daryn shook his head. His eyes were fearful, a reaction that made Mardious feel more confident in his power.

"We want them to appear weak," Mardious said. "If their superiors see that they didn't even have a chance to fight, they will believe they can never match our power. If they return with scars or blood on their hands, others might start thinking they can defend themselves."

Daryn nodded. "Sorry, boss. It won't happen again."

Mardious didn't acknowledge him. He stepped towards the injured warrior and placed his hand on the wound. The young Guardian shook with nerves.

Mardious twiddled his fingers steadily. A soft glow radiated from his healing hand. Zuke had taught him that the trick with healing someone else's wound was to return to a place of pain. There was only one event that Mardious ever thought of when practicing his technique.

"It's okay, babe," Amelia said. "Stay focused."

Pain laced through the same side of his face where the warrior was bleeding. Instead of being concerned with the minor wound, his mind trailed back to Amelia's death. The blood from her neck gushed as he remained helpless. The look in her eyes made him feel guilty.

The soft glow disappeared from his hand. There was no evidence of a wound. The warrior had even stopped shaking.

"He doesn't deserve a beautiful souvenir," Amelia said.

"Listen closely," Mardious said to the Brotherhood members around him. They stood tall in recognition. "Take these Guardians to the nearest portal gateway. Set the destination for Kimroad, and then let them pass through freely. I want them to tell the Triple Crown what happened here tonight." He unclipped a small sac of Aileron from his waist and tossed it to Daryn.

"Go grab a horse," Daryn said to Marc.

"No," Mardious said sternly. "You will take them by foot."

"But that will take over an hour," Marc said before Daryn hit him in the shoulder. They both looked to the ground.

"That's why we chose this location," Amelia mocked.

"Think of it as punishment for striking the Guardian," Mardious said simply. "Oh. And if they talk back during your trip, or if they try to start something, I don't want you to hit them. I want you to kill them."

The once-injured warrior started shaking again. Mardious couldn't help but smile.

"There's no way they'll start anything," Amelia said.

"Yes, boss." Daryn tapped Marc again, and they rushed to get the warriors to their feet.

"Don't come back here when you're finished," Mardious added. "Meet at the rendezvous."

Without another word, they started their march to the portal gateway. The warriors marched in single file, their arms and legs bound by chains. Their journey was likely to take a while.

Mardious looked around at the rest of the mayhem. Brotherhood members looted the small bank that they'd just broken into, while others loaded one of their carts with food from the grocery. A fire burnt across the street at a lumber shop. His plan was working perfectly.

"Success is in the details," Amelia said.

It wasn't as dangerous as a trip to Skyland to sneak past dragons, but in its own way leading a number of his Brotherhood to take over a small town was just as intense. Coordinating small teams to capture any Guardians before they could react, sending others to distribute sleeping potions to the locals, and then calculating just enough destruction to send fear through the rest of the realm were only a few of the challenges. But there hadn't been any surprises or mistakes. It was better than any plan that Zuke or even Sheese could come up with.

Porkchop hastily shuffled down the street into view. It wasn't a sprint or even a jog, more of a speed walk. When he was close to Mardious, he slowed his pace and caught his breath.

"We have a problem, brother." He bent over, desperate for air.

"I thought there weren't going to be any surprises," Amelia quipped.

Mardious didn't respond. He crossed his arms and waited for an explanation.

Porkchop stood tall. "We found twelve barrels of ale in the grocery," he said. "Some of our brothers and sisters went to load the ale in the cart, but others stopped them. They don't want to deviate from the plan, fearing what you might do. But a fight might break out if we don't handle it."

Mardious couldn't hide his smile. He was happy that members of the Brotherhood respected him enough to stay precisely in line with his plan. He knew they all needed to stay focused on the task at hand.

The big celebration was yet to come.

"Show me," he said.

Porkchop snorted and led the way. They passed the cart that was being loaded with Aileron from the bank, and a block down came to the cart in front of the grocery. A small circle had formed, with two men wrestling in the middle.

"What do you think we should do?" Mardious asked, rubbing his jawline and feeling his short, newly-grown beard. He'd painstakingly grown it out, liking the authoritative air it leant him.

Porkchop snorted again, keeping his eyes on the mob. "Seeing those barrels made me miss the drinks at Sugarplum."

Mardious thought about the good times he and Amelia'd had at their old job. Even though serving customers was tiresome, it wasn't all bad. Maybe it was time for them to sit back and enjoy the little things. Maybe they deserved to appreciate what they were fighting for.

"Just don't let them drink too much," Amelia said.

A few of the mob noticed Mardious approaching and stopped rallying the wrestlers. It was like a ripple in a pond; soon, more members stopped cheering, and the brawl quickly came to an end. The silence was a powerful thing.

"Where's the ale?" Mardious asked calmly.

"Over here," D'Angello said. He stood next to the cart. The barrel was on the ground.

Mardious walked over and studied the keg. It was similar to the barrels at Sugarplum, but the contents were likely different. "Has anyone tasted it?"

D'Angello shook his head. The crowd didn't say anything.

"Get me a mug," Mardious ordered.

A couple Brotherhood members sprinted into the grocery, returning a few moments later with multiple options. Mardious grabbed one, and then handed it to D'Angello.

D'Angello tapped the barrel and filled the mug. He held it out, but Mardious shook his head.

"You need to stay focused, babe," Amelia said.

"I don't want any, but you should try it," Mardious said.

D'Angello shrugged, and then gulped it down. He brushed away a foam moustache with his forearm. "Not bad," he admitted.

Mardious turned to the crowd. "Who wants to party?"

The mob cheered, but Mardious extended his arms to call for silence. "Let's take six," he commanded. "That'll leave us with enough room in the cart to load up rations. Make sure it's good stuff—we need to celebrate."

"Can we drink this one while we load the others?" D'Angello asked. He brought the mug back up to his lips.

"You have an hour," Mardious said. "You can drink while you work, but make sure the cart is full by the end."

The crowd cheered again, and then they all rushed into the grocery to grab mugs. Mardious glanced over at Porkchop, who nodded respectfully.

Properly motivated, everyone seemed to work faster. The grocery cart was filled with enough fruits, vegetables, legumes, and lentils to feed their small army for another week. The second cart was filled with enough gold to keep everyone invested and happy. The third cart provided transport for everyone, no matter how much they swayed from the effects of the ale.

The horse-drawn carts trotted through the darkness back to their basecamp in a remote part of Hazelwood Forest. The region would provide cover for them for a week before they had to move on to their next target. The road that Mardious had chosen was safe, quiet, and unpatrolled by Guardians. The thick trees provided cover to keep them in the shadows, and enough privacy to host a party. As soon as they were home, they lit their torches and cracked their ale barrels.

Instead of grabbing a drink, Mardious went to his quarters. He relaxed on a stump just outside the entrance to his shelter. The night had been more successful than he'd anticipated.

"We're one step closer," Amelia reminded him.

After his mission with the High Warrior was complete, he'd relieve himself of the position of Brotherhood leader to pursue the doorway of life. He had an idea of how much money his brothers would need in order to keep operations going after he was gone. A few more successful heists like this one, and they'd have the basis of a real enterprise. It was time to start planning the final showdown between him and his true enemy.

The members of the Brotherhood had started a fire in the centre of their refuge, added ingredients to the cauldron for a feast, and filled their mugs with more ale. Some of them sang, others danced, and a couple wrestled playfully. It was nice to see them enjoying themselves.

"They celebrate differently than we did," Amelia whispered.

Mardious closed his eyes. He imagined holding her. His fingertips on her soft skin. Her warm body pressed against his. Her tender lips igniting his love, and her bite driving him wild. He'd never forget any of the details from their heist nights.

"I haven't forgotten either," Amelia added.

Mardious smiled and opened his eyes. Porkchop strolled towards him, holding a mug in each hand.

"Are you going to join us?" Porkchop asked. He handed a drink to Mardious and sat on a stump beside him.

Mardious kept his eyes on the fire. "I have to plan our next move," he said.

"Even leaders deserve a break once in a while," Porkchop said. "Especially great ones." He held his mug out in cheers, but Mardious didn't oblige.

"If Amelia can't enjoy this drink, neither can I," Mardious replied honestly.

Porkchop sniffed the air, and then dumped out his ale. "One way we can honour those who have passed is to pour out a drink for them. It's a way of rejuvenating their memory, so they can be part of the celebration."

Mardious nodded. "I like that," he said. He poured out his ale, splashing a little on his boots.

"Two for her, so two for you," Porkchop said. He stood and reached for Mardious' mug.

Mardious stood. "I'll come with you," he said.

Porkchop focused his attention back to the fire. "They'll really appreciate it."

When they returned to the party, they were greeted with cheers. It was nice to see the Brotherhood members let their guard down a little, and not be as intimidated by his presence. The ale likely had much to do with that.

Mardious went to one of the barrels and placed his mug at the tap. He secretly twiddled his fingers and pretended to pour himself a drink. The illusion he created was a perfect substitute.

After Porkchop topped up his own mug, they made their way to the fire. Before they could sit down, someone started to chant 'Money Jane!' Soon, the entire crowd was in on the action, creating a deafening cacophany.

In response, Mardious lifted his mug high, and then pretended to chug the whole thing. His illusion spilled froth down his bearded chin and onto his clothes. He used his sleeve to wipe himself clean, and then screamed into the air. He pumped his fist, and continued the chant of 'Money Jane' while the entire crowd cheered again. He hoped Amelia heard it.

Throughout the rest of the night, Mardious refilled his illusion. He still needed to stay focused and not allow his senses to be affected by the ale. However, he used the opportunity to converse with everyone at the party. He learned more about what his brothers and sisters were like, how their ambitions were aligned, and listened to stories of their families.

He also discovered how much of an impact he and Amelia had. Some of his new brethren were grateful for the Aileron that Porkchop distributed. More had been fortunate enough to benefit from the improvements at the shelter. Others had family members that escaped to Mary Angella's new property in Kimroad, and used the time away from the Badlands to recover from addiction.

Mardious even had a conversation with D'Angello, who spoke of how different life with the Brotherhood was compared to the Tyco. Apparently D'Angello felt more respected in his new role, like he had a real voice for change. He didn't feel like he was being put in a position to do something he didn't agree with, and he didn't live in fear of making a mistake. He admitted that he loved the Brotherhood, and was grateful for the transformation in leadership.

"I told you we'd make the Badlands a better place," Amelia reminded Mardious.

After hearing everyone's story, Mardious had a new appreciation for his and Amelia's efforts to bring wealth to the Badlands, and the plan that

Porkchop had developed to spark chaos. Mardious' return to the Badlands had inspired the final changes needed to solidify widespread improvement. The plan of Money Jane had come full circle, and his home was better because of it. But was there more he could do?

As much as he appreciated his personal revelation, he began to feel more and more guilty about putting his brothers and sisters in harm's way. He even felt remorse for instilling the fear he needed in order to impose his power. It had been so easy to rule with an iron fist, but now he knew that the Brotherhood was bigger than just him. The people of the Badlands had a chance to continue to grow and prosper, even after he was done with his current mission.

Although he hadn't finalized his plans for battling the High Warrior, he knew it had to be an epic standoff. Not only would he have to come up with the perfect strategy for defeating the warrior in combat, he had to cause enough bloodshed to mark a deep stain in history.

"I don't want anyone to feel the pain I did," Amelia cautioned. "Or what you still do."

Mardious used his illusion skills to fill his mug again, and with it came an idea. Instead of using the Brotherhood in combat, he could create an army another way. He would still engage the High Warrior, but he could avoid all casualties in the process. He'd still have to put himself in harm's way, but it was a sacrifice he was willing to make if it meant preserving the lives of his brothers and sisters and protecting their families in the Badlands.

He was the only one of the Brotherhood that knew of the doorway of life. He was the only one who had a deal with Sheese in case he was captured or killed. He was someone who could afford to leave this world behind; no one would mourn him the way he still mourned Amelia.

He found Porkchop in the crowd, prepared to tell him his new ideas, but it quickly became apparent that it wasn't the right time.

"Do it again!" Porkchop exclaimed.

D'Angello leant down and slapped a sleeping Daryn as hard as he could. Daryn didn't even flinch: he remained passed out on the ground. He had clearly consumed too much ale.

Porkchop laughed again, but Mardious wasn't amused.

"Having a good time?" Mardious asked.

Porkchop wrapped his arm around Mardious' shoulder. "It's been a long road, but here we are. Nothing can stop us now. We're on top of the world!"

Mardious laughed. He liked the confidence and enthusiasm. He couldn't escape his own thoughts, though. "Nothing lasts forever," he said.

Porkchop leant his head back and swayed a little. His eyes were glassy and unfocused, but Mardious pushed on.

"The reason that Amelia and I were such a good team was because we trusted each other," he explained. "We were tested a few times, and I made a few terrible mistakes, but we stuck together through it all. We earned our spoils because of the obstacles we overcame."

Porkchop snorted, and then took another sip of his ale.

"Things are going well for the Brotherhood. The days are bright, the riches are plentiful, and the heists are fun, but I'm not confident that they'll be able to make it through the darkness. Their fellowship is new, but it's fragile. If things start going wrong, I'm afraid they'll turn on one another in a heartbeat."

"With you as our leader, nothing will go wrong," Porkchop said.

"There might come a time where I won't be around as your leader," Mardious said solemnly. "If anything happens to me, I need you to take over. You're the only one I trust to lead the Brotherhood into prosperity: to spread wealth throughout the Badlands and fulfill Amelia's dream. Are you ready?"

Porkchop snorted. "Not right now," he admitted. "But whatever you need me to do, I'll do." He patted Mardious on the back and stepped forwards. "My turn!" he yelled. He waved his palm, signalling that he wanted to slap their drunken brother.

Mardious appreciated Porkchop's loyalty. Even if he didn't remember their conversation by tomorrow, he had shown Mardious everything he needed to see. They'd come a long way, but still had further to go. Soon this stage of their plans would end, but Porkchop would take them to new heights.

"He'll be ready," Amelia agreed.

CHAPTER 21

Listen To The Way I Slay Your Crew

Mardious played his imaginary piano in accompaniment to the warm sunshine. The breeze he created blew across the pink lakes, along the beach, and over the hills. His powder carried to the four High Guardians standing around the portal gateway.

His newest potion consisted of Rosebud, ground clovers, valerian root, blue phoenix feathers, and centaur hair. It was a truth serum that kept recipients calm and obedient for a short period of time. It was the ideal tool for the first part of his plan.

"You're sure this will work, brother?" Porkchop whispered.

"It worked on you, didn't it?" Mardious couldn't help but smile.

"I'm not a High Guardian; they're a different breed." Porkchop snorted softly.

"It will work," Amelia whispered.

The potion rode the breeze and all four warriors inhaled it. Two of them were on foot, while the others were on horseback. It would take a few seconds to take effect, but Mardious was confident his plan would succeed. "Let's go," he commanded.

He left the bushes that hid them. Porkchop and five other members of the Brotherhood followed him obediently to the portal doors.

He'd led his cohort on a few more successful heists in preparation for this final battle. They robbed from the wealthy, put fear into the hearts of many, and had gained a troublesome reputation throughout the realm. They were true outlaws, living outside the rules of the common people.

Sheese did his part without even having to talk to Mardious. Wanted posters were strewn around towns and cities. Guardian patrol numbers increased around important landmarks, businesses, and banks. Mardious was the most popular man in the realm, which made him feel even better about his current quest.

One of the mounted warriors noticed his presence. She pulled out her sword, and looked like she was about to say something. But then she stopped. Her arm dropped to her side, and she sat taller.

"Told you," Amelia said.

Mardious' group caught up to him. Their footsteps were heavy, and their laughs were cocky, but he liked their confidence. They hadn't failed in any of their previous heists, and he wasn't about to let them fail now.

He stopped in front of the High Guardian that had recognized him. Her eyes had gone completely white, concealing the colour of the iris with a milky glaze. "What's your name?" he asked.

"Helena Garrick." Her voice was low and steady.

The Guardians he'd paid off had given him the correct information after all. His plan was working perfectly.

"Dismount, Helena," he commanded.

The High Guardian swung her leg over her horse's hindquarters, and she elegantly dropped to the ground. She didn't even put her sword away, just stared straight ahead.

Mardious smiled. "Now, restrain these two High Guardians," he commanded. He pointed at the other warriors standing proud.

Helena shook her head slowly. "No," she said calmly.

Mardious raised his eyebrow. Why was she disobeying his orders? Was his potion wrong? Had he used the wrong balance of ingredients? He tried not to overreact in front of his gang.

"Why not?" he asked.

"I've sworn an oath to the warriors that stand beside me in battle," Helena answered, her chest puffed out proudly. A slow smile broke across her face. "I protect them with my life, and they do the same. We stand united. Dragoon!"

"Dragoon!" the other High Guardians shouted.

Mardious stuck his arms out, ready for an attack. But the High Guardians continued to stand still. His potion was working; it just didn't have all of the desired effects he had hoped for. He would have to adjust it in the future. But for now, he was still in control.

He looked over his shoulder at his Brotherhood. "Tie these three up," he ordered. "Leave the one on the horse. We'll send him back to the Triple Crown when we're ready."

His minions followed his orders. They grabbed Helena and bound her with chains. They tied the other two together, and then moved all three High Guardians to the top of a nearby mound.

Mardious spent time with Porkchop to carefully place another potion around the stones of the portal gateway. Just like the concoction he used to isolate High Warrior Roman at the banquet of the Triple Crown, this clear liquid would ignite into a shield of fire. There was a hallucinogenic component added to it this time, making it more of a paste, designed to confuse all onlookers. It was another way to isolate the fight between Roman and Mardious when the cavalry inevitably drew near.

When everything was ready, Mardious sent the lone rider back to the Triple Crown with a message of what he had done with Helena Garrick. As he awaited the retaliation of the High Warrior, he had to deliver a speech to his clan.

"It's time for me to say good-bye," he said.

Porkchop snorted, and the others in the group looked shocked.

The plan he'd told them earlier was to take the High Warrior as a prisoner, but Mardious knew that this was the moment he'd been waiting for. This was his chance to make a statement, sacrifice himself so that his brothers could remain free, and avenge Amelia's death.

"Why, brother?" Porkchop asked.

"They're going to be sending an army," Mardious said. "I will stand alone against them, and engage the High Warrior in battle. It's what I'm destined to do."

"We will fight with you, brother," D'Angello said. "We're not afraid of death."

"I know," Mardious replied. "And you might get your chance in the future. But today is not your day. Today is not your fight."

Porkchop snorted. "You knew this from the start," he said. "Is this what Amelia wants?"

Mardious smiled. "It's about what I want. I'm here today to kill the man that murdered the woman I love. It's been too long without any meaningful retaliation for her loss. It's what is meant to be."

"But not for us?" D'Angello argued. "We miss her too, you know. Why do you get to be the only one to avenge her death? We want to do what's right. We want to be remembered, too."

A few grunts from the others reinforced D'Angello's point, but Mardious stayed his course.

"You have a more important job, brothers," he said. "You will tell everyone what has happened here today. You will remind them what one man from the Badlands can do against the entire Triple Crown. You will continue to remember Amelia. You will keep building the Badlands higher, and bring all of our people wealth. My fate, and the fate of the High Warrior, is a necessary brick in the foundation of your empire."

D'Angello sighed. He put his hand on Mardious' shoulder. "You're crazy," he said with a laugh. "I'll miss you, brother." He turned and walked away.

The other members of the Brotherhood all tapped Mardious on the arm, except for Porkchop, who wrapped his arms around Mardious in an embrace.

"I understand what you're doing, and I think it's honourable," Porkchop whispered. "Amelia is undoubtedly proud of you. But I don't want you to suffer the same fate. If you find a way out of your twisted plan, we'll be waiting for you."

Porkchop clapped Mardious on the back, then turned and walked away. Mardious was surprised to find that he was choked up. He wanted to tell Porkchop how proud he was of him, and how he would be a great leader. But he couldn't find the words in time. He just watched his brother's back as he joined the others in their hiding spot.

"Focus, babe," Amelia whispered. "They're here."

The light pulsed through the edges of the portal doorway. Mardious played his imaginary piano, and an illusionary army of a thousand black knights surrounded the gateway. Their swords were drawn, their shields were held strong, and they chanted in a thunderous manner.

Mardious moved to the mound where the three warriors were in chains. Helena knelt erect. Mardious pulled the sword from his kneeling prisoner's sheath and held it at her neck. Still fully under the influence of his potion, she was obediently rigid.

"I'm stronger, smarter, and more powerful than them, babe," he reminded Amelia.

The stone panels slid open, and before they finished disappearing into the outer frame, a Guardian in a bull-horned helmet sprinted onto the battlefield. His warrior brethren followed through the glimmer of the portal once it opened fully, but they were already strides behind. It couldn't have worked out more perfectly.

As soon as the High Warrior crossed the circular perimeter of potion, Mardious ignited it. A wall of fire encircled the entire area, stopping the army of the Triple Crown from ruining the day. Roman stopped running, and stood in a battle stance.

The black knights stopped chanting. The ensuing silence was calming.

"Do you remember this place, Roman Garrick?" Mardious shouted. He pulled the blade tighter, almost penetrating his prisoner's skin.

The High Warrior remained quiet, still as a statue. He must have been calculating his next move.

"You killed the person closest to me," Mardious yelled. "You never even gave her a chance. Your arrow ended her life in an instant. You saved the realm from Money Jane that day, but you stole my world from me."

He pressed his sword a little tighter. Roman remained motionless.

"But I'm not like you. I'm going to give you a choice," Mardious shouted. "Before we go any further, I'm going to allow you to trade places with your beloved wife. It's that simple. If you surrender right now, and lay down your sword, she'll live."

The High Warrior didn't even flinch. He still stood in a battle position, ready to attack.

"Very well," Mardious said.

He looked down, but then hesitated. He'd never killed anyone before. He'd prepared himself for the moment, and thus hadn't expected to falter. He quickly tried to remind himself why Helena's death was important.

"Did he hesitate when he fired his arrow?" Amelia asked.

Mardious glared at the murderous man across the field from him. With one quick strike, he slit the throat of the High Warrior's wife.

Her body fell to the ground. Blood oozed from her neck, but Mardious was looking to the sky, uncaring. He laughed as loud as he could, but he didn't feel happy. He didn't even feel relieved. For being a stone-cold killer, he didn't feel anything at all. He felt nothing.

The High Warrior let out a battle cry, and rushed for the closest of the black knights. As soon as he hit the first illusion, it disappeared. The warrior stumbled, and then realized what was going on.

Mardious moved his fingers faster, and created an illusion of Roman Garrick joining the fray to confuse those at the portal. He made the warrior fight the black knights valiantly, letting him strike down numerous adversaries to get closer to the hill where Mardious perched.

The illusionary High Guardian was strong and swift. His sword was no match for any of the black knights' attacks. Mardious had spent some time watching members of the Brotherhood duel, and mimicked their battle moves.

In the meantime, the real Roman Garrick marched slowly up the hill. When he got closer, he didn't have a look of bloodlust, as Mardious had expected. Instead, his eyes were pooled. Mardious could tell he was in pain.

Mardious reached to his beltline and pulled out some powder. He tossed it up, and moved his fingers faster. It hovered in the air until the perfect moment. The High Warrior breathed it in just before he made it to the top of the hill.

Mardious had planned to say something threatening, but the High Warrior didn't pay any attention to him. Roman tossed his sword to the ground, took a few more steps, and knelt beside his wife.

Roman held Helena in his arms and sobbed. He whispered something to her, and then looked up at Mardious. "I'm sorry," he said. A moment later, his eyes went completely white as the potion took effect.

Mardious was shocked. His enemy didn't even want to fight him; his loss was too unbearable. He knew exactly how it felt, and glanced towards the beach where he had held Amelia for the last time.

He remembered her choking. He thought about the look in her eyes, and how she had accepted her death. He felt his own panic and failure, and the helplessness that had caused him to lose his true love. Rage stirred within him.

"Do it, babe," Amelia yelled.

He remembered screaming at her loss. He felt tears in his eyes. This time, he screamed louder.

He held his sword high, and plunged it into the heart of the High Warrior. He felt a pulse of energy flow through his entire body: it was triumphant, wicked, and glorious.

He felt a sense of relief, as if a giant weight had lifted from his shoulders. He was happy to kill the man who had taken Amelia's life. He was impressed with himself that his meticulous scheming had come to a perfect end. All of his time and study at the Triple Crown had been worth it. All of his patience for this moment was sweetend by the taste of victory. His plan had succeeded without anyone else's advice. He felt a sense of accomplishment, and knew that his actions would send a ripple throughout history.

He laughed, but this time it wasn't an act.

Sheese was right; the quill was mightier than the sword. Because of his attention to detail, and all the effort he'd put into evaluating every angle, he didn't even have to fight the High Warrior in the end. There was no need for a physical struggle with a man twice his size. There were no surprising obstacles in his way to get what he needed. His hard work had paid off, and he felt more powerful than he'd ever been before.

He'd just defeated one of the strongest leaders in the realm.

The fire surrounding the portal doors diminished. Some wizards stood strong on the other side of the fading barrier. It seemed like hundreds of

High Guardians rushed through the portal gateway, all springing into action.

As soon as any warrior made contact with a black knight, the illusion disappeared. Some of the High Guardians clued in to the illusory knights, but others were more affected by the hallucinogen and kept fighting with fearlessness and passion.

Mardious stood still and watched the Guardians try to massacre his team. It was humorous to watch them remain so serious, when he knew they had already won the battle.

But he had won the war.

When the High Guardians made it up the hill, Mardious tossed his sword on the ground and fell to his knees. His fight was over. He'd succeeded; he didn't need to engage with anyone else. If someone wanted to kill him, he'd gladly accept his fate. If they wanted to arrest him, he'd go peacefully.

He glanced over at the bushes that the Brotherhood had hid behind. He didn't see any peeking eyes or shocked faces. He knew they'd made a clean escape.

"Put your hands where I can see them!" a High Guardian yelled. He pointed his clean sword at Mardious' neck.

Mardious raised his arms into the air and looked at the ground. He smiled again. He was grabbed, forced into the dirt, and then locked in chains. Two Guardians picked him up and dragged him away.

"You did it, babe," Amelia whispered. "Thank you."

"Rest in peace," Mardious replied.

CHAPTER 22

Death Ain't Nothing But A Heartbeat Away

A tap on the steel door down the hallway caused Mardious to open his eyes. "Sheese Lenon to see the prisoner," a Guardian said.

A few seconds later, another answered. "He may enter."

Mardious was in the last cell in a row of ten. This prison wasn't like his previous one, where he'd met Sheese and Zuke for the first time. The walls here were so clean, the stone looked white. The air smelled like roses, because the night breeze wafted through a nearby flowerbed before reaching his lone, barred window. Mardious couldn't see out of it though; it was too high.

He sat on a bed that had a steel bottom and a soft mattress. The metal frame was secured to the wall and floor, so he wasn't able to move it. Someone had tried in the past, but hadn't gotten very far, leaving one jagged, rough edge that he'd almost cut his hand on. Mardious wanted to look out the window to see where he was, but it didn't really matter. He wouldn't be in his cell for long.

The torchlight brightened as Sheese approached. It wasn't as pleasant as sitting in the moonlight, but Mardious was happy to see a familiar face. He wondered how impressed Sheese was with the execution of his plan.

There was a small, barred space at eye level so the guards could communicate with their prisoner. Sheese didn't smile. He looked around the impenetrable cell.

He quickly looked away, and then stared at Mardious. He cleared his throat. "State your name for the record," he commanded. He lifted his finger to eye level, and gestured for Mardious to get closer.

"What are you doing?" Mardious asked.

"Keep your voice down," Sheese whispered sternly.

"But—"

"Where are you from?" Sheese said loudly. He looked away again, and then moved his face closer to the opening.

Mardious was getting a little annoyed.

"I like your beard," Sheese said. "I'm here to verify your identity. With all the information I've been leaking, it seems I've gained a reputation of being something of an expert on you. More importantly though, it got me here."

Mardious stroked his itchy facial hair. It wasn't as impressive as Zuke's, but it was something. "So what happens now?"

"When I leave, I have to send High Wizard Jolene in to interrogate you," Sheese whispered. "She has a special truth serum she plans on using. She wants to know who your associates are in the Badlands, what your plans are, and other information of that nature. She's determined to destroy everything we've built."

Nerves crept in on Mardious. He couldn't give up his Brotherhood. They had stood by him when he needed them, and were going to continue to make the Badlands better. He couldn't let anyone ruin his plans and erase the legacy of Money Jane.

"Relax, I just have a few more questions," Sheese said louder. He looked away again.

"So what do I do?" Mardious asked.

"I brought you this," Sheese whispered. He turned a little, and rested his shoulder against the door. The edge of a rope made its way through the communication space. "Hurry up and take it."

Mardious grabbed the rope and pulled it through the barred opening. He coiled it along his forearm, between his elbow and palm, so it wouldn't hit the floor. It seemed odd to need rope to escape through a barred window.

"You've done an amazing job so far," Sheese whispered. "You're the only one who could have pulled this off. I want you to know how grateful I am, and how I'm going to keep up my end of our deal."

Mardious held the rope loosely. He was startled to find there was a noose at the end, large enough for him to slip his head through. As much as he'd been willing to accept his fate, holding an instrument that would bring him to Amelia was unsettling. He wanted to be with her, but he didn't feel the need to die. "I thought you were going to get me out of here," he mumbled.

"Last question," Sheese commanded.

Mardious stared at the noose and sighed.

"Hey," Sheese whispered. "You still have a lot more to do. You'll go away for a while, but when I bring you and Amelia back, we'll rule the realm together. We'll build a world full of prosperity and glory."

"Keep building," Mardious corrected.

Sheese raised an eyebrow. "Right."

"There's only one man in the Badlands I trust to lead my people while I'm away," Mardious said. "His name is Pollock Tamworth, but everyone calls him Porkchop."

Sheese looked away. "Paul. Right," he whispered. "There's a hook in the roof used for restraining prisoners. You can hang the noose from that. Tie the other end to the bed and let gravity do the rest." Sheese cleared his throat. "Looks like we're all done now," he said louder.

Mardious was confused. "Wait," he said. "You're going to continue our plans, right?"

Sheese glanced at him, and then quickly looked away again. "Of course," he whispered. "Trust me. I'll be getting a promotion soon. My rise through the ranks of the Triple Crown is inevitable. I'll keep an eye on Paul for you, and visit him from time to time." He gave Mardious a half smile.

Mardious' mind raced. He wasn't confident that Sheese would do anything for Porkchop, or the rest of the Brotherhood. Would things go back to the way they were? What was Sheese planning to do?

"I don't like this anymore, babe," Amelia whispered.

"I need to get out of here," Mardious said. "Can't you do what you did last time? We can just—"

"Why would I do that?" Sheese interrupted. The corner of his mouth curled up slyly.

"I can do a lot more alive," Mardious said. He felt like his argument was falling on deaf ears.

Sheese chuckled. "I'm surprised you haven't figured this out yet. I own this castle. I own this city. I own *you*."

Mardious took a step back. Sheese had masked his true nature before, but now there was a different layer to the scholar's malice. Mardious was finally seeing the breadth of a true mastermind.

"No one owns me," he muttered.

"I do not have a purpose for you right now," Sheese continued. "And if I try to get you out of here, I'll be exposed. I have taken all the risk to get you this far, and I can't afford to gamble any longer. There might be a time when I need you again, but I will only bring you back if you follow the plan." He gestured to the noose. "If you fail, and get interrogated by the High Wizard, then it's all over."

Mardious felt betrayed. "I thought we were in this together. You promised you'd get me out of here if I was caught, and we could try again."

"This is *my* plan," Sheese said. "I'm the one in control. The quill is mightier than the sword, but it's also mightier than magic. I was able to succeed by barely lifting a finger. True power comes from people; influencing the most people to accomplish things for you makes you the most powerful."

"I can't believe he used you," Amelia said.

Sheese's grin disappeared, and he left Mardious without saying good-bye.

"Did you get everything you need?" a Guardian down the hall asked, followed by a knock on the far door.

"That's confidential." Sheese laughed. "The High Wizard will be here shortly."

The sound of a door slamming echoed down the hallway.

Mardious stared at the rope.

"What are you going to do?" Amelia asked.

He looked up to the roof and took a deep breath. The hook didn't look sharp, but it was thick enough to support someone's weight. It was probably used for interrogation, but was also the perfect aid for his rope and noose.

He wasn't sure what Sheese's plans were, moving forwards, but he had to believe that he and Amelia would be brought back to life when the magical doorway was erected. He didn't really have any options left at this point. It was too late to do anything else, and he couldn't allow the High Wizard to interrogate him.

"We'll have to wait," he whispered. "Together."

He twirled the noose and stepped up onto the bed. He tried to push away his feelings of doubt, and focus on letting go. As much as he had liked being in control of the Brotherhood, feeling the rush of a successful plan, and marvelling at the panic he'd caused among the Triple Crown, it was all over now.

He looked up at the hook and reached as high as he could. It was still too far away, and he almost lost his balance.

"Toss the rope, and get it through the loop," Amelia whispered.

Mardious held the loose end of the rope between his fingers, focused on his goal, and threw the end like a dart. The rope missed the hook completely and fell to the floor. He dropped his hands in defeat. He closed his eyes, trying to think of what else he could do.

There was a knock from down the hall.

"You're out of time, babe," Amelia said.

Panic started to set in. He had to get the job done before the High Wizard entered his cell. He jumped off the bed and grabbed the rope. He got back into position and tried to concentrate. He decided to reach further instead of throwing it again, and he got a little closer, but the hook was still too far away.

"Zuke Hagen to see the prisoner," a Guardian shouted.

"What does he want?" Amelia sounded disgusted.

"He's not on the list," another warrior answered.

Mardious caressed the rope. He had an idea.

"Okay," the warrior said. "We'll escort him to the cell, and monitor the exchange."

Mardious jumped off the bed and rushed to the corner of the door. He started playing a joyful tune on his imaginary piano, and an illusion appeared in the middle of the cell. The moonlight offered a perfect backdrop for his cloaked figure, dangling from a rope.

Footsteps approached, and as they did, Mardious' excitement rose. He couldn't wait to see Zuke's reaction.

"Oh no," Zuke said. The light from his torch shone through the eye slit in the door. Mardious had his illusion turned so that only his cloaked back was showing, to make sure Zuke wouldn't figure it out.

"Is he dead?" one of the Guardians asked.

"Go tell the High Wizard!" Zuke shouted in panic.

"Dragoon," the two warriors said in unison.

"Wait, give me those," Zuke said. Keys rattled on a chain.

"Perfect," Amelia said.

The key slid into the lock on the other side of the door. Mardious curled deeper into the shadows. When the door swung open, Zuke took a few steps into the room and stopped. His torch dipped as his arm sagged.

"What have you done now?" He reached out, but hesitated.

Mardious wondered if Zuke was onto him. Had he recognized it as an illusion, or felt Mardious' power at work? Or was emotion clouding Zuke's judgement? Mardious gripped his rope a little tighter.

"I came here to apologize." Zuke's voice quivered. "I shouldn't have threatened you. I didn't mean to pick a fight, but I …" A sob choked him off.

"He's weak," Amelia whispered.

"I love you," Zuke said. "You're a brother to me; the only family I have. Hopefully one day I can bring you back." He reached out to grab the dangling leg, and the illusion disappeared.

Zuke stumbled forwards, but before he could regain his balance, Mardious tackled him.

They wrestled around on the ground. Mardious was behind Zuke, and already had the rope secured around Zuke's neck. He wrapped his legs around Zuke's midsection, pinning one of Zuke's arms to his side. Mardious rolled onto his back. The torch bounced off the ground and settled in the corner.

"I learned this move from an old friend," Mardious said. He gritted his teeth and pulled harder on the rope.

Zuke gasped for breath, but only managed to make choking sounds.

His free hand flailed wildly, and then reached down to his waist.

Mardious felt Zuke grab his calf. Zuke was trying to pry his leg off, but Mardious only squeezed tighter.

"Not today," Amelia said.

Mardious grunted, trying to keep every muscle in his body tight. Zuke's arm swung around again, but tapped Mardious on the forehead rather than administering a hard blow. After a few more lame attempts at trying to get free, and a couple convulsions later, Zuke's body went limp.

Mardious hung on for a few moments more to make sure Zuke wasn't faking it, and then he collapsed. His arms flopped to the ground as he tried to catch his breath.

"You don't have much time," Amelia reminded him. "The Guardians will come back."

Mardious rolled Zuke over and knelt over him. The flickering torchlight helped him see better than the moonlight through the barred window had. Zuke's eyes were open, and his expression was still. He was dead.

Mardious quickly pulled Zuke's robes off and put them on the bed. He added Zuke's golden gloves beside the garments. Then he took his own clothes off.

"Hurry," Amelia reminded him.

Mardious put Zuke's robes on, and then dressed Zuke in his black cloak. When he was finished, he was a little dissatisfied. It still looked like Zuke.

"Your scars," Amelia said.

Mardious grabbed Zuke's palm and placed it on the rough edge of the bedframe. He lifted his leg high and slammed his foot against the back of Zuke's hand, once, twice. When he pulled the limp arm up, blood oozed from an open wound in the exact place as his scar. He even smeared some blood on Zuke's arms and face; just enough to make him look more barbaric.

"You have enough time to send a message," Amelia whispered. Mardious still hadn't heard any Guardians re-enter the cellblock.

Mardious jammed his index finger into Zuke's palm, and then positioned himself at the wall. Using Zuke's blood, he drew a giant circle, and then cut through it with a line down the middle. Beside the former symbol of the Tyco, he wrote '4 Life.'

After he finished, he heard a thud from down the hall. A few murmurs meant the Guardians were back at the door.

"The rope," Amelia said.

Mardious quickly made sure the noose was secure around Zuke's neck. He slipped Zuke's gloves on. Blood and sweat mingled on his hand beneath the leather.

"Gross," Amelia said. "Are these his only pair?"

The gloves were still in good condition on the outside, but they felt old, sticky, and worn on the inside. If Mardious was going to pretend to be Zuke, the first thing he'd do is buy a new pair.

The door of the cellblock slammed against the wall. "This way," a Guardian said. The approaching stomp of the Guardians' boots was accompanied by the rustling of robes. When they stopped, Mardious was holding Zuke in his arms, sobbing like he'd just lost someone dear to him.

The High Wizard gasped. "Zuke, get away from him."

Mardious rocked a little for effect. "He was my friend." He kept his voice low and quiet, trying to imitate the real Zuke.

"He was a criminal," a Guardian said.

Mardious stopped rocking. He turned his head a little. "I know he was a madman," he replied, "but there was a time when he was good."

"It's always an ordeal to lose those we're close to." The High Wizard entered the cell and put a hand on his shoulder. "Even when we've lost touch with them. We can still honour them with—" The High Wizard gasped again. "What's that?" she asked.

Mardious turned and saw her pointing at his art.

"I think he used his blood to send a final message," Mardious said. "The edge of the bed frame … I'm sorry." Mardious turned away and sobbed some more.

"There's blood everywhere," a Guardian noted.

"Zuke, go clean yourself up," the High Wizard commanded. "We need to … figure this out."

Mardious sobbed some more, keeping his head low, and stumbled out of the cell. He passed through the hallway that led to his freedom while everyone else became occupied with Zuke's beautiful corpse.

He walked through more halls and climbed a few stairwells. He realized he was in the castle of the Triple Crown. Unerringly, he made his way to Zuke's office. He'd be able to grab some new robes there and clean himself up.

When he arrived at his destination, he closed the door and leant against the back of it. He turned and looked at himself in the mirror. He took a relaxing breath, closed his eyes, and twiddled his fingers to the tune of Amelia's favourite song.

"I liked your old robes better," Amelia said.

"Me too," Mardious admitted. He opened his eyes and met Amelia's reflected gaze in the mirror just over his left shoulder. Her hair was down, her skin was soft, and her smile was wicked.

"But it's time for me to grow," he continued. "Mardious Hood died today. His life ended in tragedy. He'll be remembered as a criminal by most, but as a respected leader by his loyal supporters in the Badlands."

He touched his chin. His beard could be fuller, but his other features were a close match to Zuke's. They both had brown eyes and dark hair. They were the same height and roughly the same weight. The heavy robes would hide all of Mardious' distinguishing scars.

"On the other hand, a new hero was born," he said. "He has the talent, intelligence, and influence to manipulate the Triple Crown from the inside. He can make a political impact, and do more for his community as a proponent of change, rather than as a general of war. He has the good looks and charm of Mardious Hood, but the acceptability of Zuke. He's Zardious … Muke?"

"No," Amelia replied. "Just … no."

Mardious chuckled. He might not be able to wander the realm as his old self, but he would be a free man as Zuke. He could continue to work for the Triple Crown, study their policies and strategies, and control the narrative. He'd grow powerful enough to own Sheese, rather than succumb to the scholar's tricks again.

"I guess we're not meeting anytime soon." Amelia sounded sad.

"We won't meet in death, but in life," Mardious replied, confident. "I trusted their plans before, but I don't anymore. There's only one person who can improve the realm, construct the doorway of life, and bring you back."

Amelia's eyes sparkled. "I agree," she said. "But I still miss you."

Mardious thought about how much had changed since he'd last held her. He was smarter, stronger, and more respected. He had inspired the people of the Badlands, and was embraced as family. He had the opportunity now to do so much more for them, to keep them safe and protected. He could expand on Amelia's dream, and make it bigger than they ever thought possible.

"I miss you too, babe," he said. "But I won't rest until I can hold you in my arms again in *this* world. I need you by my side. No one else deserves to rule, and no one else is deserving of my love."

"Are you ever going to tell me all the reasons why you love me?" Amelia asked.

"You already know them," Mardious said. He traced a line on his gloved hand, above his last souvenir from her. "But someday, I want to hear all the reasons why you love me."

"That's going to be a short list," Amelia teased. Her laugh made him smile.

He took a few more breaths, and then stood proud. It was time for him to come up with a new plan. He had his purpose in life, and he was on the right path. He was destined to succeed, because he was the only one who could.

He had already stood up to the leaders of the Triple Crown by taking down the High Warrior in combat, and escaping from interrogation and death at the hands of the High Wizard. He had discovered that his old enemies were his new brothers and sisters, and his new friends had always been his enemies. He finally saw behind Sheese's mask. But there were other ways to wear a disguise.

He focused in the mirror as his beard took full shape, and he tweaked his features to make himself look exactly like Zuke. It didn't take much. After all that time as Zuke's assistant, he knew what Zuke's responsibilities were, what his daily routine consisted of, and what his strengths and weaknesses were as a wizard. No one here knew Zuke as well as he did, not even Sheese. As much as he had joked with Amelia, he was ready to accept this new version of himself.

It was his turn now.

He stared at his true love again. It might take a little longer to see her again, but her wicked smile gave him hope. He could reach his goals with her in his heart. She made him feel alive. He couldn't wait for her to feel alive with him.

www.ingramcontent.com/pod-product-compliance
Lightning Source LLC
Chambersburg PA
CBHW060542310726
48982CB00009B/1343/J